BEWITCHING
THE DUKE

Books by Christie Kelley

Every Night I'm Yours

Every Time We Kiss

Something Scandalous

Scandal of the Season

One Night Scandal

Bewitching the Duke

Published by Kensington Publishing Corporation

BEWITCHING THE DUKE

CHRISTIE KELLEY

KENSINGTON BOOKS

http://www.kensingtonbooks.com

KENSINGTON BOOKS are published by

Kensington Publishing Corp.
119 West 40th Street
New York, NY 10018

ISBN-13: 978-1-60183-028-9
ISBN-10: 1-60183-028-9

First Electronic Edition: December 2012

ISBN-13: 978-1-60183-172-9
ISBN-10: 1-60183-172-2

Printed in the United States of America

To my sisters,
Karen, Pat, and Louise.

Thanks for all the support!

Chapter 1

Selina White paused before the Duke of Northrop's bedchamber. What was it about this room that made her tremble? She had put off this bedroom for last, even though it needed her attention the most. Slowly, she opened the door to the duke's bedchamber and slipped inside the room.

She closed her eyes for a moment to adjust to the darkness before blinking them open again. Why hadn't the servants opened the curtains in here? The duke should be arriving within the next few hours. She felt around until she found a small table. She placed her cleansing bowl on the table determined to lighten the room so she could finish her job.

Slowly she walked toward the windows and the bright sunlight that would assist her. Pulling back the heavy velvet curtains, she sighed as the vast beauty of Northrop Park opened before her. As she took in the view, a loud groan forced her gaze to the large bed.

"Bloody hell, I told Roberts no one was to disturb me until noon!"

Selina gasped and turned away from the window to stare at the man in the duke's bed. His large hands rubbed at his eyes. His tousled black hair needed a good brushing. But as his hands moved away from his face, she felt pierced by his icy blue eyes. She'd only met him one other time, but she would never forget those eyes.

"Who are you? One of the new servants?"

She almost laughed at the idea of any new servants being hired for this crumbling estate. The average age of the servants was sixty. "No, Your Grace."

He groaned and sat up against the pillows at the headboard.

He looked like the drunken degenerate she'd heard stories of for the past few years. Mrs. Roberts always disavowed those claims of the duke being nothing but a worthless reprobate, maintaining that as much as he'd loved his late wife, he could never act in such a manner. Selina doubted Mrs. Roberts's assertions. Even now, he didn't attempt to hide his naked chest. And she couldn't seem to look away, even though she knew she should. Broad shoulders melded into a strong chest lightly covered with black hair. Her fingers twitched as if they wanted to feel the sensation of his warm skin.

She must be mad!

"Have you completely lost your tongue, girl?"

"I'm not a servant, Your Grace."

He closed his eyes and leaned his head back against the headboard. "Did Thomas send you?"

Thomas? "I have no idea to whom you are referring."

"My brother. Did he pay you to join me in my bedchamber?"

She clutched the small chair near her to keep her knees from giving out. "You think someone paid me to be your whore!"

The duke shook his head. "It wouldn't be the first time."

"Perhaps not for you, but it would be for me."

"Indeed?" he said with a coarse laugh. "You enter my room with your hair unbound and your dress cut down to your breasts and I'm supposed to believe you are an innocent angel?"

"I would never do such a thing!" She stole a quick glance

down at the bodice of her dress. The man was mad, the gown completely covered her breasts.

"I've never met a woman who wouldn't do anything for the right price."

"Well, now you have. And I don't care what you believe about me or any other woman." She strode toward the table where she'd set her cleansing bowl.

"Do not leave this room until you tell me who you are and why you are in my bedchamber," he demanded.

The cold tone of his voice stopped her feet. Her mother had warned her to stay away from the house when the master was at home. Selina knew he'd hated her mother, but she never assumed his disgust would carry down to all women.

He shouldn't even be here yet. She'd been certain she could finish the herbal cleansing of the house before he arrived later today. Obviously, he arrived late last night.

"Who are you?" He started to move the coverlet off his body as if he meant to stand.

"Please don't get up," she said quickly. The last thing she wanted to see was his naked body. Although, it might prove quite interesting. *No!* She couldn't think of him that way. Absolutely not the duke. "Miss White, Your Grace."

"Miss White?" He paused and a dark scowl formed.

She only nodded.

"The wise woman's daughter? Why are you here and not your mother?"

"My mother passed on a few years ago."

"Bloody hell. Based on the smell of sage I can only assume you have taken up her practices?"

"Of course. Who else will tend to the sick on your estate?"

"There is no one sick here. I also happen to know there is a completely qualified physician in town."

"Qualified?" Selina snorted. "Qualified as a rotten sod. The man is incompetent to practice medicine."

"The man is highly educated and trained. Now get out of

my room and my house," he said in a low voice as he pointed toward the door.

"With pleasure, Your Grace."

Selina grabbed her bowl of burning sage and raced for the door. Once in the hall, she leaned against the wall and released a long breath as her heart pounded in her chest. The man was more dreadful than she'd expected. First assuming she was a whore and then almost standing up before her with nothing to cover himself. What an awful man.

"Miss White, you cannot go into the duke's bedchamber."

She looked up to see the duke's ancient butler ambling toward her. "I know that now, Mr. Roberts."

"You were in there?"

"No one told me he was here. Yesterday I was told he would arrive this afternoon. I assumed I would have this morning to finish."

"That stupid fool boy," he muttered, shaking his head. "Randall let you in this morning, didn't he?"

"Yes." Randall was the youngest footman in service to the duke, and everyone questioned his mental capacity. Selina's mother had told her that he'd taken a terrible fall when only three. He'd never been the same since.

"He knew the duke arrived last night. He should have told you." The older man leaned in closer. "Was the duke angry?"

Remembering the way the duke had looked at her when he thought she was a prostitute brought heat to her cheeks. "Of course. He tossed me out of his bedchamber."

"Oh, dear." Mr. Roberts twisted his hands together. "He's been in a foul mood since he arrived. He must have seen the condition of the house last night and it upset him."

Selina frowned. "But the estate was, and still is, his responsibility to maintain. He hasn't sent money for the needed repairs. He should be ashamed of his actions." Lack of action was more the term.

"Shh," he reprimanded as he glanced back at the duke's door. "We all know the duke has failed his responsibilities to the estate and its tenants. But you don't want to be the one to remind him of that."

"Someone should."

"Perhaps. But no one with a bit of sense would dare speak of it to him."

Selina shrugged. The duke needed someone to set him to rights. Most of the tenants were frustrated with the lack of attention their cottages received. The only thing that kept them on the estate was the generous income the duke let them retain. The fertile land provided a welcomed source of income for both the duke and the tenants.

"I fear His Grace may have taken one look at this old place and decided that having a wedding here was a dreadful idea. And if that's true there will be no hope of getting this beautiful house restored to its former glory."

One of the tenants had told her there was to be a wedding. She couldn't imagine the type of woman who would marry a man like him. Then again, she'd heard the stories of women so eager for a title they would do just about anything. The woman was most likely as shallow as he. But what would possess the man to have a wedding at his most decrepit estate? The one place he hadn't visited in eight years. "Why are they having the wedding here, Mr. Roberts? He despises this place."

"She insisted, miss. Thought it would bring happy memories to the estate instead of the ones that haunt him."

Selina had to agree with the bride. Perhaps now that he was getting married he would put away his rakish ways, refurbish the house, and have his children here. While that would be excellent news for the tenants, she had no desire to deliver the child of the duke.

"Did you finish the cleansing?"

"No. I still need to finish the duke's wing up here, and then his library and study." Her mother had always insisted the rooms used most intimately by the family should be cleansed last so they were fresh when the family arrived. Now Selina worried she might not get the chance to finish. The cleansing was one of the few rituals a wise woman still performed. Not that there were many of the women left. Generations of ridicule and threats of being labeled a witch had forced many to give up the ancient ways. Selina only knew of three other women who kept up the practices.

"What will you do?"

"I don't know."

"Walk with me down the stairs," Mr. Roberts said as he glanced over at the duke's bedchamber door again. Once downstairs, he stopped. "The duke was always a man of habit. While he hasn't been here in years, I would still wager that he takes a morning ride at nine. If you get here by then, you should have an hour to do your cleansing."

"But it might take me two days at that rate."

He sent her a paternalistic smile. "Better than not finishing at all."

"True." But after her first encounter with the duke, she wasn't certain she even wanted to complete the cleansing. She'd never met such an aggravating man in her life. But she knew her duty. Hopefully, she could avoid him and finish her work.

"I'll send a stableboy to your cottage tomorrow if the duke takes his ride."

"Thank you, Mr. Roberts."

"No, thank you, Miss White. Where would we be without you? You take care of all us servants and the tenants too."

She kissed his weathered cheek and headed for her cottage. Where would they be, indeed, she thought. She tended to their ills and delivered their babies. If only the duke understood how important her work was to the estate.

But she couldn't explain it to him. After what happened eight years ago, she needed to do her best to avoid him completely. God only knew what would happen to her if he ever learned the truth.

Colin Barrett, the seventh Duke of Northrop, stared at the closed door with a scowl. How dare that woman enter his house . . . his bedchamber . . . without his permission? He tossed the coverlet off his body and reached for the trousers he'd left on the floor last night. His valet and trunks wouldn't arrive until later in the day. Having not spent a day in this house for years, Colin was certain there was nothing in the linen press worth wearing.

After dressing, he headed for the door determined to confirm that Miss White had departed. The last thing he wanted or needed in his house was some woman who believed she held a type of mystical power or could cure all ills. No woman had such power. It was 1814; medicine belonged in the hands of educated men.

He'd returned to this house to take back control of his life. And he would start with that blasted wise woman.

"Roberts!" he shouted. Without waiting for an answer, he trudged downstairs. "Roberts!"

"I am here, Your Grace," he said from the salon.

"Did you allow that woman entrance to my home?"

Red tinged the older man's cheeks. "What woman do you mean, Your Grace?"

"That bloody wise woman!"

Roberts furrowed his brow as if in thought. "I did, Your Grace. Should I not have?"

Colin clenched his fists. "No, you shouldn't have let her inside my home without my permission."

"I do apologize, Your Grace. I assure you I shall endeavor never to let a woman like her in your home again."

Colin paused for a moment at the butler's odd choice of words. He shook his head. "Very well, then. Where is she now?"

"Now?"

"Yes, now. Did she leave?"

"Of course, Your Grace. I believe she was on her way to her home."

Colin sighed. "And which direction would that be, Roberts?"

"East, Your Grace."

"Thank you." Colin rushed out the door, intent on catching her. He walked quickly down the worn path toward the tenants' homes. A figure up ahead caught his eyes. She maintained a slow, easy gait as if she hadn't a care. She glanced around and then paused for a moment to breathe in the fragrance of a flower. Once she resumed her walk, her long, curly, blond hair blew in the breeze. He couldn't help but notice the way her hips swayed under her blue muslin skirts. God, he shouldn't be noticing that. Especially not with her.

"Miss White!" he yelled out.

She turned her head and then quickly walked inside one of the cottages.

Colin stopped for a moment. She'd heard him and yet continued on as if she hadn't. The nerve of that insolent girl! No man or woman ignored him. He strode ahead until he came to the cottage she'd walked into. Without a thought, he entered the house.

"Miss . . ." his voice trailed off as he realized his mistake. Seeing the multitude of dishes on the table and the children playing on the floor, he knew this was not Miss White's home.

"Yer Grace," a large woman said with a quick curtsy. She walked toward him with a deep frown and her lips pressed into a thin line. "W-Welcome to my home."

Oh, good God. He had no idea who this woman was. "Thank you, Mrs. . . ."

"Godwin, Yer Grace. My husband works the land for ye."

He wondered briefly at the cold tone of her voice. "Of course."

Glancing about the room, he wondered where Miss White had disappeared. "Pray excuse me, madam. I was looking for Miss White. I thought I saw her enter this cottage. I must admit, I thought this was her home."

The woman laughed soundly. "She is tending my five-year-old, Yer Grace. He got a nasty bee sting yesterday."

Why would the wise woman care about a child's bee sting? He'd been stung a few times as a child and nothing happened. A long silence stretched out.

"Very good, then. I shall wait outside," Colin finally said. He walked outside and waited for Miss White to emerge. As he leaned against a tree, he had to admit that Mrs. Godwin's attitude seemed quite odd. She hadn't even offered him tea, or the chance to wait for Miss White inside. Perhaps she was preoccupied with the children.

After almost an hour, Miss White finally opened the door.

"Good Lord, you're still here," she muttered as she noticed him standing by a tree.

"You must have known I was out here waiting for you." She'd deliberately kept him cooling his heels. Did this woman not realize who he was?

She shook her head. "I'd hoped you would grow bored with the wait." She took a step down the path as if their conversation had finished.

"I need a word with you, Miss White."

She rolled her green eyes and then turned her back to him. "Indeed. I do hope you shall attempt to keep your clothes on this time."

Colin walked closer to her as his fury ignited. The woman was walking around with her hair unbound as if she were still a child, not to mention she had the nerve to chastise a duke! "Keep my clothes on? You entered my bedchamber unannounced and yet you criticize me on good form?"

"You arrived early."

"Which has nothing to do with you being in my bedroom."

"What do you wish to speak to me about, Your Grace?" she asked with a sigh.

What did he want to speak with her about? He could not remember. There had to be a reasonable explanation for following her and then waiting for nearly an hour. "What were you doing in the cottage?"

That was not what he wanted to know. Dammit! This little hoyden had disturbed his thought process.

"Little Raymond was stung by a bee yesterday. I was just making certain everything was all right with him. His brother died of a bee sting a few years ago."

A bee sting could kill a person? He'd never heard of such nonsense. "Was he all right?"

"Yes. The mark is still a little red but he shall be just fine."

"Excellent."

An uncomfortable silence filled the air around them. He had no idea how to broach the subject. "Miss White, I do hope you understand—"

"Of course, Your Grace. You did not expect someone to disturb your peace while you slept. It is completely reasonable that you might have been irritable this morning."

Did she actually think his petulance had something to do with lack of sleep? "I believe you misunderstand me, Miss White."

"Oh?"

"I don't want you here," he said quietly. Shame heated his cheeks. But he had no reason for embarrassment. Her mother, with her assorted herbs and nonsense, had caused his sorrow. Colin had never thought that the dreadful woman's daughter would still be here on the estate. As Kate had told him, it was time to grow up and take charge of his life. It was strange to hear such a mature speech from a woman ten years younger than him.

"I understand, Your Grace. I shall stay away from your bedchamber." She started to walk away again.

"Miss White," he called out.

She stopped and looked back at him. "Are we not finished, Your Grace?"

"No." He waited until she turned to face him. "I don't want you in my home."

"Very well," she replied tightly.

"I also don't want you here any longer."

Her mouth dropped open. "I don't believe I understand, Your Grace."

"I wish for you to leave your cottage while I'm here."

"Leave?" she repeated.

"Yes. I'm quite certain you realize why I would like you to depart. I'm not asking you to leave Northrop Park permanently, only until after the wedding. Obviously, the tenants appreciate your work here. But I . . ." Dear God, she had him babbling like an idiot! "I don't want the reminder of what happened."

"My being here or not being here will not change your memories, Your Grace. The only one who can do that is you."

Colin felt his anger stir again. "It matters not. I do not want the remembrance of what happened here. And you are only a reminder of that pain. Do you understand?"

"Yes. I believe I do."

"Very well, then." He turned away believing everything was settled. She would leave and perhaps he might be able to stand living on the estate for the next two months until the wedding was over.

But as he looked up at the ancient house, all the painful memories returned.

* * *

As Selina strode away from the irksome duke, she couldn't help but glance back at him. She'd be damned if she let him chase her from her home. She had two women about ready to deliver, an elderly man who was losing his mind, and a woman sick with the wasting disease. Nothing and no one would keep her from doing her job.

Not even the Duke of Northrop.

Chapter 2

Colin walked through the house the next morning, frustrated by the condition of his ancestral home. Wallpaper was pulling away from the walls, the rugs were threadbare and covered in dust, and, based on the buckets on the third floor, he assumed there were leaks in the roof. He blew out a long breath. This was his fault. Guilt spread over him as he walked toward his study.

He had no one to blame but himself for the dreadful state of disrepair. His steward had informed him of the needed repairs but he'd ignored those letters. He'd wanted no reminders of this place. Being here now brought back all the horrific memories.

How could he have returned to this godforsaken place? Even now, he felt on edge. He'd spent most of yesterday out of the house, unable to face the memories that remained locked in these walls. It was as if it had only been a few days, not years since that March night.

Already, it felt as if the house was closing in on him. He could still hear her screams of agony, and her pleas with God to save their baby. He entered his study and his gaze focused on Mary's portrait above the fireplace. She'd been stunningly beautiful with her auburn hair and blue eyes. The longer he stared at her picture, the more his guilt ate at him. He had to get out of here . . . out of this damned house.

He should have insisted the wedding take place in London.

"Roberts," he shouted, "tell Mr. Sellers I want a horse saddled."

"Yes, Your Grace." Roberts replied from the hall.

Colin paced his room. Dust and cobwebs covered every table and corner. Of course, if he had sent more notice of his impending arrival, the house would have been immaculate. Or at least as immaculate as his elderly staff could make the decrepit place. He needed to hire more staff as quickly as possible. And workers too. The house needn't be perfect but at least respectable enough for the wedding.

It was only two months. Then everything would be fine and he could return to London. Then he would never come back to this godforsaken house again. He'd let it rot until the next duke took over. His brother, Thomas, or Thomas's son, Richard, could handle the renovations it would need then.

He strode from the room and the house to escape the memories that plagued him. A ride would ease his mind. Once he reached the stables, a fine mare was waiting for him. At least his stables had been maintained.

"Thank you, Mr. Sellers." He mounted and took the reins from the groomsman.

"Thank you, Your Grace. Aphrodite needed some exercise today."

"Then I'll make certain she gets it." He flicked the reins and headed out to the flat pasture. He'd forgotten how beautiful the Midlands were at this time of year. The sheep grazed on green grasses near a meadow of heather. The tilled fields had wheat rising from the ground. He smiled slightly as he remembered racing across the fields as a child.

He breathed in deeply, allowing the thickly scented air into his lungs. Finally, he brought Aphrodite to a halt at the rise of a hill where his property intersected with the estates of the Earl of Hartsfield and Viscount Middleton.

Colin closed his eyes for a moment only to picture the little witch who had angered him yesterday. With curling blond hair and green eyes, Miss White was not the girl he vaguely remembered meeting when she was only about ten. Now she was a beautiful woman who irritated the hell out of him. She had to be in her middle twenties now. It was highly improper for a woman of her years to walk about with her hair unbound. And why hadn't she married? Surely, she didn't mean to remain a spinster and live in that tiny cottage for the rest of her life.

He opened his eyes, annoyed with himself for even thinking about her. Her mother caused his pain. Her mother was the reason he was miserable here. Her mother killed his wife and heir.

The sound of a horse galloping turned his head toward the earl's estate.

"So the rumors are true," Hart said as he reined in his horse. He glanced to the east and then back at Colin with a frown. "You have returned. I guess the sun will now set in the east."

"Good morning to you too," Colin said stiffly.

"Excuse me, Your Grace," the Earl of Hartsfield said in a condescending tone.

"What do you want, Hart?"

Hart gave him an easy laugh. "Just making sure the rumor was true. After all, your exact words were the sun would set in the east before you ever set foot in Northrop Park again."

Colin shook his head. He had said those words and meant them until a month ago. "Kate wishes to marry here."

Hart nodded. "And you can't refuse her anything, can you?"

"No."

"She knows what happened. Why would she insist on having the wedding here?"

Colin jumped off his horse and took the reins. Slowly he walked along the knoll with Hart following him. "She has no desire to marry in town."

"You have three other estates at which she could marry." Hart stopped for a moment. "There's more, isn't there?"

"She believes having a happy memory here will help me get over Mary's death."

Hart shrugged. "Perhaps it will."

"Highly unlikely." He stopped, picked up a rock, and hurled it down the hill.

"How is she? It's been months since I've seen her."

"She is in love. Nothing could make her unhappy now," Colin said in a sarcastic tone.

Hart laughed. "Love isn't such a terrible thing, North."

Colin glared over at his childhood friend. "Love is nothing but pain and agony."

"So when does the happy bride arrive?"

"She and her mother will arrive in a month. I believe they wish to refurbish the house so it is in perfect condition for the wedding guests."

"Is there that much to do?" Hart asked with a frown.

"The house is a disaster," Colin admitted. "The roof leaks, the wallpaper is falling down, and the garden's overgrown. It will cost me a fortune to get this house up to snuff for a wedding."

"True, but at least once it's done the house will be ready for you to live in again." Hart paused for a moment. "It would be pleasant to have a neighbor out here again . . . even if it is you." He let out an easy laugh. "After all, Middleton is rarely at his home. I feel as if I'm the only one who enjoys country life."

Colin shook his head. "Once the vows are said, I will leave. And I won't be back."

"You have a responsibility to your estate, North," Hart said quietly.

"Do not attempt to tell me how to manage my estates or my duty. I performed my duty and look where it got me.

Thomas or his son can inherit this bloody house and the memories that go with it."

Colin picked up another rock and heaved it down the hill. This would be the longest two months of his life. He just wanted this wedding done now so he could return to London. Why hadn't he disregarded Kate's wishes? She and her mother could have hired all the help they needed without his assistance. But he'd never been able to ignore Kate's pleas to assist them. She'd told him she didn't feel comfortable making changes to his home without his permission.

He could do this. It was only for two months. He closed his eyes for a quick moment only to see Miss White again. Why couldn't he forget her today?

"Who do you think was the first tenant to greet me?" Colin asked as frustration rolled through his body. He wasn't about to tell Hart the circumstances surrounding the incident.

"I have no idea."

"Miss White."

Hart glanced back at the house. "But North, she's not the same woman. That was—"

"Her mother. I realize that." Colin blew out a long breath. "But it changes nothing. I'm tired of these women believing they are the reason our lands are fertile. That they are the cause of our wealth. They actually believe they know more than the physicians and surgeons."

Hart shrugged and glanced away. "Perhaps they do."

"How can you believe that?"

"Miss Featherstone and her mother saved my mother's life a few years ago. The physician said there was nothing he could do because she was dying from cancer. But with their herbs and loving care, three years later, my mother still lives. Not only that, but my mother is healthier than she's ever been."

Hart went quiet for a long moment before finally saying, "I owe them both everything."

Colin wanted to rail at his friend for his foolishness. It was God's will that his mother was still alive, not some damned women with their infernal herbs.

Selina paced the small confines of her cottage. The fury of meeting the duke yesterday had not diminished. How was she supposed to leave the estate, even if it was for only two months? There were two tenants who would deliver in the next week or two. She had to be here for them. Besides, where was she supposed to go? She'd never met her father's family and knew of no way to contact them. Her mother, like Selina, had been an only child. That left her twin friends, Mia and Tia. Although, Selina knew neither of them had room at their cottages.

She walked to the window and looked out at the gray day. She'd lived in this cottage all her life. Her mother's ancestors had lived either in this cottage or on this land somewhere. Why should she be forced to leave because he couldn't forget the past?

As she stared out the window, she noticed Mr. Sellers arrive with a horse. Selina grabbed her things and rushed outside.

"Come on, miss," Mr. Sellers said with a grin. "We don't have that much time."

"Thank you, Mr. Sellers."

He nodded to her and then assisted her onto the mare. "Just doing my part."

They rode quickly to the stables. She glanced up at the house and her heart started to pound against her chest. If the duke discovered her here today, she had no idea what he might do. There were still several rooms she needed to cleanse and it might take days to complete. But this was what she'd been raised to do. She wouldn't let one insufferable duke stop her.

After Mr. Sellers helped her down, she ran for the house. Mr. Roberts opened the door for her.

"Do hurry, miss," Mr. Roberts said. "He used to ride for at least an hour, so do what you can during that time."

She removed her short boots and dropped them by the door.

"Miss, you really shouldn't walk around in your stocking feet," Mr. Roberts admonished.

The dear old man was always trying to drum some propriety into her head. He should know by now it would never work. "I won't come in and track mud all over, causing you even more work."

Mr. Roberts only shook his head. "Very well."

"Have the footmen open the windows in the study, salon, and library. I will work there first." She couldn't go into his bedroom today. The idea of working in his bedchamber again sent an odd sensation to her belly. Far better to ignore that room for now.

"Yes, miss."

While the footmen readied the room, Selina breathed in deeply to calm her nerves. She lit the sage and blew it out. A long line of smoke billowed up from the herb. Slowly, she walked into the library and moved counterclockwise through the room, taking a few extra moments in every corner.

"No dark spirits are allowed in this room," she mumbled as she walked. "Only good will remain in this room." The smoke scented the room even with the windows open. She passed the bookshelves and looked up at them in envy. If only she had access to some of his books.

Once finished in the library, she made her way to the salon. Repeating the same actions, she concentrated on her words and not the ticking clock. With two rooms finished, she moved to his study. She had at least fifteen minutes left.

Before she started, she glanced about the room. Everything in this room was meant for him. A large, cherry desk took up one end of the room. She could picture him sitting in that leather chair working on bills and plans for the estate. At the other end, a large fireplace would keep the room warm in the cold winter months. She could imagine curling herself up in the blue velvet chair by the fireplace, reading a wonderful novel for hours, while the duke worked at his desk.

"I must be going mad," she whispered with a shake of her head.

She resumed her cleansing. But she lost her concentration due to a commotion from the back of the house. Loud voices continued to come closer until she realized it was the duke. Not knowing what else to do, she snuffed the sage and slipped behind the gold velvet curtain. Hopefully, he wouldn't notice her feet sticking out. Fear of discovery caused her heart to pound against her chest.

She took a deep breath to calm herself and listen as he came closer. His footsteps sounded different today. His gait was uneven as if he wasn't walking correctly.

"Why do I smell goddamn sage?" he shouted.

"Now, Your Grace, it's just left over from what she did yesterday," Mr. Roberts replied. "You must sit down and get off that ankle."

"My ankle is fine," he rasped.

"I could call for Miss White to look at it. I am quite certain it wouldn't take long for her to arrive."

"Absolutely not! I will not have that blasted woman in my house playing physician."

He'd hurt his ankle and still he wouldn't let her examine him? She really should help with him. She tamped down the idea of giving the man aid. He wanted her off his estate so he could rot for all she cared.

"Just get me a glass of brandy. That will fix me up."

Brandy? At ten in the morning? That was not what he needed. She couldn't ignore what she'd been raised to do. She pulled back the curtain and glared at him.

"You will not drink brandy at this hour. You need to get off that foot and elevate it."

"What the bloody hell are you doing back in my house? And hiding behind a curtain!"

She paid no heed to the glare he leveled at her. "I was doing my job."

"I told you not to come back here," he said, hobbling for his desk. "No one needs you here." He winced and sat in the leather chair.

She crossed her arms over her chest. "It appears that *you* need me."

He shook his head. A lock of black hair fell upon his forehead. "I only need you to leave. My ankle will be fine."

"Let me see your foot," she said, walking closer to him.

"Get out of my house," he ordered.

She smiled brightly at him. "There is something you should know about me right now, Your Grace."

"Oh?" His blue eyes were as hard as sapphires as he stared at her.

She closed the distance between them and then picked up his right foot. "I don't take orders from anyone." She leaned in closer until she could feel his heated breath and whispered, "Not even a duke."

She gently pulled his boot off as he clenched his jaw. "Damn you," he whispered.

"Damn me? Look at this ankle." Already it was swelling and turning black-and-blue. "You're lucky I didn't have to cut your lovely boot off your foot."

"I want you out of my house," he said again.

She glanced up at him with a little smirk. "I know you do." Returning her gaze to his foot, she shook her head. "I do not like the speed of this swelling. Mr. Roberts," she called, knowing he was right outside the room.

"Yes, miss."

"Get me some ice from the icehouse, crush it up, and wrap

it in a cloth. Ask your wife to get me some of the willow bark I gave to her."

"Yes, miss," Mr. Roberts replied before leaving them alone again.

"You have them all wrapped around your little finger, don't you?" he asked petulantly.

She pretended to examine his ankle, preferring it to the look of loathing she'd see in his eyes. "Perhaps I do. But while you are gallivanting about town without a care, I am here taking care of your servants and tenants."

He released a long breath. "I do not gallivant about town."

She looked up at him from under her lashes. "Oh?"

"No. I have responsibilities in London to attend to . . . such as Parliament."

"You have responsibilities here too," she said and then wished she had kept her mouth closed for once.

"Do watch what you say to me," he warned.

Selina stared at the swelling in his foot before gently pressing a finger into his ankle.

"Damn you," he whispered as he clutched the arms of his chair.

"I was just testing the amount of pain you felt."

"Oh? And I suppose hiding behind my curtain was part of the treatment? Do you do that for everyone or just me?"

Selina rolled her eyes and bit her tongue. "I am quite sure you know why I was here."

"Yes, I do. Now . . ." He pulled himself up out of the chair to tower over her. "Get out of my house."

"Here's the ice, miss," Mr. Roberts said as he walked into the room and then halted midstride.

"Escort Miss White out, Mr. Roberts," the duke ordered.

"That will not be necessary, Your Grace," Selina said with a smile. She walked over and took the ice and herbs from the butler. "Mr. Roberts, I just need some cloth to bind his injury."

She turned back to face Northrop. "Your Grace, sit back down this instant. My duty is to keep you healthy and standing on a twisted ankle is not good for it."

He started to rebuke her and took a step forward. He muttered a curse as he grabbed the desk for support.

"Now," she ordered.

"Very well," he said in a low voice. "Just wrap my ankle and be done with it."

"No, we do this my way." Selina crossed her arms over her chest and smiled down at him. "Put your foot on the desk to elevate it."

With a low growl, he did as she asked. She pressed her fingers over the bone and down the length of his foot. Her hands trembled slightly as she lifted his foot and moved it. What was wrong with her? He was a patient just like any other.

"I don't believe anything is broken," she finally said.

"I could have told you that. It's a sprain, nothing more."

"How exactly did you sprain your ankle while out riding?"

His cheeks reddened slightly. "It doesn't matter."

"Tell me."

"When I jumped off my horse, my foot landed on a rock. My ankle gave out and I went down." He glared up at her. "I must have looked like a complete fool to my own groomsmen."

A loud cough sounded from the doorway. Selina turned to see Mr. Roberts standing there staring at her hands on the duke's foot. She stared down at the duke's ankle as heat crossed her cheeks.

Oh, God, she had been caressing his foot.

Chapter 3

Colin watched as Miss White's face turned bright pink. Perhaps it hadn't been his imagination that her light touch felt much more like a seductive caress than a clinical examination. As soon as Roberts entered the room, her critical focus returned.

As much as she irritated him, he was certain that she took her duty seriously. This was not the first time he'd sprained this ankle. Her scrutiny of his foot showed her skill.

"I will bind your foot now, Your Grace." She picked up the linen cloth for binding and started at the arch of his foot.

When she lifted his foot, a spark skipped up his leg and all thoughts of her skill went out the door. Colin closed his eyes to get her out of his mind. That only increased his awareness of her every movement.

The scent of lavender wafted around him, enticing him. Her soft fingers moved across his calf as she wrapped his foot. He imagined her hands skimming over his body, touching his chest . . . his hard. . . . He blinked his eyes open.

Dear God, he certainly couldn't find her attractive.

Her unbound hair fell over her face as she worked on the binding. He swallowed back the desire to brush the hair away so he could stare at her face again. His gaze moved to the floor only to see her stocking-covered toes peeking out from her skirts. Why did the sight of her toes make his heart suddenly drum against his chest?

She was the wise woman. It was her mother's fault that Mary died that night. With Miss White gone, he could concentrate on the good things to come for Kate and not all the horrors he remembered.

"Thank you," he said gruffly as she tied the binding into a knot.

"You are most welcome, Your Grace." She backed a step away from him and then held out her hands as if waiting for him to rise. "You need to lie down and elevate your foot for the rest of the day. Keep ice on it for twenty minutes at a time, several times during the day. I'll come back tomorrow and check on the swelling."

"I do not have time to be resting. There are far too many things that need to be completed before the wedding." Colin crossed his arms over his chest.

"You can direct the servants from the sofa in the salon. But you will need at least two or three days off that ankle."

"I have sprained this ankle before and I know exactly what it needs," he retorted. "Now take your leave."

"As you wish." She walked back to the windowsill and picked up her ceramic bowl with the burned sage. "May I at least continue with this?"

"No. I do not need my house cleansed." He'd had enough of her fussing about him. All he wanted was her out of his house now. She brought back memories that needed to be forgotten. And desires he couldn't act upon.

"Very well then. Good day, Your Grace." She turned and left without another word.

Colin sat back in his leather chair and blew out a long breath. He needed to get rid of her forever. The longer she stayed on the estate, the more his memories would eat into him. Perhaps once she left he could be happy here again. Her departure might free him of the strangling recollections so he might enjoy his home again.

Determined to find her and tell her at once that she must leave immediately, he stood and took a step. Pain shot up the length of his leg. "Dammit!"

As much as he didn't want to admit it, she was right. He needed to take a day or two off his foot. "Roberts," he shouted.

"Yes, Your Grace," Roberts said as he reached the entrance to the study.

"Get me a cane and help me into the salon." Dammit. He hated feeling like an invalid in front of his servants.

"Of course, Your Grace. I'm so glad you are taking Miss White's advice."

"I am only doing exactly as I have done every time I've wrenched my ankle over the years."

"Of course, Your Grace."

Miss White. He swore that if he heard that name one more time today, he would dismiss the person who said it. *Miss White.* He didn't even know her Christian name.

"Roberts," he asked as they hobbled toward the salon, "what is Miss White's name?"

"Selina, sir."

Selina. A lovely name for a beautiful woman. He shook his head quickly. He could not allow his thoughts to go there again. She was just as bad as her mother.

He needed her gone immediately.

Selina approached the house with trepidation the next day. The duke reminded her of a wounded animal, ready to strike out at anyone trying to help him. She would need to handle him with extreme care. But no one, not even the Duke of Northrop, would dissuade her from her duties on the estate.

The door opened as she approached. Mr. Roberts stood in the doorway with a frown.

"Good morning, Mr. Roberts. How is he today?" she asked softly, in case he was within hearing distance.

"He's a dreadful patient, miss. Bad-tempered, drinking, and swearing. At least he did stay on the sofa yesterday."

"And today?"

"He's in his study."

"I do need to see him. I must check the swelling."

Mr. Roberts opened the door and let her inside. Once inside, she handed a small bag to him. "This is for your wife."

"Thank you, miss. She's feeling completely well now."

"Tell her to take it in a cup of tea once a week."

"I will. Now, just let me see if His Grace is receiving callers."

"Nonsense," she replied, walking down the long corridor. "I shall announce myself."

"That's highly improper, miss." Mr. Roberts whispered, "He'll hate that."

She smiled back at the butler. "I know."

Selina tiptoed to the threshold of the study. Glancing inside the room, she noticed the duke sitting at his desk with his foot propped on a stack of books. At least he'd listened to her about elevating his foot.

She hesitated at the door, watching as he read a piece of correspondence. His black brows drew into a deep frown and he muttered something she couldn't hear. He was truly one of the most handsome men she'd ever seen. His broad shoulders filled the chair. She bit down on her lower lip, remembering the sensation of her fingers on his bare leg yesterday. He was all muscle and strength. It was a pity he was betrothed. He would have made a wonderful lover.

She smiled at the thought. Being a wise woman, no one cared if she married or had a child without the bonds of matrimony. The only priority was bearing a child . . . not just a child, a daughter to teach the ways of the healers.

While she hadn't taken a man to her bed yet, she thought

the duke might not be a bad first choice. But she would never do such a thing with a married man or even an engaged one. Pity that. She had a feeling he would be rather fine in bed.

"Is there some reason you are here today?" the duke asked roughly.

Selina blinked and heat crossed her cheeks. "I apologize, Your Grace. I was woolgathering."

"Indeed? Or attempting to determine the best way to announce yourself?"

"A little of both," she said and then walked directly into the room. Putting aside her mad desire for a man she could never have, she placed her wool satchel on the desk. "I am here to check on the progress of your foot."

"And if I say no?" He stared up at her with those icy blue eyes.

His intense look almost intimidated her . . . almost. "Then I would have to take your foot like this," she said, lifting his foot into the air and then placing it against her belly, "and unwrap your ankle with no assistance from you."

She could have sworn she heard a low growl from his throat. Ignoring the sensation of his bare foot on her stomach, she focused her attention on his ankle. "The swelling is down from yesterday."

"I am quite well."

"How many times have you sprained this ankle?"

"At least five," he replied. "The first time I was twelve when I fell out of a tree."

Selina shook her head. "It must never have healed properly. Who wrapped it then?" She felt him tense under her fingers.

"Your mother," he said in a low voice.

"Oh." Selina said nothing else. Thinking back, she realized that was about the time her father had died. Mother never completely recovered from his death. It was not long after her father's death that the drinking began.

"Perhaps there was nothing else she could do," she finally whispered.

"Or perhaps my stepmother should have called a physician to wrap it correctly," he retorted.

She remained silent and pulled out fresh linen from her satchel. After binding his foot again, she gently placed it back on the stack of books. "Do keep ice on it again today."

"I know what to do for my foot, Miss White."

"Excuse me, Your Grace," Mr. Roberts said from the threshold. "Miss White, Mrs. Graham asked that you attend to her mother as quickly as possible."

Selina gathered her things. "Of course," she replied.

"Is there something wrong with Mrs. Graham's mother?"

"I won't know until I get there," she lied. After all his talk about a physician's abilities and training, she wasn't about to admit that she was most likely going to watch a woman die tonight.

Colin sat at his desk with his foot propped up as dusk enveloped the estate. A cool breeze fluttered the curtains. He glanced over at them only to notice a woman sitting on the edge of the reflecting pond. Why would Miss White be sitting out there at this time of evening?

For a long moment, he just stared. The wind blew her blond tresses in front of her face. She quickly brushed the hairs away. He felt entranced when she was near. It made no sense. She was the exact opposite of Mary.

"Excuse me, Your Grace."

He glanced over at the door where Roberts stood with a grim look on his face. "What is it?"

"Mrs. Fitzhugh passed a short while ago."

"Mrs. Fitzhugh?"

"Mrs. Graham's mother, sir. She had been ill for months." While he'd read the rambling letters his steward sent him every month, he had no real knowledge of his tenants. Their passing had meant nothing to him. He looked back out at Miss White and wondered if she was responsible for the woman's death. She had left here to attend to her. And yet, the wise woman couldn't heal her. "Thank you, Roberts."

Wincing, he stood and reached for his cane. He ambled through the French door and down toward the pond. At first, she didn't notice his approach; she continued to stare down into the water. When a twig snapped under Colin's foot, she looked up and shook her head.

"You should not be on that ankle, Your Grace."

"And you should not be on my land, Miss White," he retorted and then sat on the edge of the pond to get his weight off his ankle. He did his best to conceal from her the pain he felt. She'd probably give him some damn herbs for the ache.

"I was assisting a tenant." The breeze blew her muslin skirts about her slim calves.

"I heard Mrs. Fitzhugh passed."

She nodded.

"Perhaps a physician—"

"Could have hastened her death? Yes, I'm sure that fool man in town would have done just that."

"And yet, you couldn't help her either." He folded his arms over his chest.

A slight smile lifted her full lips upward. "You do not know the first thing about Mrs. Fitzhugh or her condition."

"Do inform, *Dr. White.*"

"Very well, the woman was eighty-five years old and had lost her husband of over sixty years only last year. Once he had passed, she lost her will to live. She had loved him since they were both children. She couldn't imagine life without him."

Colin couldn't help but snort. "And that is why you are not a physician. You believe nonsense such as people dying over broken hearts."

"And no part of you died when your wife passed?"

Her barb hit its mark. "How dare you mention my wife! How I felt after she died is not your concern."

"Then what exactly is your diagnosis for poor Mrs. Fitzhugh?" She cocked a brow at him as if daring him to answer.

He laughed slightly. "I would not dream of playing at doctoring. That takes training and education."

"And I am simply an uneducated woman."

"Education or not, you are a woman."

She narrowed her eyes. "A woman could never be a physician, could she?"

"No," he replied simply. "It is far too taxing."

"You pompous ass," she said as she rose. "You have no idea the number of lives I have saved."

"Purely accidental." He had no idea why he continued to verbally spar with her. Perhaps it was the fact that he could. In London, the women would never disagree with anything he said. But they all wanted the same thing from him: marriage.

As she walked away, he realized how much he'd enjoyed taunting her, watching the color rise to her cheeks in anger, and the way her eyes flashed emerald.

Dear God, his brother was right. He needed a woman.

Chapter 4

The next afternoon Selina arrived at the duke's home with a different tactic in mind. She would not attempt to engage the narrow-minded man in any form of conversation, especially none concerning what she did at the estate. She would check on his foot and then leave. And she most certainly would not caress his foot or leg in any manner.

As she approached the enormous house, she wondered if this visit was even necessary. He was able to walk to the pond yesterday. Surely, by today he would be even more capable of putting weight on his ankle.

Perhaps she should forget checking in on him and go see Mrs. Thomas. The woman was already due to deliver any day. Selina paused on the gravel-lined drive and thought about the matter at hand. Her mother would have told her to perform her duty whether the pompous ass wanted her assistance or not. Still, she could go visit Mrs. Thomas and then come back to see the duke. Having made her decision, she turned to walk away until a low chuckle stopped her.

"Don't tell me *Dr. White* is leaving without checking on her patient?"

She whirled around to see the duke leaning against a tree with his arms folded over his chest. Her breath caught as the breeze fluttered his black hair. She wanted to slap that arrogant look off his face. But since she could not do that, she would force him to put up with an exam from her.

"I thought I had forgotten something but I was wrong." She walked closer to him until a hint of sandalwood drifted by her nose. "We need to go inside so I can check on your foot now."

"My foot is fine and I would like you to leave now."

Her heart pounded, not just at his attitude but far more likely at his nearness. Spying the cane leaning against the tree, she said, "I see you are still using the cane. Therefore, I insist on examining your foot again today."

"Indeed? Exactly how do you propose to do that when I am standing on my foot?"

"You really should not be on your foot, Your Grace. If you promise to go inside and prop your foot up, I will not touch your foot again."

He gave her a half smile. "Touch? Or caress?"

Mortification heated her cheeks until they burned. "I did not caress your foot."

"Yes, you did," he whispered, leaning in closer to her. "Even Mr. Roberts noticed."

Oh, dear Lord. This man was a dreadful person for mentioning such a thing to her. "I am leaving now, Your Grace. Good day."

She turned back around and noticed Randall running toward them. He at least wouldn't notice anything between her and His Grace.

"Miss White, Mrs. Thomas needs you now."

"Who is Mrs. Thomas?" the duke asked from behind her.

"She is the wife of one of your tenants. She must be ready to deliver." Selina opened her small valise to make certain she had everything she would need for a birth.

"Oh," he said in a stilted voice. "You must be off then."

"Off? I will need to run to make it on time. After four

babies, this one may come before I get there." She closed her valise and raced down the drive.

Colin watched Miss White rush from the estate. His stomach suddenly ached. He strolled to the large reflecting pond where two swans paddled. Sitting on the concrete edge, he watched the birds swim.

Turning around, he stared up at his ancestral home. Built two hundred years ago, it was a massive structure with more rooms than he would ever need. His mother used to hold large country parties here and filled the numerous bedchambers.

For over an hour, he sat and looked at the house and grounds. Children should fill some of those bedrooms and run across the manicured gardens. There should be happiness here, not sorrow.

Days like today, Colin wondered how his father would have advised him. Would the old duke understand Colin's reluctance to live here? Considering his father remarried eighteen months after his mother's death, Colin doubted the old duke would understand. Colin picked up a flat rock and skipped it across the water. He was certain his father would have told him to perform his duty as duke and mourn his wife for a year. Then find a new one and forget the first wife.

Only it had never been that easy. Mary had been a very special woman. He'd never met a woman since who cared for people the way she had. He'd never loved a woman other than her . . . and never would again. She had taken his heart to the grave with her.

His mind turned to the green-eyed woman who seemed to bother him far too much. She forced images into his mind that had no purpose and would only cause him frustration. He closed his eyes and remembered the way her breasts pressed against the fabric of her dress as she stood her ground with him. Her unbound hair had caressed her cheeks making him want to move the hair and let his fingers graze her skin.

He blinked his eyes open in anger. The last woman he wanted in his bed was that little hoyden. He had to get her away. The temptation was far too great with her nearby. He felt guilty for asking her to leave while he was here but it was his estate and therefore his right. He had an obligation to Kate to make this wedding wonderful. He could not do that with Selina near, inciting his anger with her talk of medicine and herbs and her tempting scent driving him mad with desire.

She had to leave.

There was no other choice if he was to keep his sanity.

"What are you doing out here again? I told you to keep that foot elevated."

Colin closed his eyes against the instant irritation he felt at being disturbed. It wasn't the interruption that bothered him, but who disrupted his peace.

"What are you doing here, Miss White?" he bit out.

"I always come to the pond after a child is born."

She sat down on the wall and removed her short boots. She then reached under her skirts and pulled off her stockings. Colin stared at her delicate feet for a moment as awareness shot through him. She shivered as she dipped her feet into the water. The woman had no sense of propriety at all. Didn't she understand showing her shapely calf to some men was an invitation to trouble?

"The cold water would be good for your foot," she said casually as if unaware of how inappropriate her actions were.

"My foot is fine." His gaze dropped to her slender bare legs rising from the water.

She tilted her head up and stared at the sky. Slowly, she released a sigh. He stared at the long length of her neck and wondered if it would taste soft and sweet. Colin swore to himself. He had to stop that line of thinking.

"It didn't take long with Mrs. Thomas," he commented, remembering the hours of agony Mary endured.

"I barely made it in time. Mrs. Thomas was already to pushing when I arrived. Ten minutes later, the baby was born."

She made it sound so easy. Colin knew it wasn't always so. "Why do you come here after a birth?"

She shrugged again. "I don't know. It's just something I've done since my first delivery. After the excitement of helping a new life into the world, being here calms me."

"I take it Mrs. Thomas and her child are well?"

"Yes," she said with a wistful smile. "A healthy baby boy."

Colin looked away as pain seared his heart. Mary had been so insistent that she would deliver a boy for him. And she'd been right.

"What's wrong?" she asked softly.

"Nothing." He swung his legs around and stood. As long as she was here, he would never be able to forget what happened here. "Enjoy your peace . . . while you have it."

"While I have it . . . what do you mean?"

"I want the cottage cleared out in the next week and you gone," he said roughly.

She turned around and stood with her hands on her hips. "How could you think to do such a thing? My family has been here as long as yours. My mother and grandmothers have kept your family safe from harm, helped birth your heirs, you included, and tended your family when sick."

"You are not a physician. You dabble in herbs and call yourself a healer. I don't need a healer here. And I don't need *you* here." He turned to leave but stopped at the sound of her overconfident laugh.

"You need me more than any of your relatives did, Your Grace."

He looked back at her trying to ignore the tears shimmering in her eyes. "I don't need you."

"I won't leave here. I have just as much right to be here as you do."

"Miss White, if you have not vacated the property within a week, I shall send for the constable."

"You will do what you must," she said softly. "And so will I."

Selina strode back to her cottage determined not to let him run her off her property. He could call the constable or even the regent. She would never leave her family home. She flung the door open so hard it bounced against the wall, rattling the dishes in the cabinet.

She walked into her bedroom and opened the trunk at the bottom of her bed. As she rifled through the mess of papers and things, tears blurred her eyes when she could not find what she needed. That document had to be here somewhere! Without it, she might have no choice but to leave her home.

The late afternoon turned to evening. She opened the bottle of wine Mr. Thomas had given her as payment for her services this afternoon. Two glasses later, she went back to her search. There was still the bottom drawer of her desk to investigate.

She opened the drawer and sifted through the old papers. She finally found what she'd been searching for and now he would never be able to make her leave. She sipped another glass of wine for fortification and then was ready to face her demon again. Armed with ammunition, she headed back to the duke's house. No one would forcibly remove her from her cottage.

A footman opened the door for her. "Welcome back, Miss White," Randall said with a grin. "Shall I announce you?"

"No, thank you, Randall. Where is the bastard?"

Stilted footsteps sounded from upstairs. "The bastard is right here, Miss White."

She glanced up to see him glaring down at her. Did he actually think he could intimidate her by standing up there? He had a lot to learn about her.

"I believe I asked you to leave," he said as he crossed his arms over his chest.

She marched up the wide marble staircase, only grasping the rail once for support. "Hah! I have all the proof I need, right here," she said, waving the paper in front of him.

He shook his head. "You embarrass yourself, Miss White. Please leave before I call the footmen to escort you out." He turned away and walked toward a long corridor.

"Not until you read this paper."

He said nothing but continued to march away from her.

Selina followed him quickly. "Don't you dare walk away from me!" Spying a small pillow on a chair, she picked it up and hurled it at him. She smiled as it hit him directly between the shoulder blades. But her quick slice of happiness faded when he turned around with an ominous look on his face.

He strode toward her with his fists clenched. She wanted to run but her legs seemed unable to move. Just as he reached her position, she turned to run.

He caught her immediately and pushed her against the wall. "Who do you think you are to come into my home uninvited and order me to read some blasted paper you've found? I am master here and you . . . are nothing."

Selina gasped at the force of his words. Her eyes widened and her breath quickened. He stood only inches away from her and her senses filled with him. A hint of sandalwood drifted past her nose as he stood over her. *Nothing!* He thought she was worthless. He had no idea of her importance.

"I am your wise woman, Your Grace," she said slowly, enunciating each word with purpose.

"No," he whispered harshly, "you are not. You are nothing but a leech on my property. I want you gone."

"I have a paper that proves my right to stay."

He yanked the paper out of her hand and opened it. His lips twitched as he scanned the document. He handed the worn page to her and said, "You may know about herbs but you know nothing about the law."

"What do you mean?"

He backed away from her with a shake of his head. "That paper gives your great-grandmother the right to live here into perpetuity."

"Exactly! Since I am her granddaughter, I also have that right."

"No, Miss White. Only your great-grandmother had that right. It does not give her progeny the same right." He started to walk down the corridor again. "Good evening."

Selina couldn't move. All these years she'd assumed she had the right to live on this land. But she didn't. The duke could demand she leave for any reason. Whether it be blaming her mother for the death of his wife and child or the inane idea that as an uneducated woman she shouldn't be attempting to heal people. She clutched her stomach in pain. She'd never questioned her right to live here. This land was her home too.

There was nothing she could do now. Tears blurred her sight as she staggered to the staircase.

Slowly, she walked down the stairs. Randall's face was pale as she passed him.

"I'm so sorry, Miss White," he whispered with a quick glance up the stairs.

"Thank you, Randall."

"It's gotten dark, do you want me to have a footman escort you home?"

She knew the estate was safe for her to walk even at night. Every one of the tenants was her friend. "No, I shall be fine."

She glanced back up the steps to see the duke staring at her.

"At least take a lantern, miss," Randall said so quietly the duke wouldn't hear.

"No, thank you, Randall," she replied loudly. She glanced up at the duke, who stood at the railing glaring at her. "I know my way around this estate better than anyone . . . even the duke."

Chapter 5

"When you are duke, every tenant is your responsibility."

The sound of his father's voice echoed in his ears. Colin knew she'd aimed her barb directly at him for being gone so long. She dared to imply that she knew the land better than he did. He'd raced over the countryside as a child. He knew the dips and peaks in the land, where the rabbit holes were and the fox dens.

Staring at the closed door, he realized that she had walked out the door without a candle or escort. "Randall, follow her home."

"She told me not to, Your Grace." Randall looked down at the marble floor.

The man was afraid of the woman. *Dammit.* He didn't want to follow her but it was his duty. He winced slightly as he walked down the steps.

"Open the door, Randall," he demanded.

"You're going out, sir?"

"Yes. You should have insisted she take a footman with her," Colin chided. "There are wild animals out there." Not to mention tenants he didn't even know any longer. Any one of them might try to harm her.

"I'm sorry, Your Grace. It will never happen again."

Colin breathed in the fragrant June air. He could just make out her yellow muslin as she walked along the tree line. Foolish woman didn't know enough to stay away from the trees where the animals might be hiding.

Not wanting to get into another argument with her, he trailed behind her. The full moon cast a white light on her golden hair. Her full hips swayed under her skirts suddenly spreading lurid thoughts into his head. With her fire, he could only imagine what she would be like in bed. Lusty. Wanton.

Christ. What the bloody hell was wrong with him? He didn't desire the termagant. He wanted her off his property. He wanted her and the memories she brought gone.

Or did he just want the temptation she wrought removed?

"I know you're back there but I do wonder why."

"Until you leave my property, you are my responsibility."

"No, I am no one's care. I am nothing, just a poor woman with no home. I am certainly not your burden."

Guilt sliced into him, but he pushed the feeling down. He walked a few steps behind her as the scent of lavender filled the air. He knew it came from her. The scent had swirled around him during his rage in the hall. She was as she'd said, just a poor woman and now he was taking her home away from her.

But he would not give in to the guilt. He'd had enough regrets for his actions over the past eight years. "I will speak with the Earl of Hartsfield. He seems to have great respect for his wise women. I am certain he would love to have another."

"Stupid man," she mumbled under her breath.

"Excuse me?"

"Hartsfield already has two wise women. Why would he need another?"

Colin went silent for a moment. "At least he will take you in."

"Oh, then it must be for the best. After all, one of my

ancestors has taken care of this estate and your family for centuries but you obviously don't need one."

He blew out a breath. "There is more to this than that."

She turned around sharply, almost running into him. "And what exactly is it?"

How could he begin to explain his reasoning when he didn't know himself? It was simpler to give the answer she would assume. "I cannot have the reminder here."

"Reminder of what?"

"Why my wife and son died," he muttered, staring off into the forest. "I need you to leave so I don't have to relive it every day that I'm here."

"Until you realize there was nothing," she paused briefly, "my mother could have done, you will never heal. It was God's will. I see it all the time. People die before they should and there is nothing I can do about it. God knows I wish I could."

God's will.

How many people had tried to tell him that? But he knew it wasn't God's will. It had not been God who insisted Mary deliver at the estate. He'd wanted his heir born at the estate just as he'd been born here. He was the reason Mary died that day. She'd wanted to remain in London near her mother for the birth. But he'd insisted that his heir would be born at the ducal estate. Just as all the previous dukes had been born here.

Miss White turned back around and headed for her cottage. "Good night, Your Grace."

"Good night, Miss White."

Once he saw that she was inside and a candle flickered, he headed back to the estate . . . alone with his guilt.

Two days had passed with no sign of Miss White. Not that he'd had time to even think about her with the workers arriving daily to get the house in order for the wedding. But today, he left instructions for the foreman and then departed for a ride.

He flicked the reins of his gelding and headed toward her cottage. As he approached, he saw nothing to indicate she was in residence. Perhaps she had already found accommodations elsewhere. He slowly jumped down and walked to her window. Peering in, he noticed a bowl on the table and the embers in the fireplace. It appeared she'd made no effort to start packing her things.

He would have to speak with her again and insist she make arrangements. Or perhaps it was time to do that for her.

He climbed back on Zeus and headed toward Hart's lands. As he rode, he nodded to several tenants, only to have them turn their backs at him. What was that about? He could only guess that they were displeased that he hadn't visited yet. But with the workers arriving daily, he had to make certain they knew what needed to be done. Tomorrow, he would make the effort to greet his tenants.

Urging Zeus to a run, he flew across the countryside. He had missed getting a good ride every morning. Finally, he slowed his horse to stop when he reached Hart's stables. He climbed down and handed the reins to a lad.

"Give him a good rubdown, boy," Colin said and tossed him a coin.

"Thank you, sir."

"That's Yer Grace," an older man said and whacked the boy on the backside of the head.

Colin shook his head as he walked toward the door.

"Yes?" a butler said after opening the door.

Colin realized that he must have been gone far too long if his friend's butler didn't recognize him. "I'm here to see the earl."

The butler waited for a card.

"I don't have a card, my good man. I am Northrop."

The butler's blue eyes widened. "Excuse me, Your Grace. Come right in."

Colin followed the man down the gallery filled with family portraits until they reached Hart's study.

Hart looked up with an easy smile. "To what do I owe this honor, North?"

"I need to speak with you in private."

"Of course." Hart walked toward the door. "Do you want coffee? I just asked them to bring me some."

"Yes, thank you."

Hart called for a servant to fetch them coffee and two cups. The servant returned with remarkable speed and placed the tray on a table near the window. Hart poured two cups and then handed one to him. Colin took the drink and sipped it slowly. Warmth spread throughout his body as he drank the slightly bitter brew.

"How is the refurbishing coming along?"

"Slow. It might be hard to have everything ready before the wedding."

Hart smiled. "Kate won't mind. She is a very even-tempered young woman."

Her temperament was one of her finest attributes. She would make a wonderful wife. In that sense, she reminded him of Mary.

"Now, what really brings you here?" Hart asked as he placed his cup down on the table next to him. "I doubt you came all this way to chat about your house."

"I'm wondering if you can do me a favor."

"Of course, name it."

"Do you have space on the estate for another tenant?"

Hart eyed him suspiciously. "I do. Are you looking to keep a mistress here?"

"God, no. I just want Miss White off my land."

Hart shook his head. "Don't do that, North. You are begging for trouble if you do."

"I am sick to death of everyone telling me how much these women do for us. I want her off my estate." Colin finished the rest of his coffee and then placed the cup on Hart's desk. "Will you take her or not?"

"Of course. I'm sure Miss Featherstone will be happy for the company. And Mrs. Featherstone will appreciate the help."

"Exactly." And Colin was pleased that he had this mess finally settled. "I shall tell her to be packed by Friday."

"Shall I send a man for her?"

"No, one of my men will bring her and her things over." Colin stood and nodded. "Thank you."

Hart shook his head. "I still believe you are making a mistake, North. Miss White has done nothing but good for your tenants."

"Not for me," he muttered.

"They will hate you for forcing their wise woman to leave. Most of them believe these women keep them safe from harm and the land bountiful."

"Then they are fools," Colin remarked.

"Very well, anyone else I can take off your hands? A good footman or two, maybe?"

Colin smiled. "Highly unlikely you would want any of my elderly servants. Just take the wise woman."

"As you wish."

With that settled, he could get on with his life. Already, he felt as if a weight had been lifted off his chest. Now, with Miss White gone, he could concentrate on the wedding.

Selina felt the bulging belly of Susan Wells and attempted not to frown. The baby was due any day but Selina hadn't felt a movement in the past few minutes. "Has the baby been moving a lot?"

"Not as much this week but I'm not sure there's anywhere to go."

Selina smiled at the young woman. First babies were always the hardest and sometimes they didn't cooperate. "Well, perhaps he is just sleeping for me today."

God, she hoped that was all it was, but she didn't have a good feeling. She hadn't lost a baby in over two years. There was nothing worse . . . except losing the mother too. "I will stop by tomorrow and see if we can't wake him up."

"Probably as soon as you leave, he'll be kickin' up a storm," Susan said with a laugh.

She prayed Susan was right. If there was still no movement by tomorrow, she might have to brace Susan for the worst. A knot tightened in her belly. She packed up her things, said her good-byes, and walked home.

She'd spent the past two days trying to figure out what she would do if the duke upheld his threat to make her leave. Mia's small home was full with her mother living there too. Tia's cottage on Viscount Middleton's land was smaller than Selina's home.

A deepening sadness invaded her mind. She didn't want to leave the tenants who needed her. And with her worries about Susan, Selina felt as if she couldn't leave the poor woman stranded. It might take Mia two hours to get here, longer at night. Anything might happen to Susan and the baby by then.

As she arrived home, Mrs. Roberts sat on the bench in front of the cottage window. "Mrs. Roberts, is everything all right?"

"Yes, my dear. I came by with some fruit tarts to thank you for the herbs you sent." Mrs. Roberts hoisted her sturdy frame out of the bench and walked toward Selina.

"Thank you. Would you care for some tea?"

"Oh, I would at that. I've been up since dawn, baking for all the workers the duke has here. It's nice to get away for some peace. They are a noisy bunch of men."

Selina smiled and opened the door for her. "At least the house is finally being put into order."

"True." Mrs. Roberts set the tarts on the table and started fussing with the fire. "I'll get the fire started while you fetch the water."

Selina kept several jugs of water on hand. She reached for one and poured the water into a pan. Once Mrs. Roberts had the fire started, they waited for the water to boil. Selina readied the tea and pulled out plates for the tarts.

"You will have one, won't you?" she asked Mrs. Roberts.

"I shouldn't . . . but maybe just a small one."

Selina poured the tea and then sat down at the small table. "How is everyone at the house?"

Mrs. Roberts looked down at her tart. "Everyone is horrified by the duke's actions, my dear. We all believe he may have lost his mind."

"He is the duke and can do as he likes," she replied and then took a bite of the flaky crust. "This is wonderful."

"Thank you." Mrs. Roberts sipped her tea. "We do not understand why His Grace would want you gone. Your kind has been here forever."

Her kind. She was nothing more than a woman with some knowledge of herbs and healing. Yet the tenants thought her some kind of magical being who could heal every illness. "He is a modern man with modern notions."

"What do you mean?" Mrs. Roberts asked.

"He believes physicians and surgeons have the answers. After all, I am just an uneducated country woman. I might be able to read but I have never been to university. How much could I possibly know? And what could I possibly know about healing people?" Selina sipped her tea and sat back.

Mrs. Roberts tilted her head back and laughed. "I'll take your uneducated knowledge over one of those arrogant physicians any day."

Selina smiled back at the older woman. "Thank you."

"What will you do now?"

Selina shrugged. "I honestly don't know."

Mrs. Roberts leaned in closer until her large breasts pressed against the table. "I heard he went to Hartsfield."

"For what reason?"

"To get permission for you to stay on his lands."

Selina covered her mouth with her hand. She blinked away the tears that threatened to fall. Finally, she moved her hand. "What did the earl say?"

"The duke told Mr. Roberts that he wanted a wagon to be in front of your home on Friday for the trip over to the earl's land. So I can only assume the earl gave his permission."

Of course, Hartsfield would do that. "What am I to do?" Selina mumbled.

"That's the reason I'm here, Selina." Mrs. Roberts smiled at her. "We have a plan."

"We?"

"The servants and I came up with a plan so that you won't have to leave."

Selina smiled at the kindhearted lady. "I don't have any choice, Mrs. Roberts. His Grace can evict me."

She waved a pudgy hand at Selina. "Pish-posh, girl. What did the duke really say?"

"He told me to leave the cottage."

"Exactly. And so you shall."

Selina suddenly felt like thumping her head on the table. "If I must leave then I will have no choice but to go to the earl's land."

"Selina, he told you to leave the cottage. He never told you to leave his land."

Thinking back Selina was certain he had told her to leave his lands. But she desperately wanted to hear Mrs. Roberts's plan. "But all the tenants' cottages are occupied. There is nowhere else I can go."

Mrs. Roberts laughed. "There is an entire house with only a few people living in it."

"Northrop Park?"

"He never said you couldn't live there."

"Once he discovers me there, he will have me removed immediately," Selina countered.

"And that might take months. That house has fifty bed-chambers. We could move you to a new room every night if needed and he wouldn't discover you for months. That will give you time to show him your worth."

Selina looked up at the plain white ceiling. She knew it had nothing to do with her worth. "But he doesn't want me here."

"That man doesn't know what's good for him. Did he ever say you couldn't help his tenants after you leave the cottage?"

Selina shook her head and then brushed a lock of hair out of her eyes.

"So if he sees you in the house, just tell him you are there at one of the servants' request. If he sees you on the property, you are there to help out one of the tenants."

This was so wrong. She knew why he wanted her off his property. And she had no doubt that when he said he wanted her gone from the cottage, he meant departed from his property. Nonetheless, she had a duty to this land that took precedence over his wishes.

"Are you certain I won't be discovered?" she asked hesitantly.

"There are only a few servants he brought with him from London. The majority of us have lived here our entire lives. The few new servants will take orders from Mr. Roberts or myself. Every one of us will help keep you safe."

"What about during the wedding?"

"That will only take up to a fortnight. We will hide you elsewhere if they need all the bedchambers."

"What about after the wedding?"

"Once the wedding is over, he'll go back to London. Mr. Roberts heard him say so."

Selina took a long breath in and held it for a moment. Slowly she released it and made her decision. No one would force her to renege on her duties to this land and its people. Not even the Duke of Northrop.

"Very well, Mrs. Roberts. I believe we can make this work."

Chapter 6

Colin tried to listen as his steward discussed the cost of wheat this year, but his attention was elsewhere. It was Friday. The wagon should be at her cottage. Within a few short hours, she would be on her way to Hart's lands. There she could live happily for the next two months. Perhaps she would be so content there she would decide to remain on Hart's estate for good.

And he could forget her and all that she represented.

Therefore, he should return his concentration to his steward.

"As such, Your Grace," Mr. Hughes said, "I recommend reducing the percentage of wheat the tenant farmers receive."

What did he miss? "Excuse me, Mr. Hughes, I am not quite certain I understand why you would have me do such a thing."

"Sir, you will greatly increase your profits if you reduce their percentage. Even half a percent decrease to the tenants would increase your wealth substantially." Mr. Hughes closed his ledger as if their conversation were finished.

"Mr. Hughes, this estate is my most profitable already. Part of the reason for my success here is that I give a very reasonable portion to my tenants and they continue to work the land as if it were theirs. I will change nothing."

Mr. Hughes glanced down at the desk. "Yes, Your Grace."

Colin watched Hughes's face as he attempted to say more but did not. "What else, Mr. Hughes?"

"Sir, it's just that you have sent away our wise woman. There is a chance that with her gone, your lands may not produce as they did in the past."

Colin banged his fist on his desk. He was so damned tired of everyone on this land treating her as if she was some sort of goddess. "Miss White does not toil on this land. The tenants do. They will continue to do so for generations whether Miss White is here or not. She has no mystical powers. Her departure will not impact our crop output."

Mr. Hughes nodded. "If you say so, Your Grace."

"You don't believe me?"

"I should take my leave now." Hughes stood and gathered his things.

"Speak your mind, Hughes."

Mr. Hughes stared down at his boots. "If the tenants are unhappy that you've sent away their healer, they may take their displeasure out on you. They might deliberately set out to ruin the wedding, or worse, the crops."

"They would do no such thing," Colin said harshly. Although, as he thought back to the day he entered Mrs. Godwin's home, the reception had not been cordial. And then there was the way most of the tenants turned their backs on him when he rode past. None of that mattered, he decided. This was his land and he would do what was needed. "Good day, Mr. Hughes."

"Good day, Your Grace."

Dammit! Colin picked up a teacup and hurled it toward the fireplace to ease his frustration. The sooner she left, the better. Just to make sure she really intended to leave, he decided to verify her whereabouts.

He strode to her cottage. The dark clouds overhead suited his mood perfectly. As he walked, he realized his ankle must be completely healed. It didn't even ache with the approaching rain.

He stopped a short distance away and watched the scene. One of his wagons sat in front of the house as many of the tenants assisted her with her things. She brought out a small trunk and placed it in the back. As if she knew he stared, she turned and spied him. She only shook her head and walked back into the house.

He approached the house slowly. Several of his tenants nodded but none muttered much more than a quick greeting. He felt their anger as they loaded her possessions. Perhaps Mr. Hughes might be correct with regard to the tenants' reactions.

"Did you come to check on me?" Miss White asked as she brought out a satchel.

"I came to say good-bye," he said as a slice of guilt knifed him in the stomach.

"Very well then, good-bye, Your Grace." Her emerald eyes shone with unshed tears. She dropped the satchel in the wagon and then walked back inside.

He knew there was nothing more to say, and yet, he had no desire to return to the loneliness of his home. He heard a quick giggle as someone said something to her. The sound of her laugh warmed his heart.

Gradually, he walked away, knowing he was not welcome there. He stopped at the reflecting pond and looked over the land that was his only because he happened to be born at the right time and fathered by the right man. Had his father been a tenant on the land, he'd be assisting Miss White instead of forcing her to leave.

If he had any sense, he would stop her. But glancing up at the empty house, the memories were still too raw for him. Forcing her to leave was the best option for everyone. With her gone, he could concentrate on the upcoming wedding. For once, happiness would be the overwhelming emotion in the house, not the continual sadness that draped every room.

So why did he feel like he'd just made a huge mistake?

Selina looked about her empty cottage as sorrow enveloped her. This was the only home she'd ever known. While the servants' plan to keep her hidden in the house for two months might work, he still might discover her. And if that happened, she'd never be able to return here again. But she had to try. What he didn't know after he left would not hurt him.

"Is that everything, Selina?"

"Yes." She brushed away a tear that fell but another just took its place.

Mrs. Roberts embraced her. "It will be all right. You'll be back in your home in no time."

"Thank you, Mrs. Roberts."

"We have the two books you requested, your herbs, and your personal things up in a bedroom on the third floor. His Grace has the west wing on the second floor. He'll never know you're living right under his nose."

Selina nodded and gave the kind older lady another squeeze. "Thank you for all your help."

Mrs. Roberts let out a husky laugh. "We're not about to lose our wise woman. The duke has no idea how much you do for us all."

And he never would, she realized. With this plan, she had no way of showing him the duties she performed for the estate. Not that it would matter to him. He believed only men made good doctors. Healing needed knowledge, and education, and, according to the duke, a penis. After a final look around, she walked outside and closed the door to her cottage. Instinctively, she knew she'd never be back to live there again.

"We shall head out toward the earl's estate in case the duke is watching," Mr. Evans said in a hushed tone. "Once we reach the woods, you and David will get out and walk back to Northrop Park. Randall will be at the back of the house to let you inside and show you to your room."

A nervous energy filled her. If this went wrong, she would end up living with Mia and her mother forever. But this plan would work, as long as they all were careful.

Mr. Evans continued, "I will go on with your things to Mrs. Featherstone's home. They arranged for your possessions to be left, out of sight, in the stables."

They had worked on the plan for two days and now that it was time to implement it, Selina worried what would happen to the people involved if they were caught. The duke would likely evict them for disobeying his commands. She couldn't be responsible for that.

"Maybe I should just go live with Mrs. Featherstone," she said softly.

"Absolutely not," Mrs. Roberts said as she approached the wagon.

"Mrs. Roberts, think what might happen to you and your husband should the duke discover you were a part of this scheme," she implored the older woman.

"He will never find out." Mrs. Roberts looked at the other men involved. "But if any of you men feel unsure of helping out Miss White, just speak up."

Mr. Evans and his son both shook their heads. "If not for you, Miss White, my wife might be dead from that fever last year," Mr. Evans said.

David laughed. "My mama says I wouldn't be here if not for yer mother helping with the delivery. I owe ye everything."

"Very well, then," she said. With all this support, they would make their plan work. With a flick of the reins, the wagon rumbled down the road. Selina cast a quick glance back in the direction the duke had left, but there was no sign of him.

A slice of disappointment slid through her. Why should

she be unhappy that he wasn't here to watch her leave? It made no sense. Had he been there, she would have felt angry that he did ensure that she left. Perhaps she was just going mad. That seemed the most likely explanation.

After a short drive, Mr. Evans stopped the wagon. She and David climbed down and made their way through the small copse of woods toward the house.

"Randall will give a sign that the master is locked in his study," David whispered as if the duke might be directly behind them.

He locked himself in his study. She wondered why he would do such a thing. "What is the sign?"

"He will chase the swans out of the pond."

Selina almost laughed. Unless Randall walked into the pond, she doubted those stubborn birds would go anywhere. They waited for close to an hour and then they saw Randall flapping his arms as he attempted to make the swans fly. He finally stepped into the pond and ran toward the birds. Only the swans wanted no part of this and turned on Randall, honking and flapping their wings.

"We need to go save that boy before they attack him," Selina said with a laugh.

With a breath for courage, Selina ran for the salvation the enormous house would bring her. As they raced past Randall, David yelled at him to get out of the pond. Once they reached the terrace, Selina stopped near a statue of Venus. She caught her breath and noticed Mr. Roberts standing by the terrace door. He waved for her to come inside.

"The duke is in his study," Mr. Roberts said as he ushered her up the back staircase.

"Why does he lock himself inside?"

"I believe when things are troubling him, he may take to the spirits."

Her heart went out to the man who mourned his wife so deeply that after eight years, he still couldn't get over her. She wondered if his upcoming marriage was only out of duty to produce an heir. How sad that his new wife would never know the love he gave to his first wife.

What was wrong with her? This was the man who had evicted her from her home and she was feeling sorry for him! Not for a moment longer, she decided. Some people might consider her softhearted, but she would harden her heart where he was concerned. He hadn't a thought for her, and she would do the same for him.

She followed Mr. Roberts up the stairs to a third-floor bedroom. He opened the door to what might be a bright room . . . on a different day. She glanced out the window and noticed the clouds had finally given way to the rain they held.

"Here you are, miss," Mr. Roberts said with a kind smile. "When the duke is out of the house, you're free to come down. I'll have a footman send up a tray for your meals."

"What if one of the tenants needs me?"

"All the footmen who watch the door know you are here. It's only those snooty London men we need to watch out for. If you are needed at a home, we'll let you know straightaway."

"Thank you, Mr. Roberts."

"If you need anything, just ring." Mr. Roberts closed the door behind him, cloaking her in her secret chamber.

Selina smiled as she looked at the bed that would be hers for a short while. The cherry four-poster bed was huge compared to the small bed in her cottage. The bedchamber was nearly as big as her entire home. For a brief moment, she wondered what it would be like to live in this luxury every day. She couldn't imagine having a maid wake her in the morning with a cup of chocolate on a tray. Or dressing in fine silk gowns for a ball.

She wasn't meant for that type of life.

As she glanced about, she realized that while beautiful, this room was her prison for the next two months. While Mr. Roberts had told her she could come downstairs if the duke was out, she really didn't have access to the rest of the house. She couldn't entertain her friends in here.

But it would all be worth it, she tried to convince herself.

Once he left for London with his bride, she would be free again.

Colin walked out toward the reflecting pond as darkness settled over the estate. He'd lived alone for the past eight years, other than when his stepmother and sister paid a visit. After the first year of mourning, he had not come to enjoy the solitude, but he at least could tolerate it. So why did he feel such dreaded loneliness at this estate?

Was it just the idea that his wife had died here? Or could there possibly be more to his morose feelings tonight?

It certainly wasn't because he'd made Miss White leave.

She needed to be gone while he was here. He needed no reminders of eight years ago. There were enough memories here that would never leave. And he needed the temptation she brought as far away as possible. He'd promised himself that he would never put his heart at risk again. While he doubted he could fall in love with such a woman, he did desire her.

He sipped the last of his brandy and placed the snifter on the concrete edge of the pond. For a long moment, he stared up at the stars. He wondered if there were any other planets out there like this. Was there another man a million miles away staring up at the stars wondering the same thing? Colin shook his head. Perhaps that third brandy was one too many tonight.

He glanced back at the house as a candle flickered from a third-floor bedroom. Who would be there at this hour? He had never asked his servants to clean round the clock in preparation for the wedding. As he watched, a figure dressed in white passed in front of the window. The woman didn't stop long enough for him to make out who it might be but he knew whoever it was, she was not one of the elderly servants he had in service.

As he stared up at the window, the figure passed by the window again. She moved swiftly, unlike most of the servants in the house, so he discounted the idea that one of them might be upstairs. He knew exactly who that woman was . . . Mary. Or rather, the ghost of Mary. There was no other logical explanation, not that believing in spirits held much logic. He stared up at the window, unable to look away. The specter never returned to the window and within a few moments, the room went dark.

The house was more than just a vessel for bad memories. It contained her spirit. She'd never left. No wonder he always felt so uncomfortable in the house.

Having this wedding here was a dreadful idea. Perhaps he could write to Kate and tell her so. Not that he could inform her that the house was haunted. She would think he needed to spend some time at Bedlam.

And perhaps he had.

But there was no other explanation for seeing a woman in the room upstairs. Either she was a ghost or he really had gone mad. Both thoughts left him cold.

He had to find out what was going on up there. He raced up the two flights of stairs and then stopped in the hall. Thinking back, he couldn't remember exactly in which, of the many windows, he had seen the apparition. He stood still and listened. Not a sound could be heard from any of the rooms. No chains rattling, no footsteps, or moaning. Absolute silence filled the area. As if to prove he wasn't mad, he opened the doors to two bedchambers and found nothing but dark rooms with white coverings.

He really was going insane.

* * *

Selina spent the first few days in her bedroom prison. Several times during the day, Mrs. Roberts would join her and they would chat. But for the most part, her day was dreadfully dull. The tenants were all quite well and didn't need her services. The duke seemed to spend his days in his study. According to Mrs. Roberts, he never left the room and looked quite peaked. Selina thought about checking on him but knew he would not appreciate her interference.

After eating a lonely dinner tonight, she sat at the table next to the window and longingly stared outside. Dark clouds filled the horizon warning of an impending storm. A knock on her door broke the silence.

"Miss, it's Randall," he whispered from the hall. "Please let me in."

Selina rushed to the door and let him in. "What's the matter? Did the duke see you bring up the tray?"

"No," he said with a laugh. "It's Mrs. Wells, miss. It's her time."

"Of course," she replied. "I'll get my things."

Quickly she packed her satchel and herbs. She prayed this would go smoothly. She had been able to sneak out for a short time yesterday morning to call on Susan. Selina had still felt no movements from the baby. Susan was optimistic and said she was certain she'd felt a few slight kicks.

"I'll escort you out of the house," Randall said with a smile. "But I can't accompany you."

"There's no need, Randall. I don't usually have someone with me."

"All right, miss." Randall opened the door, and peered right and then left. "It's clear."

Feeling like a spy in the war, she tiptoed down the corridor, trailing Randall. Once outside, she raced toward Susan's small home. As it was a first birth, Selina would most likely spend the night there. Rain sprinkled down on her but she ignored the cool sensation.

Several candles blazed in the small cottage. Selina knocked on the door and Susan's mother opened it. "Oh, thank God, you're here, Selina. I fear this won't go well," Mrs. Jones whispered. "It's only been three hours but she's in terrible pains."

"Let me check on her."

Mrs. Jones led her past Mr. Wells who looked as if he might faint. "Outside, Mr. Wells. Miss White is here now," Mrs. Jones ordered.

Once inside the bedroom, Selina pressed her lips together. Susan appeared pale and sweaty. "Susan, how are the pains?"

"Awful," she gasped. "You said they would start slow but they didn't. I want to push already."

Selina thrust away her emotions and set to work.

Colin walked the length of his library as he sipped his brandy. No matter what he'd tried today, he couldn't get the image of that specter out of his mind. He looked down at his snifter of brandy. Perhaps he was drinking more than normal. Although, he didn't think that was the cause of his delusions. He had seen someone or something upstairs. For the past few nights, he had gone to the pond and stared up at the house. He had seen nothing to make him believe there was anything unnatural upstairs.

A knock sounded on the door to the library. "Come in."

A pallid Mr. Roberts entered the room. "Excuse me, Your Grace."

"What's the matter, Roberts? You look white as a ghost." Did he really just say ghost? He had ghouls on the mind tonight.

Roberts looked away. "It's Mrs. Wells, sir."

Mr. Wells had been the blacksmith on the estate for ten years but Colin didn't remember hearing about him marrying. "What is wrong?"

"She delivered a stillborn girl tonight, Your Grace."

He closed his eyes against the instant pain he felt. This was his fault again. He forced Miss White to leave. She might have been able to help Mrs. Wells. "I will speak with them in the morning. Thank you for letting me know."

"Good night, Your Grace."

"Good night, Roberts."

Damn her!

No, damn him.

This was his fault for forcing her to leave. His servants and tenants would despise him for evicting her. They would never forgive him. Just another thing to blame on him. The tenants and servants loved her. And with good reason; she took care of them far better than he had the past eight years.

Selina. With her curly, blond hair and emerald eyes.

He had to stop thinking about her.

If it wasn't guilt he felt, then he thought about her physical attributes. Her full, pink lips that just begged to be kissed. Or her breasts that would just fit in his hands. There was something dreadfully wrong with him. He didn't want her on his land.

But he wanted her in his bed.

He walked the length of the room again. Why wasn't this brandy making him tired? Or easing his frustrations?

If not for the rain, he would have taken a walk. He walked to the terrace door and opened it. Rain continued to fall but not as hard as earlier. A figure with blond hair caught his eye. She paced the length of the reflecting pond. He blinked to make sure he wasn't dreaming or worse, imagining a spirit again.

It had to be her. But what was she doing here? She should be ensconced in Mrs. Featherstone's warm home tonight, not out in the cold rain.

He placed his glass on the table and headed out into the

night. As he approached her, she looked up, shook her head, and then held up her hand as if to stop him.

"Please just let me have my one place to calm myself," she all but shouted at him.

Taken aback by her frantic tone, he slowed his pace. "What is wrong, Miss White?"

"Just leave me alone," she sobbed and then wiped at her face. "I should have prepared her for the possibility," she mumbled. "I should have told her this might happen."

Colin took a few steps closer, drawn to the pain he saw in her eyes. "What happened, Selina?"

Her lower lip trembled as she stared at the water. "She was a beautiful baby. Blond hair and blue eyes. Lifeless blue eyes," she cried.

Mrs. Wells's baby. "Were you here for the delivery?"

"Of course I was here." Her sadness turned to anger, directed at him. "Did you think if you forced me to leave that I would give up my duties here? Did you think I wouldn't run here and help the people I love?"

"I honestly never thought about it," he whispered. The wind blew tendrils of blond hair over her face. Without a thought, he brushed them away.

"You can't stop me from doing my duty to this land and the people who live here. I won't stop. You'll have to send me to prison because nothing else will stop me," she shouted her frustrations at him.

But her words never reached his ears. All he saw was the pain in her eyes and he wanted to comfort her. Ease her troubles. Make her understand all his reasons for wanting her to leave.

He stepped closer and pulled her into his arms. Expecting she would push away, he wrapped his arms around her tightly. Her head landed on his chest and after a quick pound to his chest, she wept.

"Why?" she mumbled. "Why does God have to be so cruel sometimes?"

"I don't know," he said against her hair.

"It's not fair. She'd had such an easy time of it. No morning sickness, no problems at all. Why didn't the baby survive?"

"Shh," he whispered, unable to think of a word to say that would comfort her. He closed his eyes only to relive his own anguish at the loss of his wife and child.

"I didn't feel movement the last few times I saw her. I should have prepared her for the outcome."

He had no idea what to say to her so he continued to hold her close.

"Why couldn't I have saved her?" She looked up at him with tears in her eyes.

Unable to move for a long moment, he just stared at her. She needed his comfort, his warmth, and God knew he needed the same from her. Slowly, he brought his lips to hers.

A gasp of shock was all he heard from her. He moved over her lips as desire crept over him. Waiting for her to push him away, he tentatively slid his tongue over her full lips. Her hands moved to his chest but instead of forcing him away, she wrapped her arms around his neck.

Wanting nothing more than to take her pain away, he tugged her body against his. They were both soaked from the rain but he didn't mind. Their heat warmed them. Passion flared as he skimmed his tongue over the crease of her lips again. Only this time, she opened for him.

The sensation of her velvety tongue on his almost sent him over the edge. He wanted to lay her down on the wet grass and make love to her for hours. As she responded to his kiss, he heard a low moan from her throat.

God, this wasn't right. He couldn't want her like this. He couldn't make love to her all night. But his body wouldn't listen to reason. He trailed his hands down her back and cupped her buttocks.

She moaned again as he pressed her hips to his growing erection. He wanted to slip into her warm depths and watch her face as she reached her climax. He wanted to release his pent-up frustrations and feel that moment of pure pleasure.

He wanted—

She thrust him away. "Oh dear Lord, what were you doing?"

He blinked and shook his head. "What was *I* doing? I believe you were doing it too."

"That may be, but I am not engaged!"

Chapter 7

Selina raced to the woods to get away from the duke. Hiding behind a tree, she watched as he searched for her. She prayed the darkness would conceal her position. She didn't want to hear his reasons for kissing her. Or face the fact that her body betrayed her.

"Selina, come out of hiding. I need to take you home," he said, impatience lining his voice. "It's raining and I believe we would both feel better if we talked about what happened in dry clothing by a warm fire."

A warm fire with him near would lead to far more than a simple chat. With rain still falling, she could barely make out his form even though he was only a few feet away. She remained completely still to keep her hiding place secret.

"Dammit, Selina!" he shouted. "Where the bloody hell are you?"

The angry tone of his voice was just one more reason to keep quiet. At least now it sounded as if he was going deeper into the copse of trees. With him farther away, he might not find her tonight. If he did, he would surely tell her that his kiss meant nothing. He'd only been trying to make her feel better.

He was nothing more than a rake. All the rumors she'd

heard about him over the years were true. She felt a pang of pity for his impending bride.

She stilled her thoughts and listened for him again. A twig snapped a distance away and then she heard a muttered curse. Knowing this might be her only chance, she broke away from the trees and ran toward the house.

Randall opened the door as she approached the house. "Is everything all right, Miss White?" he asked hesitantly.

"Yes," she replied with a quick glance back toward the pond. "I'm just wet from the rain."

"I shall call for a bath," he said and then walked down the hall to fetch the footmen.

"Thank you, Randall." She hastily made her way up the back staircase to the third floor before the duke arrived back home. She closed her door and leaned against the hard wood as all the emotions of the night surfaced. Covering her face with her hands, she mumbled, "How could I have let him kiss me?"

She'd been so upset about Susan's baby and then seeing him had only made her angry. And yet, those few moments in his arms gave her comfort and warmth and for some reason she felt certain he'd understood her pain. If it had ended there, she might not have thought any more about it. But she'd felt his reaction to their kiss when he pulled her hips tightly against his. His arousal had been long and hard, and she'd wanted to rub against him like a wanton.

She had wanted him tonight.

She couldn't deny that she found him attractive in a dark brooding manner. But tonight was different. If she hadn't come to her senses, she might have let him take her up to his room and make love all night long. That idea was mad. She would never become involved with a married man. While the duke had yet to say his vows, a betrothal meant a contract to marry.

Besides, how could she think of such a thing when she knew he hated her?

Slowly she undressed, but as she did, one thought wouldn't leave her mind. If he hated her as he appeared to, why did he kiss her?

It made no sense.

As she reached for her night rail, she wondered about that.

He forced her to leave the estate because of her mother, but could there have been another reason? Could he desire her and think it best to remove her from his presence so he wouldn't be tempted? She laughed aloud at her fanciful imagination.

After a few minutes more of pondering, she finally decided their kiss had been nothing but a quick lapse in judgment. Tomorrow, he would be kicking himself for kissing the wise woman . . . if he wasn't already. She'd tasted the brandy on his velvety tongue. Too much drink was likely the explanation for his behavior.

Although, she could hardly blame brandy on her reaction to his heated kiss.

But what woman wouldn't respond to the kisses of a handsome man? Besides, while he might be a rake, he was still a gentleman. He would most likely even apologize if she saw him tomorrow. And she would be gracious and accept his apology without condemning him. It was simply a mistake on both their parts.

A soft knock interrupted her thoughts. As footmen brought in the tub and buckets of water, she walked to the window and stared out. Had he returned yet? What if something had happened to him while he'd been searching for her?

"Has the duke arrived back home?" she asked one of the footmen.

"I don't believe he left the house tonight, Miss White. He's been in his study all evening."

Oh, dear God, no one knew he'd left his study. "Ask Randall to check on His Grace. I thought I saw him near the pond when I was coming back from Mrs. Wells's home."

"Yes, miss."

Once they were gone, she blew out all but one candle and slipped into the steaming water. A soft sigh escaped her as her cold muscles finally relaxed. He would be fine, she told herself. So why couldn't she believe that? He'd been born and raised here. He knew this estate better than most. But if something happened to him, it would be her fault for not speaking up when he had called out for her.

She washed quickly and then dressed in her night rail again. Standing near her bed, she bit down on her bottom lip, worried that she had caused the Duke of Northrop harm. She blew out the candle and walked toward the window. Pushing the curtain back slightly, she stared out into the dark night. At least the rain had finally stopped.

Selina spied a figure by the pond and then gasped. For a long moment, she could only gaze down at him as if in a trance. She blinked, quickly pushed the curtain in front of the window, and moved away. Her hand shook as she reached for the servants' bell. He'd been staring up directly at her.

Her hiding place had been discovered!

Colin stared up at the window on the third floor. His body trembled from the cold, wet clothing he wore but his mind raced with insane thoughts. Perhaps his mind was playing with him again. Trying to clear his mind, he looked away and then back to the window. The image of the woman was gone as quickly as the flickering light had disappeared.

Even as chilly as he was, he sat on the pond wall and continued to stare up at the window for a few minutes. When nothing reappeared, he counted the number of windows over and then decided to act. He raced back to the door of his study and then headed for the stairs.

"Your Grace, you're all wet," Randall exclaimed.

"Yes, I am, Randall."

"Wait," Randall said as Colin reached for the first step. "Your Grace, can you look at something?"

Colin growled. "Can it wait?"

Randall's face crumpled. "I'm sorry, sir. I just . . ."

"What is it?" Colin asked, approaching the young man.

Randall pushed up the sleeve of his jacket and pointed to a small mole. "Do you think this is something I should ask Miss White about?"

Remembering that Randall wasn't the brightest man in his employ, Colin mentally counted to ten for patience. "It's a mole, Randall." He pushed up the sleeve of his own jacket. "See, I have several on my arm too."

"So, I don't have to worry about it?"

"No, Randall."

Randall let out an exaggerated sigh. "Thank you, Your Grace. Shall I call for a bath for you?"

"Not yet," he answered as he turned back to the steps. He climbed the marble stairs, cursing his wet boots for slowing him down.

"When then?" Randall mumbled.

"Later."

Colin didn't stop until he reached the third floor. He counted off the rooms and then hurled the fourth door open so hard it bounced off the wall and swung back toward him. The room was completely empty. But as he walked inside, the smell of a recently blown out candle wafted past his nose. Mixed with the acrid smell was a hint of lavender.

Someone or something had been in this room tonight. He moved toward the linen press and opened the cabinet doors.

It, too, was completely empty. He spun around. There were no cloths on the furnishings. He was not losing his mind.

"Your Grace, what are you about wandering up here this evening?" Mrs. Roberts walked into the room. "Why, you are soaked to the bone! You need to get those things off before you catch your death."

He looked over at Mrs. Roberts and frowned. "I was outside and noticed a candle flickering up here. I came up to investigate."

Mrs. Roberts looked down at the floor. "I apologize, Your Grace. Miss White gave me some herbs for my gout and they make it hard for me to sleep. I thought I would get a start on freshening up the rooms on this floor. I didn't mean to disturb you."

"I did not realize you were having issues sleeping." The plump old face of Mrs. Roberts was not what he'd seen in the window.

"It's better than the pain of the gout," she replied with a hearty laugh. "Come down and let me call for a bath for you."

He nodded. Perhaps a bath would help clear his mind. After spending almost two hours searching for Selina, he'd finally given up. She did indeed know this land better than he. Although, he hated the idea of her walking all the way back to Hart's estate in the dark . . . alone. He should do something about that but the only sensible option was having her return here. And that kiss tonight proved he desired her far too much to allow her near him again.

He followed Mrs. Roberts down the stairs to his room and waited for his bath. Hearing the floor creak above him, he ignored the sound. There was no spirit in this house. It was only his imagination. The floor creaked because it was made of wood, which expanded and contracted depending on the weather.

The only thing he couldn't explain was the face in the window.

It had been there. And he knew without a doubt that the

face had not been Mrs. Roberts's. The woman's face was much younger and thinner than his housekeeper's face. He raked his fingers through his wet hair. The woman, like the sounds, was his imagination.

God, he could not wait for Kate and her mother to arrive. Even though having them here would drive him mad, at least it was a madness to which he was accustomed. The emptiness of this house had to be the cause of his foolishness. Well, that and a petite blond who was driving him insane.

Chapter 8

A loud knock on her bedchamber door woke Selina at seven the next morning. The servants knew she didn't enjoy getting up early. There must be another tenant who needs her, she thought.

"Selina, please let me in."

Hearing the worried tone of Mrs. Roberts, Selina assumed the worst. Perhaps their quick bedchamber move last night didn't work and the duke had discovered that she was living under his nose. "Come in."

Mrs. Roberts walked into the room and went directly to the linen press. "Get up, girl," she said as she pulled out a cotton dress.

"What is going on?"

"His Grace just called for Zeus to be saddled. He said he was heading to the earl's lands. We can't take the chance he means to go to Mrs. Featherstone's house and check on you."

"Why would he do that?"

"He confessed to Mr. Roberts that he had seen you last night by the pond and that you had run away. The duke said he'd wanted you to stay the night here because of the rain and darkness. He searched for over two hours trying to find you last night."

"Two hours?" Selina whispered.

"Yes. He finally decided you must have returned to Mrs. Featherstone's cottage." Mrs. Roberts laced up Selina's stays. "He appeared very worried."

Or worried that she might tell someone that he kissed her, she thought. "I doubt he cared whether I made it to Mia's house or not."

Mrs. Roberts draped the green cotton dress over Selina's head. "Of course he cares. But he is a troubled man. When I found him in your room last night, he looked slightly mad. He was soaked to the bone from searching for you."

She'd barely slept last night from the guilt of leaving him in the rain. Selina nodded. "Thank you again for all your help last night."

"Selina, you must be more cautious with the candles."

"I will not use them unless I know he has retired." As Mrs. Roberts buttoned up her dress, Selina asked, "How did you get everything out of that room before he arrived?"

"Randall detained him for a few moments. Just long enough to get the tub out of your room and into the bedchamber across the hall."

Selina smiled, remembering the commotion of five footmen, Mrs. Roberts, and a few maids all getting her items out of the room before the duke arrived. This was not safe for them. "I really should consider moving to Mia's house. It is not right that I put you and the other servants in a position that could cost you your jobs."

"Hush," Mrs. Roberts scolded. "You will do no such thing. Just remember to pull the bell five times like you did last night should we need to move you quickly."

"I will, thank you." Selina adjusted the bodice of her dress.

"I can't make it all the way to Mia's house before the duke. He will have a head start on me."

Mrs. Roberts pulled Selina's hair up into a tight chignon. "No, he will need to dress and eat first. He always eats a large breakfast. While he does that, Mr. Sellers has a lad who will ride with you until you are at least halfway to the earl's lands. He will take your horse and you will start walking toward Northrop Park as if you are coming to check on a tenant."

Selina blew out a breath and then started to dress. "What do I tell him if he sees me and stops?"

"Tell him you are going to check on Mrs. Wells."

Something she had to do today anyway. He wouldn't question her motive. "Very well."

Once dressed, she headed for the stables where a stable-boy waited with a horse for her. "We'll ride for thirty minutes and then I'll take yer horse back through the woods so His Grace don't see me."

"Thank you, James."

They rode out quickly, heading toward the Earl of Harts-field's lands. Selina wished she could ride like this all the time. It would make getting to the tenants' homes so much quicker, but she couldn't afford a horse. Once they reached the earl's property, she stopped her mare and jumped down.

"Here you go, James," she said, handing him the reins. "Be safe and don't let the duke see you."

"I will, miss."

As she walked back toward Northrop Park, her heart filled with warmth at all the tenants and servants were doing for her. They were putting their own lives at stake to help her. She owed them everything and could only pay them back by heal-ing them when sick.

She pulled the pins out of her hair and rubbed her head. There was nothing worse than having her hair up in a chignon. It gave her headaches.

After walking for a few minutes, she heard the sound of a horse galloping closer. She looked up to see the duke gaining on her. His coattails flew out behind him as he rode. She paused for a moment and stared at the handsome man approaching her. A spark of excitement coursed through her.

He slowed his pace when he caught sight of her. "What are you about this morning, Miss White?"

The horse stopped close enough that she could pat his head. The friendly beast nuzzled her cheek. "I am walking to Mrs. Wells's home."

"At this hour?"

"By the time I arrive on foot, it will be close to nine. I'm quite certain she will be awake." If the poor woman had slept at all last night. Selina dreaded going back to the house. She had lain awake for hours last night, attempting to determine what had happened during the pregnancy. No answer had ever come to her. And when she wasn't thinking about Susan Wells, their kiss occupied her thoughts for hours. Even now, she couldn't help but stare at his molded lips and wonder how it would feel if he kissed her again. Enough of that nonsense, she scolded herself. He was betrothed.

"You have no horse?" he asked softly.

Selina rolled her eyes. "How would I afford one, Your Grace? The tenants pay me with what they have . . . a chicken, a bottle of wine or gin; they don't have much."

He climbed down from the large chestnut horse and stood next to her. "I have never thought about it. Of course, I tried to find you last night so you might have stayed at my home. It wouldn't be so long of a walk from there."

"It would be highly improper to stay overnight at the home of an unmarried man," she retorted.

"Hmm." He sounded terribly unconvinced.

"What do you mean by that?"

"I just don't envision you as the type of woman who cares so much about propriety."

She stopped walking and stared at him. "I cannot believe you said that about me!"

"Indeed. Most women your age would never be seen in public wearing their hair down. Only a woman's husband should see her hair unbound and flowing down her back."

Heat instantly burned across her cheeks. "I have no maid to assist me with my hair."

"Ahh," he said, looking up at the blue sky. "Lack of funds. Still, I cannot believe it's all that difficult to put your hair up into a chignon. A few twists and pins should do it."

Her jaw tightened in frustration. But there was nothing she could say in her defense. There was no reason for not putting up her hair, except that she liked it down. "The pull of my hair gives me headaches. Something a man would never understand."

He nodded. "I see."

She did wonder why he hadn't mentioned their kiss last night. If nothing else, he should offer her an apology. A proper gentleman would do that, she reasoned.

"I need to continue on," she said.

"May I walk with you?"

"I cannot stop you from walking your lands, Your Grace." Perhaps he needed time to determine the best way to say he was sorry.

"I suppose I should speak with both Mr. and Mrs. Wells," he said stiffly.

"Very well, then." Selina moved forward and he kept pace with his horse trailing behind.

After a few minutes of silence, he finally asked, "Why do you do this?"

"Do what?"

"Care for the sick, deliver the babies and everything else you do."

"Who else will?" She cast him a sideways glance, noting the way his coat cut across his broad shoulders.

"A physician, perhaps?" he offered.

Selina laughed. "The only physician is in the village and he's a drunken sod. I wouldn't let him touch a soul on this property."

"But why *you*?"

"Because I am of the same blood as my mother and her mother before her. This is what we do and have done for centuries."

"But couldn't someone else do it?" He held up a hand to stop her interruption. "I mean what if something happened to you? Or what if you wanted to go to London for a fortnight?"

Selina laughed. "London? Why would I want to go there? All those people in that small space, it must be rife with disease."

Colin looked at her in confusion. Had she never been to London? Was it possible that she'd never seen the most important city in the world? Why did he have a sudden urge to show her everything in town?

"London is beautiful," he said slowly. "There are museums and parks, the opera, and wonderful shopping. Why wouldn't you want to see London?"

She laughed again. "And there is poverty and sickness. Why would I want to see that? If I need to buy something, I go to the village. But here I have all this," she said, sweeping her arm at the vista.

He couldn't fault her eyesight. His lands were beautiful rolling fields that seemed to go on forever. Looking around, he realized just how much he'd missed visiting this particular estate.

"Thank you," he said softly.

She stopped and then looked up at him with a frown.

"For what? That kiss? I most certainly didn't mean to let you kiss me."

He laughed gruffly. She wanted an apology for their kiss. "I was saying thank you for taking such good care of my tenants and servants."

"I am just doing my job, Your Grace."

"When we are alone, I wouldn't mind if you called me North or Colin."

"No, Your Grace. That implies an intimacy that we should not have."

He smiled again. In fact, he couldn't remember smiling this much in one day in years. "Hmm, perhaps it's an intimacy that would help us to get along with each other better."

"I highly doubt calling you by your Christian name will help us get along." She started walking again and he tagged along.

"I do believe you're wrong. Already, we are having a pleasant conversation and all it took was a kiss."

She turned on him with her eyes flashing like emeralds. "A kiss you stole. A kiss for which I never gave my permission—"

"Asking permission for a kiss takes all the excitement out of it. If I were to ask you for permission to kiss you right now, the kiss would be as dull as a Sunday sermon."

She put her hands on her hips. "Some Sunday sermons are very awe-inspiring."

"Indeed. Perhaps I am wrong." He frowned. "But how would I know if I am? I believe there is only one way to discover if my theory is correct." He bowed deeply in front of her. "Miss White, would you allow me a kiss?"

"No!"

His lips twitched. "Of course not. Why would anyone want to suffer from a dull kiss?"

"That is not my reason at all," she exclaimed. "You are betrothed. You are here planning your wedding and yet you kissed me. As it is, you still owe me an apology for that kiss last night. It was completely improper."

As he stared down at her heart-shaped face, the urge for another kiss overwhelmed him. "I shall never apologize for that kiss, Miss White. You needed comforting and I needed . . ."

His voice trailed off as he thought about what he needed. He needed to know that someday he might feel human again. And for some odd reason, the kiss of a wise woman gave him that feeling once more. Why would the one woman he should despise cause him to act so . . . so . . . much like a libertine?

"Exactly what did you need, Your Grace?" she asked in a knowing tone.

"Nothing important," he mumbled in reply.

"Humph."

"And I'm not betrothed," he said softly.

She halted. "You are not to be married?"

He almost laughed at her gape-mouthed expression. "No. And if I was, I would never dishonor my betrothed by kissing another woman."

"Oh," she said with a frown. She took a step and then spun around. "Then who is getting married?"

"My sister, Kate."

"Oh."

They walked a few more minutes in silence until they came upon the Wellses' cottage. For once, he seemed to have struck her speechless. He rather liked that. He slid a glance to her and noticed she still seemed to be unable to utter a word. Had she really thought that he was the one getting married? He would have to ask her about that sometime, but not now. His stomach ached as he stopped and stared at their home. He supposed that as duke he should be the first to give his sympathies. But he didn't want to. He wanted to run from this place.

"I don't want to go in."

Colin turned his head and stared at Selina. "Why?"

"This is my fault. I should have warned her when I didn't feel any movement."

"Why didn't you?"

"I don't know," she cried. "I was so upset with you returning and then evicting me from my home. I know that's no excuse . . . I guess I thought I'd have a few more days."

His heart went out to her. They would both have to face their demons when they walked inside that house. "Perhaps doing this together will make it a little easier."

"How so?"

"Hold my hand." He held out his left hand for her. After a moment of hesitation, she joined her hand with his. "Together we are stronger than apart. I'll give you strength . . . and you'll give me strength," he whispered the last part.

She squeezed his hand. "Thank you," she said softly.

Colin blew out a long breath and then knocked on the door. Mr. Wells opened the door and let them in.

"Welcome to my home, Your Grace," Mr. Wells said in a quiet voice.

If the man noticed Colin holding Selina's hand, he said nothing. Colin felt a tremble in her. "We came to give you and your wife our deepest sympathies, Mr. Wells. I know how hard it is to recover from the loss of a child."

"I'm certain *you* do," Mr. Wells said. "Unfortunately, my wife isn't taking this well. The physician came from the village and gave her laudanum."

"The physician?" Selina whispered so softly Colin almost didn't hear.

"Yes, Miss White. My wife wanted another opinion on why the baby didn't make it." Mr. Wells turned away from her. "Had she listened to me, the physician would have been here for the birth."

"And what did he say?" Selina asked.

"These things happen sometime. That it was God's will. He also said he would have let my wife know if he hadn't felt any movement so he could have prepared her for the worst possible outcome."

God's will. How he hated that saying. He looked over at Selina's pale face.

"I'm so sorry," Selina whispered, blinking back tears. "May I at least speak with her for a moment?"

"No, we don't want you here," Mr. Wells replied. "From now on the physician will assist us when we need medical attention."

Colin wanted to rail at the man for speaking to her in such a manner. But how could he when he felt the same way?

Chapter 9

Selina wiped a tear from her cheek as she strode toward the reflecting pond. She'd needed to get away from the Wellses' house as soon as she finished speaking with Susan. Even though she needed to be alone, she had no doubt that Colin would soon follow.

Colin?

Why was she suddenly thinking of him as Colin? One kiss in the rain and suddenly he was Colin? Or was it the fact that she now knew he was not betrothed and therefore she could welcome his advances if she chose? She fisted her hands in frustration. He was still the duke. He had evicted her from her home.

She did not want him.

She shook her head, determined to get the annoyingly handsome man out of her mind. She glanced behind her only to notice him gaining on her. The tails of his black coat were blowing back from the wind that whipped across the fields. He held the reins of his horse as the animal trotted behind him.

If only she could return to her cottage and be alone for a short while. Ever since she moved into Northrop Park, she'd barely had a moment of privacy. The servants seemed to think she needed constant companionship and normally stayed with her until she went off to bed. Now the duke had taken a sudden interest in her duties here, which should please her but did not. His presence was disruptive on so many levels.

"Selina, wait for me."

She ignored him and continued walking to the pond. She finally stopped and put her hand in the cooling water.

"Why didn't you wait for me?"

Selina brushed her wind-whipped hair out of her eyes. "I saw no need. We'd finished giving our condolences to the Wellses so I left."

He grabbed her arm and turned her to face him. His blue eyes searched her soul for answers. "It's a hard thing for a man . . . or a couple to lose a child. He was angry, that's all."

"I know that. This is not the first child I've lost. I just haven't lost a child in . . ." Her voice trailed off as she remembered the one delivery that still haunted her. For years, she'd attempted to put that one mother and child out of her mind, but it never seemed to work. She stared at the water wondering if the memories of that night would ever leave her.

"I'm sorry," he whispered.

"I should take my leave now. I'm quite certain you must have other things to do with your time than talk with me."

He released a long sigh. "I suppose I do."

"Yes. With the wedding approaching, you should make certain your workmen are doing their jobs." She started to walk toward the earl's lands. "Good day, Your Grace."

"Selina, wait."

She turned at him with a frown. "Wait for what?" She really had no time for delays. Today was the solstice and she had many things to do.

"I'll have a horse saddled for you to ride back to Hart's lands. It's a very long walk and you must be tired." He paused for a moment as if in thought before adding, "You do ride?"

"Yes, I ride." She supposed he didn't know Mr. Sellers gave her use of one of the mares whenever she needed it.

"Perfect."

The idea that he wanted to ease her discomfort had a strange warming effect on her. Why would the man who supposedly hated her want to make life easier for her? It made no sense. Then again, ever since he kissed her last night, she felt completely turned around when he was near.

"Thank you, Your Grace."

He smiled down at her until a deep dimple lined his left cheek. "In order to get that ride, I insist you call me Colin."

Right about now, she would call him a god if that's what it took to ride instead of walk. "Very well, Colin. I shall take you up on your offer."

They walked to the stables and found Mr. Sellers berating some of the lads for not brushing out a horse correctly. He glanced up at Colin and her with his mouth gaping.

"Good morning, Your Grace," he said, quickly recovering from his shock.

"Good morning, Mr. Sellers," Colin said. "I would like a gentle mare saddled for Miss White." He glanced down at her. "I also would like her to have access to the same mare any time she needs it."

"Yes, Your Grace," Mr. Sellers replied. "James, go get Daisy saddled for Miss White."

The lad nodded and then ran off to the stables.

"Your Grace," Selina started and then moved away from Mr. Sellers's hearing distance. "I do believe you are being far too generous."

He only smiled. "Consider it the apology you so desire and I refuse to give."

"As you wish, Your Grace." She pulled a piece of cloth from her skirt pocket and then tied back her hair.

"Very good. I will accompany you to Hart's lands. I need to speak with him anyway."

She walked back toward the stable and waited for James to bring out Daisy. Within a few minutes, James led the black mare out of the stable. He helped her up and she waited for Colin to mount his horse.

They started off at a slow pace as Selina enjoyed the ride. She leaned forward and patted the mare before looking over at Colin. "How did she get named Daisy?"

Colin laughed. The idea that a majestic black mare had been given such an innocuous name always made him chuckle. "My younger half sister named her."

"I had completely forgotten to ask how she is," Selina remarked. "I haven't seen her since she was . . ." she shrugged, "maybe eight or nine."

"I didn't know you knew her."

She laughed softly. "I think she wanted to be a wise woman. She would follow my mother and me around as we visited with the tenants."

"I doubt you would even recognize her now. She will be here soon."

"Of course, for the wedding."

They rode along in silence for a while. He slid a glance toward her and knew he'd made the right decision. Her small breasts bounced in rhythm to the horse's gallop. How could he be attracted to the one woman who made him completely insane?

He needed to get his thoughts off her before he did something rash like kiss her again or admit the truth.

"The weather has been pleasant lately," he said, shaking his head at his inane comment.

She glanced over at him and nodded. "Yes."

She apparently wasn't about to make this easy on him. There had to be some topic of conversation they could have without getting into an argument. Before he could come up with another topic, he saw Hart's estate. Thank God.

"I need to go this way toward the Featherstones' cottage," Selina said, inclining her head toward the right. She pulled up on the reins, coming to a halt. "Thank you for the use of your horse."

As she started to jump down, he said, "No, you may keep the horse at Hart's stables. I will speak to him about it."

"Thank you, Your Grace."

"Colin," he said firmly.

"Thank you, Colin."

He watched as she galloped toward the Featherstone cottage. He couldn't seem to take his eyes off her as she rode. All the unwelcome thoughts about her returned with great speed. The idea of her riding him seemed paramount in his mind.

With a shake of his head to clear his unsolicited thoughts, he headed to Hartsfield Manor. Once there, he quickly found Hart examining his empty fountain.

"Is there a problem?" he asked as he walked toward his friend.

"Damn thing isn't spouting water like it should."

"Why don't you have one of your men fix it?" Colin asked with a suppressed laugh.

"Why would I do that? It's a beautiful day. There is no point staying inside staring at my books."

Colin did laugh that time. He knew how much Hart despised working on the estate books. His friend would always prefer to be outside, preferably tinkering with things.

"What brings you here?" Hart asked as he examined the fountain.

"I accompanied Miss White."

Hart frowned deeply. "Odd, I haven't seen her around the estate much."

"Apparently, she still spends much of her time tending to my tenants and servants."

"Ah, so all you did was make it harder for her to perform her duties." Hart examined the mouth of the cupid where water normally spouted.

Hart's remark added another spoonful of guilt onto the mountain Colin already felt. "I suppose I did. Anyway, I left Daisy with her for her use. You do have room in your stables, don't you?"

"Of course, first your wise woman and now your horse. I shall take good care of both."

Hart's quip sent a streak of resentment through him. He didn't want Hart taking care of Selina. Nonetheless, the remark was nothing to feel jealousy over. Colin knew Hart had feelings for Miss Featherstone, but still the sensation of jealousy continued to grow. It made no sense. She was the wise woman. A peculiar one at that.

"Hand me that wrench," Hart said.

Colin handed him the tool and watched as he twisted the wrench around a nut. "I take it you found the problem?"

"Just a loose nut. That should take care of it." Hart climbed out of the fountain and gave the order to start the water again. They waited for a few minutes as the water flowed smoothly out of the cupid's mouth.

"Join me for luncheon," Hart said.

Colin agreed and before he knew it, luncheon turned to dinner and a little too much brandy.

"Tia is joining us tonight, isn't she?" Selina asked Mia as they gathered wood for the fire.

"Of course she will be here. She hasn't missed a solstice yet."

After arriving at Mia's house, Selina discovered Mrs. Featherstone had taken ill with a fever. Tonight would be the first solstice ritual the women had ever performed on their own. "Are you nervous?" she asked Mia.

Mia flashed a smile. "Yes. What if we do something wrong? My mother will have my head."

"We have been doing this since we were children. I'm certain we shall get everything correct." Selina picked up a piece of wood and dropped it in the cart. "At least with your mother absent, I don't have to call you two by your given names."

"Oh, but what English girl doesn't want to be named after a Greek goddess?" Mia asked with a touch of sarcasm. "I'll never understand what she was thinking."

"True, but Damia is rather a pretty name."

Mia shook her head. "It's far better than my poor sister's name."

Selina had to agree with that. Hestia was not the prettiest of names but the shortened version of Tia suited the woman just fine.

Mia looked down at the cart and said, "That should be enough. Did you bring a sacrifice?"

Selina felt the heat of embarrassment cross her cheeks. "I pilfered one of his books when I was in the house for the cleansing."

"It is supposed to be something of meaning to him. It should be given by him."

"Well, that is not about to happen. He is barely civil with me. It is a book of sonnets that I found on a table in the library. I'm sure he's read it, but I doubt he'll miss them. What did you bring?"

"The earl sent me a lock of his hair for the fire."

Selina smiled, wondering if her friend would ever see that the earl was smitten with her. "That should work. That leaves Tia."

"That girl will probably show up empty-handed just like last year."

"As a matter of fact, I happen to have a handkerchief that belongs to Middleton," Tia said from behind them.

They both turned and hugged the third wise woman. While Tia never seemed to recognize the importance of her position, at least she put in an appearance when needed. The wild redhead looked nothing like her brown-haired twin, except for the soulful brown eyes they both received from their father.

"Let's get the fire ready for tonight," Mia said as they pushed the cart up the small hill.

Every year on the summer solstice, they performed the same ritual their mother and grandmothers had for centuries. Standing at the intersection of all three properties, they marked off twenty paces and drew a circle around them. During the ceremony, each wise woman would stand in the circle on the land where she belonged.

They tossed the kindling down and then stacked the wood around it. The fire had to be large enough to cover all three properties. They lit their lanterns and waited for midnight.

As the air cooled and darkened, they finally lit the bonfire. Each woman chanted a blessing for the land, the rain, and the crops just as their mothers had before them. Circling the fire, they sprinkled grains for a healthy harvest into the fire and watched as they sparked upward into the night sky.

Selina smiled as the embers shimmered in the air. It would be a good growing year. And hopefully, the tenants—and the duke—would be healthy.

"Ready the sacrifices," Mia said over the crackle of the fire.

Selina picked up the book of sonnets but as she did a sense of foreboding swept over her. She opened the cover of the book and leaned closer to the fire in order to read the inscription.

To my dearest husband,
    Happy Birthday! I hope you love this book as much as I do. With all my love,

                                                                    Mary

The book fell out of her fingers as if already scorched by the fire. She couldn't sacrifice this book. Slowly, she bent down and picked up the volume. Now she had nothing to sacrifice. The sound of a horse galloping closer forced her gaze toward the earl's lands.

"Oh, dear God, not now," she whispered.

Seeing the fire on the horizon, Colin propelled his horse to a run. He prayed it wasn't his home on fire due to some carelessness of the workers. But as he approached, he saw the women standing around a huge bonfire and anger filled his mind.

Did they not realize the danger of building such a large fire? Even though there had been some rain lately, it was still dangerous. These "wise" women were putting all three estates at risk.

He urged his horse faster until he reached the fire. After tying his horse to a tree, he stalked the group of women.

"Good God, women, have you no sense?" he shouted. "That bonfire might spark a wildfire."

The Featherstone women both gasped as he approached but Selina stared at the ground with a guilty look on her face. Then Mia Featherstone laughed. "Your Grace, we have several buckets of water in case a spark catches. We have been doing this for years . . . centuries."

"What are you ladies doing here? It's almost midnight." His gaze reverted to Selina. In her hands she held a book, most likely some volume of unholy pagan rituals.

"Your Grace, it is the summer solstice. You are welcome to watch us but please let us finish the ritual," Mia Featherstone said softly.

"I do not want any part of this on my lands," he replied, staring at Selina, who wouldn't return his gaze.

"We are almost finished, Your Grace," Mia replied. "All we have left is the sacrificial burning."

"The what?" Did they actually toss a sheep or some other animal on the fire?

"We sacrifice an object belonging to the lord of the land," she said. "The earl offered a lock of his hair. Viscount Middleton offered a handkerchief."

He crossed his arms over his chest and slowly walked up to Selina. "And exactly what did I offer?"

"Nothing, Your Grace," she mumbled.

"But I thought you had a book," Tia said in a questioning tone.

Selina shot her friend a glare. "I was wrong." She moved her hands behind her back.

"Give me the book, Miss White," he ordered.

"I already said I don't have a book."

"The one in your hand." He held out his hand, waiting for her to place the book in it.

"Your Grace," she started as she brought her hand in front of her. "Please, don't be angry. Once I saw the inscription, I knew I couldn't burn the book."

Colin frowned as he took the book from her. Glancing down at the cover his anger exploded. "You thought to burn this book?"

"No," she mumbled. "Not once I saw the inscription."

"Where did you get this?" he demanded as the other two women backed away.

"It was on your desk in the library."

He lifted her chin to look her in the eyes. "You were in my house and stole from me?"

"You left me no choice in the matter. I knew if I came to you and explained the situation you would have laughed at me. Or worse, called me some kind of witch because we believe in these rituals whether you do or not."

Somewhere deep in his brain, he knew she was right.

Nonetheless, he couldn't grasp the fact that she almost burned the last gift ever given to him from his late wife. He treasured that book.

"Don't ever step foot on my property again," he growled and then turned away from the fire.

"Your Grace, I am dreadfully sorry," she cried. "I promise I wasn't going to burn the book. I saw the inscription. I know what she meant to you."

He turned back and glared at her. "You have no idea what she meant to me. Unlike many of the arranged marriages in society, I actually loved my wife."

"I'm so sorry," she said softly. "Please, let me continue to help your tenants and servants."

"No. Don't set foot on my property again."

Selina watched him ride away as tears filled her eyes. Damn that stubborn man. Why couldn't he realize that all she wanted to do was help keep the lands fertile? While it might seem like a silly ritual to him, it was important the tenants know it had been performed.

"What are you going to do?" Mia whispered as she put her arm around Selina's shoulders.

"Nothing. I will not stop helping those people. I don't care if he calls the constable to drag me away. They need me." Selina inhaled deeply. "I won't stop performing my duty."

Mia nodded. "Will you be coming home with me?"

"No. I'll go back to my room at the house." She gave her friends a watery smile. "He will depart as soon as the wedding is over. All I have to do is avoid him for another few weeks. How hard can that be?"

"Another few weeks?" Mia whispered. "The wedding is six weeks away. Do you really think you can evade him for that long?"

"I have no choice," Selina admitted. With all the workers

about now, he was all over the house. She rarely left her room because she feared he would discover her.

"Do you really think that's wise?" Tia asked. "Why not come home with me? In fact, you could be the wise woman for Middleton's lands so I can leave for London."

"You're not going to London, Tia," her sister said firmly.

"I am and no one will stop me." Tia brushed a lock of red hair out of her eyes. "Selina can stay at my cottage while I'm gone. That way, she is out of the duke's ire."

"No," Selina said. "I will not be evicted from my lands."

Mia cleared her throat. "They are actually his lands, Selina."

She frowned at her friend. "I know that. But still, I will not leave."

Chapter 10

The next few days were uneventful as Selina did everything she could to stay out of the duke's sight. Unfortunately, the man didn't seem to leave the house often enough that she could roam either the house or the estate. She was not a woman who enjoyed sitting around doing nothing like the ladies of the upper crust. She paced her large room, pausing by the window for a breath of fresh air. She desperately needed to be outside, riding or walking, anything to feel less constricted than she did in this house. While it was a lovely room, every day it felt more and more like a prison to her.

Finally, a knock on the door broke the tedium.

She opened the door just a crack only to find Randall in the hall.

"This just came for you, miss." He slid the paper through the opening and then nodded his head. "Shall I wait for a reply?"

Selina stifled a laugh. "No, if I need to return a message, I shall ring for you."

"It is no problem to wait, miss."

"Randall, go back to your position before the duke wonders why you are not at your station."

His eyes widened as if he hadn't thought of that possibility. "Very good, miss," he said, nodding.

She closed the door and then moved to the window where the light was better. She smiled as she opened the missive and read Mia's note. There was a traveling fair in town and she begged Selina to meet her there this afternoon at one.

Selina glanced at the clock and nodded. She had an hour to determine the best way of escaping the house without Colin noticing her. After changing into her light yellow muslin dress, she walked to the door. She cracked it open and looked both ways before running to the servants' staircase. He certainly would never use them but it didn't stop her from peering down the steps before creeping down them. When she reached the second floor, she stopped. This was one of the most likely places he would be this afternoon.

Voices echoed from down the hall. She breathed in deeply to slow her racing heart. As the voices diminished, she peeked around the corner. Seeing no one in the hall, she rounded the corner and continued to the lower level.

Again, she stopped and listened for voices. As no sound reached her ears, she slipped down the hall searching for an exit that wouldn't reveal her to the duke. She departed from the library door to the terrace. Finally, she could breathe. Even if he found her here, she could use the excuse that she was here to see a servant.

As her heart finally slowed its staccato beat, she walked across the lawn and headed toward town. It would take her an hour on foot, but for the chance to see her friends, it was worth it.

By the time she reached the outskirts of Cheadle, she could hear the noise from the churchyard and square. A rush of excitement pushed her lips upward. She'd attended this fair since she was a little girl. She still remembered her father hoisting her up on his shoulders so she could watch the happenings. One time she even saw a man with a monkey on his shoulder, holding on just as she had with her father. After that day, her father had always called her his little monkey. She wiped away a quick tear that fell down her cheek. She still missed him.

"Selina!"

She turned at the sound of Mia's voice. Her friend rushed to greet her with a hug. "I'm so glad you were able to come," Mia said.

"Me too. I had to sneak out of the house so he wouldn't see me," she said with a slight giggle.

"There you two are," Tia said as she approached them. "You must try these almonds. They are the best I've ever had."

Selina took one from the bag and then chewed the nut. "Is that cinnamon?"

Tia nodded. "Yes!"

"Let me have one too," Mia said as she reached into the bag. After she popped one into her mouth, a slow smile lit her face. "They are delicious!"

"What have you seen so far, Tia?"

"There is a magician and a fortune-teller over at the square." Tia leaned in closer. "They weren't allowed on the church grounds. But the juggler and the menagerie are in the churchyard. They even have a lion this year."

Selina smiled. "I must see that!"

Mia nodded as she took another almond from her sister. "And we need more almonds."

Selina and Tia laughed.

Selina hadn't felt this relaxed since the duke had returned. To be with her friends without the worry of him seeing her made her feel lighter. She glanced around the area one more time just to be certain he hadn't decided to come to town.

"Who are you looking for?" Mia asked with a knowing smile.

"I don't want to even think about him today."

Tia laughed. "The duke would never come to a fair.

That is far too unsophisticated for a man of his station. He's probably back at the estate reading a treatise on our tea exports from India."

Her friend was most likely correct. Selina almost laughed aloud at the idea of Colin sitting before the fortune-teller looking for some wisdom. Although, she wondered what the woman would say to her. There was only one way to find out.

"I have decided to have my fortune told," she told her friends as she walked toward the decidedly frightening woman.

"Good luck," Mia called. "We shall be at the menagerie."

As Selina approached the woman, she slowed almost to a stop. The woman wore a scarlet dress with a multitude of colored threads shot through it. Atop her head was a black and gold turban. The woman suddenly turned her head and stared at Selina. The fortune-teller frowned her wrinkled face. Black kohl lined her tired eyes lending her an exotic yet daunting look.

The woman crooked a finger at Selina. "Come along. Others will be here soon and you must be first."

Why would she need to be first? A nervous shiver made her body quake. "I haven't decided if I want to have my fortune read yet."

"Of course you have decided. I knew the moment you broke away from your group of friends that you would want a reading."

Selina took a step closer and then stopped again. What was wrong with her? She never let a person intimidate her. Not even the duke himself could manage that feat.

"Come along," the old woman complained. "I don't have all day."

She swallowed down her trepidation and pulled out the seat across from the woman. "My name is—"

"I know who you are," the woman said in a harsh tone. "I

am Madame Czerwony." She took Selina's hands into her own. "And you are the wise woman."

"I am just a healer."

The older woman shook her head. "No, my dear. You are one of the few left in these lands."

Selina was surprised by the woman's words. No one believed in the tales of the wise women. "Can you tell me of my future?"

The woman, with her one blue eye and the other clouded by a cataract, stared at her until Selina felt forced to look down at their joined hands. "No," the woman finally answered. "I don't think you would believe me."

"What do you mean?"

"You're already a wise woman. But someday you shall also be a very great lady."

Selina suppressed a laugh. There was nothing great about her . . . nor would there ever be. "I doubt that very much."

"Of course you do," Madame Czerwony said with a slight shrug.

"How will I become such a lady?"

This time the old woman cackled. "The same way they all do. You shall marry into it." She leaned in closer and whispered, "And if you do, you will be forced to give up many things. So think carefully about whether or not it's worth the sacrifice."

Selina blinked back tears. She was no great lady and never would be. Why would this woman tell her such nonsense? She pulled her hands out of the fortune-teller's and rose. "Thank you."

She reached into her purse and pulled out a few coins. Her hands shook as she tossed the money on the table.

The woman was wrong. Still, as she walked away from the seer and toward her friends, her body trembled. There was something about that woman that frightened her and Selina had no idea why.

* * *

"Come along," Hart grumbled as he led Colin toward the stables.

"Why are we going into town?"

"Because you need to have some enjoyment while you're here. Kate will be arriving in a week or two, so your life will be nothing but preparing the house and yourself for the wedding. This is your last chance at freedom for a few weeks."

His friend knew him far too well. Once Kate arrived, his thoughts would be on the wedding and, more than likely, the memories of his marriage to Mary. Perhaps a day without worries would be helpful . . . possibly even amusing. "Very well, then."

Hart's brows rose slightly as he let out a quick laugh. "I honestly thought I'd have to drag you there."

Colin shrugged. "You are right. I shall have too many things on my mind in the next few weeks to enjoy myself. So this is my last day for a pleasant outing."

They waited outside the stable for Colin's horse to be brought out. As they passed the time, Colin noticed a rider on the horizon and wondered who could be visiting today. The rider approached the stables just as the stableboy handed the mare's reins to Colin.

"Middleton?" Colin said, surprised that his neighbor and friend was even out in the country.

"Shocked to see me out here?" He laughed as he removed his hat and brushed his dark blond hair back off his forehead.

Hart chortled. "You love London. What brought you out here?"

Middleton shook his head. "Family issues. And summer does become a bit oppressive in London."

"We're off to the village. Will you join us?" Hart asked.

"Of course. I hear there is a fair in town. Perhaps a pretty girl, eager to please a lord, for each of us. Or maybe we should pretend we are of lower class and find some amusement there?"

It wouldn't be that far of a stretch for Middleton, Colin thought. The son of a second son of a viscount whose father had gambled away what little fortune he had, Middleton only inherited the title after a few oddly suspicious accidents in his uncle's family.

"Let's be off," Hart said.

They rode toward town and talked about the lands they grew up on, the current weather and the conditions of the crops. Once they reached Cheadle, they left their horses at the livery and walked toward the square.

The eyes of the villagers immediately went to the three lords walking through their town. Colin glanced around and felt slightly uncomfortable, as if they were intruding where they shouldn't. A few people nodded to them but said nothing in greeting.

"Perhaps this wasn't a good idea," Colin started.

"Nonsense," Middleton replied. "There is no reason we cannot be here."

Hart nodded. "For once, I agree with Middleton."

Middleton laughed so loudly several people turned to stare at them. "You are only here for one reason."

Hart's cheeks reddened slightly.

"And what would that be?" Colin asked.

"There is no reason I want to be here other than to get you out of your crumbling house."

"Of course," Middleton said with a smirk. "It has nothing to do with the fact that Miss Featherstone was meeting her sister and Miss White here today."

"Exactly," Hart grumbled. "It has nothing to do with that."

Selina was here? Colin scanned the crowd seeking out the woman he couldn't seem to stop thinking about. The same woman who fired his anger and his passion. A flash of blond hair caught his attention. Was she really having her fortune told? Based on her frown, she didn't seem to care for what the old woman was telling her.

"And who might you be staring at, North?" Middleton asked.

"The fortune-teller." He looked away from Selina to avoid any further probing questions from Middleton. "Shall I have my future foretold to me?"

"I highly doubt that charlatan can read anything," Middleton said. "Look at that poor girl's face. She looks like she might just cry."

Colin glanced back at Selina and noticed that she did indeed appear visibly upset by her encounter with the old woman. Should he confront Selina and ask her what was wrong? He shook his head. That was the last thing he should do. She was a strong woman who could take care of herself . . . and everyone on his estate. Far better than he could.

Still, he felt a need to be there for her. Watching her rise from the chair across from the fortune-teller, he made a quick excuse to his friends and started walking toward her. He could hear both men chuckling behind him and for once, he didn't care. She needed someone to talk to and maybe she would want to confide in him.

He cut her off as she attempted to cross the road to get to the church. Clasping her elbow, he led her to a quieter area away from the crowd. "What's the matter?"

"How dare you just . . . just . . ." Her voice trailed off as her chin quivered.

"What happened with the fortune-teller?"

Immediately, her face hardened and all visible signs of her distress vanished. "Nothing happened. The woman is a liar."

"Then why did you look so upset?"

"I did not look upset. I just don't appreciate paying someone to lie to me."

The breeze brought the fragrance of her lavender soap toward him. Once again, he felt his body react to her nearness. This was madness. He could not be attracted to her. Yet, no matter what his mind thought, his unruly body rejected the logic.

"What did she say?" he finally asked her.

"It matters not." She blinked a few times as if still holding back tears. "She is a charlatan."

He led her toward the stream where few people roamed. "Then why does it matter if you tell me?"

Her green eyes widened. "Because you of all people would only laugh and ridicule everything she said."

Was that what she thought of him? He would mock her because of the old woman's tales? "I wouldn't do that."

"Of course you would." She turned to walk away. "Me, a great lady," she mumbled as she moved, "that is an impossibility."

Colin watched as she returned to her friends but her words wouldn't leave him. What had she meant by what she'd said? Had the fortune-teller told her that she would be a great lady?

"Perhaps there is only one way to find out."

He strode toward the old woman's table only to find a young woman leaning in closer to the fortune-teller as if she couldn't miss a word. The fortune-teller's black and gold turban bobbed as she nodded in reassurance to the younger woman. The medium glanced up and noticed him waiting for her.

"That is all I see," she abruptly told the younger woman.

"Thank you, Madame Czerwony. I will take your advice to heart."

"Of course you will, Miss Reilly. Run along, now. I have an important man to see now."

Miss Reilly turned and gaped. She curtsied quickly and said, "Your Grace," before dashing from the table.

"Your Grace," Madame Czerwony said softly. "Why are you here this fine afternoon?"

Colin walked to the table and sat in the deserted chair. "I would like to know what you said to a . . ." How could he describe Selina to this woman? ". . . a friend of mine. It upset her greatly."

"I do not believe it is any of your business."

"She is my . . ." The words trailed off.

"Your wise woman, Your Grace?"

How did she know that? "Yes."

The old woman shrugged. "That she is, but that does not mean you have the right to interfere."

Of course, she was correct in that matter. He had no rights at all where Selina was concerned. And worse, he had no idea why it even mattered to him. He tried to tell himself he would have done the same for any of his tenants. If he knew his tenants, which he did not.

Still, he couldn't let the subject drop. He had to discover why she'd been so upset by the fortune-teller's words. "I shall pay you three times your normal fee."

A slow, wicked grin crossed her face. "Only three times? I believe five is a more appropriate sum for me to reveal a confidence."

Colin knew he was being cheated but if that's what it took to learn one of Selina's secrets, it was worth it. "Very well."

He pulled out the money and tossed it across the table. "Now, tell me exactly what you said to her."

The old woman cackled. "I only told her she would be a great lady. And I warned her that in becoming that person she might have to give up a great deal. So she needed to think about if it would be worth it."

"That's it?" Why would that upset Selina? "There was nothing more? No warnings of an early death? Misfortune coming her way?"

"No, Your Grace. I see a long life for that girl. If she makes the right decision."

"And what would be the right decision?"

Madame Czerwony shook her head. "Only she can know that." She cleared her throat and then sipped from a glass. "Now be off. Unless you want to pay me to read your fortune?"

Colin almost laughed at the idea of paying the charlatan more money. "Thank you," he said as he rose from his seat.

Chapter 11

The next few days, Selina stayed in her room and hoped no one needed her. It was only six weeks until the wedding, and if that meant staying in this room every minute except when a tenant was sick, then she would do just that.

If only the warm summer air didn't call to her. She longed to walk the fields to the tenants' homes or better yet, ride the fields with her hair blowing in the breeze. Six weeks. *Six excruciatingly long weeks.* She could manage. She had no choice.

A loud commotion at the front of the house drew her to the window. She had cracked the window open just enough to let some air in so now she could hear servants talking. An elegant black carriage had pulled up in the drive. Behind the carriage, a wagon filled with trunks came to a halt. Several servants milled about until the carriage stopped. Then they went straight to work.

The door opened and an older woman with gray hair stepped out. Wearing a handsome burgundy driving gown, she looked as if she were ready for a drive through Hyde Park instead of a trip to the Midlands. The servants all bowed to the woman as a younger woman stepped down and stared up at the house with a frown.

"The bride has arrived," Selina mumbled but continued to stare down at the group. She briefly wondered why Colin wasn't outside greeting his guests.

"Welcome home," she finally heard him say.

She inched closer to the window in order to spy his position. He walked forward and bowed over the dowager duchess's hand before moving to his sister.

"You're here early. I'm afraid now you'll have to put up with all the noise of the workmen."

Instead of bowing over her hand, he embraced Kate warmly. It was fascinating to watch the interaction between him and his half sister. He appeared to love her very much.

"Oh, Colin," the younger woman whined. "That was the most dreadful ride ever. We actually stayed at an inn where the only choice for a meal was a meat pie. Can you imagine? A meat pie. I'm terribly sore after the long drive. Please tell me the servants have hot water waiting for me so I can bathe."

Before Colin could say a word, she continued her complaints. "I swear those roads were so bumpy. I thought my head would hit the ceiling of the carriage. And the rudeness of . . ." Her voice trailed off as they walked into the house.

Selina smiled. She was slightly surprised at how spoiled Kate seemed now. His sister had always been a pleasant girl. Perhaps that's what London did to people.

Selina moved away from the window to her soft bed. She frowned as she leaned back against her pillows. Would Colin ever consider marrying again? He truly should for the benefit of the estate. While his brother might already be married with a son, Colin's heir should inherit the dukedom. But she was certain he still hadn't completely recovered from his wife's death, so she doubted he was ready for marriage again.

She wondered what it would feel like to be loved as his wife was during their marriage. She imagined he would be attentive to her, listen to her questions, and answer without disparaging her.

Gently she touched her lips. Would he be just as attentive in bed? Selina thought back to that kiss they shared by the pond. Oh yes, he would satisfy his wife's every desire.

Colin shut the door to his study and walked to the brandy decanter. He poured a large snifter and then moved to his desk. Finally, he had some peace again. The women in the house were driving him mad and they'd only been here for a few hours. How would he handle them for six weeks?

And worse, the one woman not in the house would not leave his mind. He sipped his brandy and leaned back against the leather chair. He looked down at the book and caressed the leather cover. Perhaps he had overreacted that night when he'd become so incensed with Selina. But it was all he had left of Mary.

Still, Selina had looked sincere when she told him she wouldn't burn the book. So why hadn't he believed her? Because she was a witch. Perhaps not in the usual sense of the word but she had cast a dreadful spell over him. He wanted her when he knew he shouldn't. If that wasn't witchcraft, he didn't know what was.

A knock scraped at the door.

"Come in," he said loudly. He cringed slightly when Kate walked into the room with a happy smile. He rose from his seat, thankful his thoughts regarding Selina hadn't had their usual effect on his manhood.

"Do you mind if I join you in a brandy?"

"You know I don't mind."

She took a seat closer to the fireplace and then smiled up at him. "Come sit near me. It's been over a month since I've seen you."

"I take it the nap and bath did wonders for your disposition?" He walked to the brandy and poured a small snifter for her.

She laughed softly. "I must apologize. I was not in the best of moods when I arrived this afternoon."

After handing her the glass, he stared at her for a long moment. She'd always had a habit of tapping her fingers when something bothered her. Right now, all her fingers were tapping a staccato beat against her glass.

"What's wrong, Kate?" He took the brown chair across from her.

She stared down at her glass. "We are going to move up the wedding date."

"Oh?"

"Please don't be upset. I told Mother to write to you, informing you of the change but we were so busy with everything. And please don't worry about the house, none of that matters."

He stared at her for a long moment. His gaze settled on her flat belly. "Is there a reason I should know about?"

"I want to be married, Colin," she said with a laugh and then brushed a lock of dark brown hair out of her eyes. "Besides, more people will be able to attend if we have the ceremony in July instead of August."

He supposed that made sense. Many people left the heat of London after the Season and headed for their country estates. This wouldn't be too out of the way for many people. "What date then?"

"The eighth of July."

"That's only two weeks away!" He assumed she meant closer to the end of July, not the beginning.

"Everything is set. The workers will be finished with the major items on your list, won't they?"

He blew out a long sigh. The date change should make him happy. After all, now he would be able to leave Northrop Park much sooner. "Yes, they only have a few more days to finish the roof repair."

"Excellent! See, this will be perfect."

"That means people may start arriving within the week," he said aloud.

"Yes, but if we need more staff, Mother and I can hire some temporary workers from the village."

"We might need to do just that." He leaned in closer. "My staff is getting aged. They can barely see the dust on the tables. But I dare not let them go."

"Why not?"

"They've been here since long before I was born." He laughed and she joined in. It was comforting to have Kate here.

"Tomorrow, I will check the upstairs bedrooms and make a list of where people will stay. Because we moved up the date, we decided on fewer guests so we won't need all the bed-chambers. I'll have the entire thing organized by tomorrow night."

While many people considered Kate spoiled, he knew it was only due to her station. She was a master at organization. Just having her here would produce a successful wedding. "I'm very glad you're here," he said softly.

"So am I. London is becoming unbearable with all the unmarried women going on about not making a match this season. It's wonderful to be away from it all."

"Good." And within three weeks, he'd be able to leave here and stop thinking about Selina.

"Good morning, Selina," Mrs. Roberts said loudly, jarring Selina from a restful slumber. "Here's your tea and toast. I must run."

Selina pushed her hair out of her eyes. "Why are you in such a rush?" Normally, Mrs. Roberts helped her dress and then stayed to chat for at least an hour.

"Oh my, you haven't heard." Mrs. Roberts stopped by the end of the bed.

"I saw the carriage arrive yesterday."

"Indeed, Lady Kate and the duchess are creating so much more work. They moved up the wedding. Now it's to be the eighth of July." Mrs. Roberts's eyes widened. "That's a fortnight early. We have so much to do!"

They moved the date. In just over two weeks, Kate would be married and Colin would leave for London or one of his other estates. As Mrs. Roberts left the room, Selina pushed her plate away. Suddenly she had no appetite. She rose and walked to the window. Glancing down, she noticed Colin and his sister riding off toward the fields.

She continued to stare at him as he rode. She could imagine the strong muscle of his legs pressing against the horse. His hands would reach over and stroke her hair . . . the horse's mane, she meant. Dear Lord, there was something dreadfully wrong with her.

The day slipped to another, then another without Selina having the opportunity to leave her room. The servants were so busy they barely said two words to her when they arrived with a plate of food. Today, Mrs. Roberts had forgotten to come up and help her dress. The tedium was driving her mad. She would have to find a way to escape the house today.

Noticing the gray day through the window, she decided to wait until later. Perhaps the weather would clear.

With nothing else to do, she picked up a book and returned to bed. After a few hours of reading and dozing, she heard the handle of the door squeak. She ducked under the covers to hide herself from the footman who normally brought her lunch. She couldn't be seen in her night rail at noon.

"What in the world is going on in this room?"

Selina went completely still, hearing the soft feminine

voice. That was not the footman or any of the maids that she knew.

"Come out from under those covers this instant!"

Slowly, she pulled the coverlet down until she could see who stood in her room. Selina's face heated as she stared at Colin's sister.

"What are you doing sleeping here?" Kate's mouth gaped slightly. "Oh my! Are you his mistress? Did he actually have the nerve to bring you here when people will be arriving for my wedding in the next week?"

"No! I am certainly not his mistress," Selina remarked. Why did that seem to be the general consensus? The first day he arrived he'd assumed she was here for his pleasure. "How could you think he would do such a thing to you?"

The younger woman continued to stare at her. "Then who are you?"

Selina blew out a breath and closed her eyes. "My name is Selina White. I'm—"

"Selina! I didn't recognize you! I haven't seen you since I was ten. You were always so kind to me and let me tag along with you and your mother." Kate spoke so quickly Selina could barely keep up. She raced to the bed and quickly hugged Selina. "I'm so happy you're here. I asked about you yesterday and Colin said you were living with Hart's wise woman."

"Lady Katherine . . . Kate," Selina paused, staring at her. "You are all grown up."

Kate tilted her head and smiled shyly. "Thank you, Selina. It's always been Kate to you. But I still don't understand what you're doing up here."

Selina bit down on her lip trying to determine what to tell Colin's sister. She was so sick of not having anyone to speak with she couldn't help but blurt out the truth. "He doesn't know I'm here."

"He doesn't know?" Kate burst out laughing. "I asked

about you at dinner last evening and he about bit my head off. He only said you were at Hart's."

"Oh, Kate, you mustn't tell him I'm here."

"He really doesn't know you're living in his house!" Laughter erupted from her again. "That is brilliant."

"He evicted me from my cottage," Selina said coldly. She explained how the servants had come up with the plan to hide her upstairs.

Kate's brow furrowed. "I know he holds your mother responsible for Mary's death but he should not blame you."

Selina looked away but nodded.

"So you've been living here for close to a fortnight and he hasn't realized it yet." She giggled softly. "What are your plans?"

"Mr. Roberts told me he plans to leave as soon as all the wedding guests depart. Once he's gone, I'll move back to my cottage. From what I've heard, I doubt he'll ever return to Northrop Park."

Kate nodded with a smile. "I believe I can keep your secret, but only on one condition."

"And what would that be?"

"That you come to the wedding."

Come to the wedding! "I can't do that. A few nights ago, he told me to never step foot on his property again. He will be furious if I attend."

"I know," Kate said with a giggle. "He has been so detached for the past eight years that it's nice to see him show some emotion even if it's anger. At least that means he's feeling something."

"At my expense!" Detached? The man was a rake. Then again, perhaps remaining unemotional with all those women was the only way he could seduce them all.

"Perhaps," she said with a shrug. "But you will promise me you'll attend or I shall march downstairs and inform him you're up here."

Selina shook her head knowing she was defeated. "All right, you win."

"I always do." Kate sat up as if to leave. "May I visit you during your imprisonment?"

"Please," Selina replied. "The servants are so busy with the wedding being moved up that I have no one to talk to all day. Most of the tenants are well so there is nothing to do. If I leave I fear your brother will discover me."

They talked for over two hours. Kate told her all about London, the Season, and her betrothed, John. Selina admitted that she had originally thought Colin was the one to marry soon.

"Colin marry?" Her laughter died off as she shook her head. "I doubt that will happen ever again. He just won't let go of the past."

The small interactions they'd shared had made Selina wonder if he would be happy married again. He missed his late wife so dreadfully.

"But shouldn't he marry at least for an heir?"

Kate shook her head slowly. "After what happened, I don't think he would ever let his heart open to another woman. He would rather Tom's son inherited." She glanced over at the clock. "I must go now."

"Thank you for visiting with me."

"I shall come back later. We'll play cards and become fast friends again."

Selina smiled as Kate left the room. She prayed Kate would keep her secret for the next two weeks.

After two days of having his stepmother and sister underfoot, Colin needed to get away. They were driving him mad with wedding plans. He assumed a ride would set him to rights again.

He walked to the stables but Mr. Sellers was not around.

Instead of waiting, he ambled inside toward Zeus. A familiar whinny stopped him cold. He turned toward the black mare and let her nuzzle his shoulder.

"What are you doing here, Daisy?" Could Selina have been so angry with him that she returned the sweet mare? The woman could be more stubborn than any person he knew.

"Your Grace, what are you doing here?" Mr. Sellers said with a slight gasp when he noticed the mare.

"When did Miss White return Daisy?"

Mr. Sellers coughed and glanced away. "A few days ago, Your Grace."

"Did you attempt to convince her to keep the mare?"

"Of course, but she refused."

"Saddle Daisy and Zeus. I shall return Daisy to her."

"Yes, Your Grace." Mr. Sellers whistled for the stableboys. Two came running as Colin walked back into the yard.

A few moments later, one of the boys raced to the house. He spoke to Mr. Roberts and then ran back to the stables. Colin wondered briefly what that was all about? With a shrug, he decided it might be best if he didn't know.

With the horses saddled, he headed out toward Hart's lands and the wise women. He'd promised the horse for Selina's use.

By the time he arrived at Mrs. Featherstone's cottage, he felt exhilarated by the fresh air and lack of female chatter. He jumped off Zeus and tied the horses to a post. The door opened before he even walked toward it.

"Good afternoon, Your Grace," Miss Featherstone said. Her cornflower dress blew out around her ankles.

"Good afternoon, Miss Featherstone. Is Miss White at home?"

She bit down on her lip and glanced toward his lands. "No, Your Grace. I . . . I believe she is visiting some of the tenants."

"I see." Was she visiting Hart's tenants or disobeying Colin's orders and calling on his tenants?

"Would you like to leave a message for her?"

"No. I believe I shall wait for her."

He glanced over at Miss Featherstone's worried face. "It might be a few hours, Your Grace. You can always write her a note. I will make certain she receives it."

"How kind," he remarked. "But as I said, I shall wait."

Miss Featherstone's gaze continued to scan the lands, mostly his lands. "Would you like to come in for some tea? My mother is home and would enjoy the company."

"No, thank you. I will wait out here. The air is refreshing."

Her gaze darted between the fields and the line of trees. "Of course, Your Grace. I believe I shall try to find her for you."

"Oh, Miss Featherstone, there is no need for that." Colin had no doubts that she was trying to protect her friend. But he wanted to see from which direction Selina arrived.

He sat on a small stump and waited for over an hour before he saw her coming from the direction of the tenants' cottages. Hart's tenants. He stood as she walked closer to him. Her green eyes sparkled like emeralds and burned him with their fury.

"To what do I owe this honor," she sneered.

"I came to return your horse," Colin said. He suddenly wished for their animosity to be over. Remembering the walk they took to Mrs. Wells's home, he wished they could return to that level of almost friendship.

"Daisy is your horse and should be kept at your stables, not Lord Hartsfield's. That is why I sent her back. But do not worry, Your Grace, I didn't take a step on your lands. I asked one of the earl's stableboys to return her."

She attempted to storm past him but he caught her wrist. He stared down at her delicate fingers.

"I told you Daisy was for your use. I have plenty of horses in my stables."

She tried to pull out of his grip to no avail. "No, thank you, Your Grace."

He knew there was only one way to appease her. "I must apologize for my behavior the other night. I'd had too much brandy and when I saw the book in your hand . . ."

"Once I noticed the inscription, I knew I had to return the book to you," she whispered.

"Again, I apologize." He slowly released her wrist but immediately missed the warmth of her skin.

"May I call on your tenants again?"

He closed his eyes and nodded. Why was this woman getting under his skin when no other had in eight years? He couldn't stand to see disappointment in her eyes. Or know he'd hurt her feelings.

"Thank you, Your Grace."

He opened his eyes and smiled. "I believe we agreed you would call me Colin in private."

"This is hardly private. Anyone might overhear us and assume things about our relationship that are not true."

"You are indeed a wise woman, Miss White." And a woman who seemed to have bewitched him. He had to find a way to break that spell before he did something disastrous.

Chapter 12

Selina waited until dark before creeping back into the house. While she may have gained access to his lands, he would still be furious to discover she lived right under his nose. Or maybe that was above his nose. She giggled slightly as she tiptoed up the servants' stairs to the third floor.

Opening the door to her room, she found a plate of cold chicken and bread. She kicked off her boots and then sat at the small table to eat. She devoured the food, after saying a quick prayer of thanks for Mrs. Roberts's support. Once finished with dinner, she moved to a chair near the window and reflected on the day.

With permission to roam his lands restored, she should feel happy and settled. But all she could remember were the turbulent emotions she'd felt with his long, tapered fingers clutching her wrist. His possessive grasp had sent tingles of longing through her body. And knowing he wasn't engaged only made things worse. There was no reason to deny the desire she felt for him. If offered the opportunity, she would welcome his advances.

Selina laughed softly. As much as she might feel a passion for him, she knew he did not reciprocate the feelings. She picked up her wineglass and sighed. Now that was a damned shame.

A slight knock scraped across her door. "Come in."

A young woman not more than twenty tentatively entered the room. "Miss White?"

"Yes."

"Oh, thank God," she said, rushing toward her. "You must come with me quickly."

"Who are you?" Selina asked. This was not one of Colin's maids.

"I'm Ann. Lady Katherine's maid. She needs you. Something's wrong with her." The girl's blue eyes implored her to hurry.

"What's wrong with her?" Selina asked as she picked up her bag with herbs and other assorted remedies.

"She's bleeding bad, miss. At first I thought it was just her monthlies but now I'm not so sure."

The breath expelled from her lungs. They moved up the wedding date. And now she knew why. "We must hurry."

As they raced down the servants' steps, she asked, "When did she start bleeding?"

"Just after dinner. She's cramping too."

She ran down the hall. "Which room?"

"Fifth door on the left, miss."

Selina refused to wait for the girl who seemed unable to keep up with her pace. Just as she reached the main hall, she ran into a hard body. Large hands gripped her shoulders and kept her from falling. Not now, she thought.

"Get out of my way, Colin."

"What's wrong with my sister?" he demanded.

"I won't know until I see her. But the last thing she needs is her brother hovering over her bed. Go back to your study, I'll let you know after I've seen her." Selina twisted out of his grip and moved past him. She reached for the door handle only to have his hand pull hers away.

"I am calling for the physician."

"Do what you think is necessary," she shouted as her anger increased. "It will take the man an hour to get here, assuming he's sober. Right now, I'm the only one here with any experience in these matters. Now, please let me do my job."

He opened the door. "I will be waiting in my study."

She strode into the room and took in the scene before her. The dowager duchess sat on the side of her daughter's bed crying hysterically. Selina placed her bag on the nightstand and turned toward the woman.

"Your Grace, please move yourself to the chair by the window. And if you cannot keep your emotions to yourself, I shall have a footman remove you."

The older woman looked up at her with tears in her eyes. "This is my daughter. Who are you to tell me where I can or cannot sit?"

"I am the woman sent here to help your daughter. Now please move, Your Grace."

"Humph," she said and then moved away from the bed.

"Kate, look at me," Selina said softly.

"That's Lady Katherine to you," the duchess retorted.

"Do be quiet, Mother," Kate moaned. "Oh, Selina, it hurts so much. I'm losing the baby, aren't I?"

"What baby?" her mother exclaimed.

Selina cast Kate's mother a glare. "Shh." She then sat on the bed and felt Kate's forehead. "How many of your monthlies have you missed?"

"I just missed my second month."

"Were you bleeding before today?"

Kate nodded and wiped away a tear. "I've been spotting for three days."

She examined her new friend and tried her best not to let her tears fall. Seeing the amount of blood loss, she whispered, "I'm so sorry, Kate. I believe you may have lost the baby."

Kate held her hand against her mouth as her tears flowed down her cheeks. "Only John knew. That's why we pushed up the wedding, so I wouldn't be showing. We figured we could just say the baby was born early."

"I'm so sorry," Selina mumbled again as she prepared some herbs to ease Kate's pain.

"Don't tell Colin."

Selina turned back to Kate. Her friend's face was pallid and sweaty but it was the look of anguish that made her agree. "I suppose that news is up to you to tell him."

"He must never know. After what happened to Mary, he cannot handle another loss of this kind. Please, promise me you won't tell him."

"You are my patient and moreover my friend. If you insist that I don't tell him then I shall honor your request." She had no idea how she would do such a thing. He would demand to know what was wrong with Kate. "I will tell him it's just a feminine issue. Men never know what to say to that."

"Thank you, Selina." Kate's cold hand clasped Selina's.

Selina spent the next few hours helping Kate. Other than giving her some herbs for the cramping, there wasn't much she could do for her. But as midnight neared, she knew she had to tell Colin something.

"I will check on you tomorrow, Kate." Selina covered her friend with a light blanket. "Try to sleep." Thankfully, the herbs would help with that too.

"Thank you, Selina." Kate's eyelids dropped shut.

"I will stay with her tonight," her mother whispered. "Thank you, Selina. I must apologize for how I acted when you came in the room. It was just the shock of it all." She paused and tilted her head slightly. "You're just like your mother, a loving wise woman."

Selina nodded and headed for the door. With a deep breath for support, she walked down the black-and-white marble-tiled floor to the study. Before she reached the room, she could hear muttering from inside. Her heart went out to him. Slowly, she opened the door.

"Well?" he demanded.

"Well, indeed." She ignored his question and then strolled to the brandy decanter on the table in the corner. Seeing the half glass in his hands, she poured only one snifter.

"Selina, what is wrong with my sister?" His tone had softened slightly, as if he understood her strained emotions.

"She's having some feminine issues," she lied, staring at the amber liquid in her glass.

He paced the room, raking his hand through his black hair until it all but stood on end. "She's miscarrying, isn't she?"

"You knew?" Her heart ached with his pained expression. She wanted to comfort him. But she had no right to do that. "I promised her I wouldn't tell you . . . but since you have already guessed the truth, I can only confirm it."

"I suspected. Why else would she change the wedding date? I shouldn't have let her ride the other day. That's what did it. I'm sure of it."

"There is no way of knowing what caused the miscarriage. Sometimes these things just happen."

He stopped midstride and closed his eyes. "Why?"

Selina sipped her brandy, hoping for a little fortification from the spirit. "I don't know, Colin. Many women lose babies in the first three months. Sometimes that's nature's way of taking care of a baby that wasn't growing properly."

"But why did she do it?" He finally sank to a chair and drank the rest of his brandy.

She snatched the glass and then refilled it for him. Handing it to him, she said, "Why does any woman take the chance before marriage? She is in love with him. She was swept away by desire."

Their fingers grazed each other when he reached for the glass. He stared at her until she had to look away. His probing sapphire eyes disquieted her until she felt the need to move away from him. She took the seat across from him.

"Desire," he grumbled. "It only leads to pregnant women and loss."

"Not always. Neither of us would be here today if our parents had ignored their desires."

He lifted the glass to his lips and sipped from it. "Perhaps," he said softly.

"There's no perhaps about it," she replied. She drank down her brandy and savored its comforting warmth. She wanted to forget this night. And all the other nights that ended the same. Death had cast its dark spirit into her heart.

Colin stared over at the beautiful woman across from him. His desire for her seemed all-consuming lately. He wondered how she would react if she knew.

"Would you do it?" he whispered.

She blinked and then warm green eyes stared at him. "Do what?"

"Have sexual congress before marriage?" Good God! Why was he asking her such a personal question?

"Yes," she answered with no hesitation. She rose and walked to the window, looking out at the dark night. "But I'm in a different situation than your sister."

"How so?"

"I am expected to have children. A girl in particular. No one here cares how the child comes to be, whether in the bonds of marriage or not. The only thing that matters to them is that I have a girl to whom I will teach the healing arts." She let out a low sigh and leaned her head against the window frame.

"But don't you care?"

She shrugged. "It would be nice to have a man who loved me and accepted me for who I am." She glanced back at him. "But those are the exceptions. Most are like you, who don't understand why I give up so much of my time to help others. Or those who believe medicine should be left to educated men."

Colin sipped his brandy again and stared at his drink. "Why do you? Every time I ask you about it, you tell me it's your duty. Is there more to it than that?"

"Yes!" She moved away from the window.

As she passed him, a hint of lavender swirled in the air. "So why else do you help everyone?"

"Because no one else will," she said emphatically. Returning to her seat, she leaned forward, close to him. "That physician in the village is dreadful. He scares more people than he helps."

"All right, but why *you*?" he asked again. "There are many other women who live on the land who could learn what you know. So why you?"

Her gaze fell to the floor. "Because I have an obligation to do this for the others." She looked up at him intently. "Because seeing how my assistance helps someone is an incredible feeling. Watching as a new baby, that I helped bring into the world, looks up at his mother is the most heartwarming sensation in the world."

He smiled slowly. "So you love what you do?"

"Of course I do."

"But what about on a night like this when things go wrong? How do you deal with the emotions?"

She cast him a gentle smile. "That is life. There is good and bad. No matter how hard I try I can't save everyone."

"I might believe you if I hadn't seen how upset you were over Mrs. Wells's loss."

She blinked furiously as if reliving the memory. Colin instantly regretted the remark. He had been enjoying her company tonight and with one comment, he'd brought back the memories of her emotional night by the reflecting pond.

"Some days are harder than others," she whispered. "Seeing a child die is the worst."

He knew that all too well. He closed his eyes as the memories returned as if it had happened yesterday, not eight years ago. "Why can't I forget?" he whispered.

A warm hand touched his thigh. The idea that she would touch him to comfort him warmed his frozen heart.

"Because you loved her," she said softly. "But maybe it's time to let go."

He opened his eyes to find her on her knees in front of him. Her green eyes were wet with tears for him. "I don't know how."

A large tear fell on his knee. "Your wife would never have wanted you to lock away your heart. She would have wanted you to love again, Colin."

He looked away from her unable to face the pity he saw there. "You can't possibly know that."

"No woman who truly loved her husband would want him so lonely." She dropped her head on his knee. "You need to return to London and find a woman who will love you."

He leaned his head back against the chair and sighed. While he'd done much to ruin his reputation over the past eight years, he knew nothing was so awful that couldn't be forgiven with his title. The women of the *ton* would be overjoyed to have a chance to become the next Duchess of Northrop. But he doubted one would come to love him as Mary had.

His hand reached down and caressed Selina's head. Her tears had stopped but her head still lay on his thighs. He wanted to grasp her arms and then pull her onto his lap. Only that would lead to things he should not even consider. Kissing her that night by the reflecting pond had been a mistake. A glorious, passionate error.

Or was it?

That night he'd felt alive again. It had been the first time in eight years that he'd truly desired a woman. He wanted Selina in his bed. But how could he ask such a thing from her. As if sensing his desire, she rose and moved away from him.

He caught sight of her toes sticking out from the hem of her dress and smiled. She had no sense of propriety at all.

"Where are your shoes?"

She stared down at her feet as pink tinged her cheek. "I-I left them at the door. They were muddied."

"Muddied? We haven't had rain in a week."

"Well, I found a patch," she said with a nervous laugh.

He smiled over at her. There was something about this unconventional woman that made his heart feel lighter. "I would appreciate it if you stayed with me tonight."

Her green eyes widened slightly. "What do you mean?"

His fists clenched when he realized her mistaken meaning. "I meant stay in the house. So that if my sister needs you tonight you are close."

She stared at the floor. "Of course. I will relieve the duchess so she can sleep."

Colin rose from his chair and held out his hand to escort her to Kate's room. He had to get Selina out of the study before he offered to take her to his room. *Distance.* He had to keep a strict distance between them.

Chapter 13

Selina walked up the stairs with Colin directly behind her. She was a coward. There had been abundant opportunities to offer herself to him while in the study and she'd said and done nothing. She would certainly understand if he rejected her. He might not even find her attractive in that manner.

And yet, she thought he might. Even now, she could swear he was watching her hips sway as she walked. What would he do if she just turned and moved into his arms? As she reached the top step, she realized nothing would happen. He clasped her elbow and led her to his sister's room.

"Good night, Selina," he whispered near her ear.

She shivered. "Good night, Colin."

"Thank you again for taking care of my sister."

She seemed only able to nod. Walking into the room, she saw the duchess sleeping in the bed with her daughter. Not willing to disturb either woman, she quietly departed the room. She covered a yawn with her hand as she headed to the stairs.

"Where are you going?"

Selina blinked and stared at Colin. "They are both asleep. I didn't want to disturb them."

"I asked you to stay," he said, walking closer to her.

"I will ask a footman to make a room up for me. I told you I wouldn't leave."

"Come with me," he said, taking her hand. "There is a room already made up."

He led her down the hall toward the west wing. She remembered Mrs. Roberts telling her that his suite of rooms was in this wing. Could he be ushering her there? He stopped before a door and then swung it open.

Selina ambled into the room and her mouth gaped. She entered a large salon with two divans, four gilt chairs, cherry tables, and a large fireplace.

"The bedroom is through here." He opened another door and she entered a room nearly twice as large as her room upstairs. A huge four-poster bed dominated the back wall. The lavender bedcovers made her realize this was not his room after all.

"If you need anything I am right next door." He bade her good night and walked to a small door on the same wall as the bed.

Connecting rooms! This was the duchess's room. His late wife's room! This was the last place she should stay. "Colin, I'm not certain this is the room I should sleep in tonight."

With his hand on the knob, he shook his head. "She slept in another room. She never used this room except to dress. The room is only made up because the servants believe it should always be ready in case I bring a bride home. Good night, Selina."

"Good night, Colin," she whispered.

Once the door shut, she remembered that she still wore her dress. It was one of the few that buttoned down the back. The maids were exhausted from the house cleaning and upheaval this evening. It wasn't that improper to ask him to help her, was it? Before she could change her mind, she knocked on the door to his room.

He answered it so quickly she wondered if he'd been standing right next to the door. "Yes?"

"My dress buttons down the back," she said, suddenly thinking she should have slept in the dress.

He nodded with a sigh. "Of course, just turn around."

She presented her back to him. His knuckles scraped across her skin at the top of her dress. She trembled. His warm breath caressed her shoulder as the first button came undone. Her breath quickened.

It was nearly two in the morning and yet she felt quite awake. She could only imagine him slipping the dress off her shoulders and untying her stays. If only he would . . .

"That's the last button," he said. "Do you want me to untie your stays?"

"Yes," she replied in a breathless voice. She could have sworn he groaned slightly. Without a doubt, this was the most improper thing she'd ever done. She slid her dress down her arms just enough that he could untie her stays. His fingers quickly loosened the ties on her stays until she would be able to get the garment off herself.

"That should do," he said in a gruff voice.

"Thank you."

What would he do if she turned and let her dress drop to the floor? Would he be consumed by lust and take her in his arms? As the door closed behind him, she realized that the decision had been made for her. After carefully placing her dress over a chair, she walked toward the huge bed. She lay down and wondered what he was doing in the room next door. She laughed softly at her musings. He was no doubt already fast asleep. And she should be the same. Except every time she closed her eyes, she remembered the sensation of his lips on hers that night by the pond.

She tossed the coverlet off her and then walked to the window. She glanced out into the dark night. From this window, she could look down at the reflecting pond. Moonlight illuminated the white swans with their heads tucked into their feathers. At least they could sleep.

She turned and stared at the connecting door. All she had to do was walk over there and open the door. Then she'd know if he desired her or not.

Colin dressed the next morning before his valet came to wake him. Not that he had slept last night. After practically undressing her, all he could think of was her. He could not get involved with a woman like Selina. It was madness.

And yet, that was all he'd thought of for hours. He'd even walked to the door that connected the rooms and held onto the handle. But his principles would not let him open that door. She deserved better than a man who couldn't put his past behind him.

Determined to put her out of his mind, he walked downstairs to breakfast. He entered the room expecting to see his stepmother. Instead, Selina sat at the table wearing the same dress he'd removed from her last night. She looked over at him with a shy smile.

"Good morning, Your Grace."

"Good morning, Selina. Are you enjoying your toast?" He took the seat across from her.

"Very much so," she replied. "I haven't looked in on your sister but I will as soon as I'm finished. Then I shall get out of your way."

"You're hardly in the way," he said as a footman placed a plate of eggs and ham in front of him. He had an overwhelming urge to find an excuse for her to stay. Perhaps he should twist his ankle again.

"You have enough going on with the wedding plans."

Mr. Roberts cleared his throat to get Colin's attention. "Your Grace, this just came for Lady Katherine. The messenger said it was very important."

Colin picked up the letter and stared at the seal. It was from her betrothed. "Why do I feel like this is more bad news?"

"He couldn't possibly know about the incident from last night," she whispered.

"I need to give this to her. Excuse me." He walked up the stairs slowly. After a quick knock, his stepmother bade him entrance.

"Is Kate awake?" he asked softly.

"Yes, I'm awake. And I'm not dying, Colin. You can speak in a normal tone of voice." Kate sat up slowly. "What's the matter? You look like hell."

"I shall take my leave to change my clothing," his step-mother said and then left the room.

Other than being slightly pale, Kate looked very well rested. He would have to thank Selina for that. "You have a letter from John."

Her face lit up like a small child who'd just received a sweet. "Let me see it."

He handed the note to her and then sat in the chair nearest the bed. He watched with dread as her brows furrowed and tears welled in her eyes. "What's wrong, Kate?"

"His mother died three days ago. He's in mourning and shouldn't marry me for another three months. He thinks we should run to Gretna Green, regardless of his mourning period."

Colin clenched his fists. "What do you think?"

"There's no point in rushing the marriage and suffering the consequences of the gossip it would cause."

"Are you certain?" he asked softly.

She stared up at him and nodded. "You know, don't you?"

"I was suspicious when you moved the wedding date. When Miss White told me it was feminine issues, I assumed you lost the child."

"Yes." She brushed away a tear.

"I'm sorry, Kate."

"I just wish I could be there to comfort him. He was very close with his mother. I will write to him and tell him there is no need to elope now."

There was nothing else he could say to her. What was it about this house that caused so much misery? There had to be some way of changing it. "Miss White would like to check on you. Should I send her up?"

"Please." She placed the letter on her nightstand and lay back against the pillows. "I'm so glad she was here last night, Colin."

"Me too." But he did wonder how she'd arrived so quickly. "When did you call for Miss White last night?"

Kate shrugged. "I'm not certain. Why?"

"I had only just heard that you were unwell, and by the time I arrived upstairs, she was here."

Kate's cheeks reddened. "I didn't want you to know yet. And I believe she was checking on a tenant."

"Very well," he said, allowing the topic to rest.

"If you wouldn't mind, I would like her to stay a few days. She has been a great comfort and a dear friend to me."

As much as he didn't want the temptress in his house any longer than necessary, he couldn't deny Kate her comfort. "Very well," he finally answered.

He left his sister in search of the wise woman. Only his stepmother sat at the dining table and she'd said Selina was not there when she arrived. He then checked the bedchamber to no avail. Perhaps she had already left.

"Mr. Roberts," he asked, walking back down the steps, "have you seen Miss White?"

"She walked toward the library, Your Grace."

Colin strode down the long marble hall to the library. He found her staring at the books. "Were you looking for something in particular?"

She gasped. "You frightened me, Your Grace."

He stepped closer to her. "Did you want to read something?"

Her green eyes sparkled. "You would allow me to borrow a book?"

"Of course." He took another step closer until the scent of lavender swirled around him. "So, which one has caught your interest?"

"Well, this one is definitely interesting." She pulled out an old book and handed it to him.

He laughed. "*The Malleus Maleficarum.*"

"Have you read it?"

"No, have you?"

"I have no need to read such a biased book." She stared at the lettering on the book. "But I do wonder how it ended up in your library."

"It's not that hard to determine. How better to claim your wise woman is not a witch than by having the witch-hunting manual of the day in your personal library. I would guess that one of my great-grandfathers was determined to protect the woman."

"How unusual," she commented sarcastically.

He opened the book and smiled. "Not if he loved the woman."

She took a step back. "Are you saying that one of your great-grandfathers kept one of my great-grandmothers as his mistress?"

"It's quite possible." Colin had no idea if there was any truth to that or not. There had always been some gossip about a wise woman becoming the duchess a few hundred years ago. But he'd always put that off as foolishness.

Selina shook her head. "I need to check on your sister. Was the letter from her betrothed good news?"

"Unfortunately, no. John's mother died so he needs to push back the wedding date until after his mourning period." Colin placed the book back on the shelf and slowly turned around to face her. "Kate would like you to stay a few days. She said you have been a great comfort to her."

"If that is acceptable to you, I would like to stay."

"Thank you."

"I should go see to her."

Colin sighed. He doubted this would work but he felt there were no other choices. Ever since he realized that Kate had miscarried, he'd thought of little else. And seeing that odd specter a week ago had made him wonder if Selina couldn't help with that too. "Selina . . ."

"Yes?"

He closed his eyes. "Would you please complete the cleansing of the house?"

"Of course," she replied easily. "But I do wonder why you wish me to do so now."

He walked away from her and sat in a chair. "I want this house to be rid of the bad memories. It seems like nothing good ever happens here."

She glanced around as if to determine if they were alone. "Colin, I can't guarantee that cleansing the house will rid it of the memories. Those are in your mind, not the house."

"At least try."

"I will get started on that after I see to your sister."

"Thank you." He looked over to see the slight smile on her face. "Will the cleansing work on spirits too?"

"Spirits?" she asked with a slight frown. "Do you mean like ghosts?"

He nodded sharply.

"I suppose it might," she replied with a shrug. "I honestly don't know for sure. Why, do you think there is a ghost in the house?"

He closed his eyes for a long moment. "I saw her."

"Her?"

"Mary. A few times, upstairs on the third floor. I was outside at the reflecting pond and I saw a woman in white walk past the window."

Selina's eyes widened. "Indeed?"

Seeing the shocked look on her face, he knew he had to say something to calm her. He needed her to stay the night and she might bolt if she thought the house was haunted. "I am quite certain there is nothing to be afraid of, Selina. I've never heard the servants even speak of the specter."

"Of course, you're right."

Hearing a bit of humor in her voice, he wondered if she didn't believe in ghosts. Not that it mattered. Until he'd seen Mary's ghost, he never believed either. At least she didn't appear to be frightened of the idea of staying in a haunted house.

"I will check on Kate now." She turned and walked out of the room with a slight grin on her face.

Why had he agreed to let her stay again? He must be suffering some grave form of madness. Now for the next few days and worse, the long nights, he would think of her.

Selina walked up the stairs attempting not to laugh aloud. A ghost! He'd thought she was the ghost of his late wife. She sobered. It was rather tragic, actually.

After checking in on Kate, Selina returned to her room to wash and change into a clean dress. She pulled her sage out from the nightstand where she kept it. Today, she would cleanse the rooms on the third floor again, ghost or not. She giggled slightly again. She hoped if he knew she was performing the ritual, it would give him some peace.

While the sage might help remove the negative spirits in the house, she wondered if it would help Colin. She doubted it would make any difference since his issues stemmed from the negative emotions he carried inside of him.

If only she could help him with that.

She lit her sage in the ceramic bowl and headed for the west wing. The rooms had yet to be made up for the wedding so the furnishings were still covered with white cloths. She walked through each room wondering what was underneath. She peeked under a few cloths in each room. Based on the ornate style of the wall coverings and the gilt furniture, most of the rooms must have been decorated by Colin's grandmother.

She refocused her thoughts on the task at hand and chanted about removing the negative spirits in the house. So intent on her work, she walked out of one room directly into Colin. He laughed softly as she looked up at him.

"Why are you up here?" he asked. "I thought you would have started downstairs."

She needed a quick excuse for starting up here. "It's always best to start at the highest floor and work my way down."

"Why is that?"

Why indeed? She needed an explanation that would give him some comfort. "The negative spirits only move down and then out the door."

"I see." He cleared his throat and then said, "Would you mind if I watched what you do?"

"It is your home, you may do as you like." Just the idea that he would be following her around sent a nervous energy through her.

"I will come with you."

For the next few minutes, she tried to ignore the man next to her as she walked through the room. Even though he remained quiet, she could hear his every breath. Her hands trembled slightly as she lifted the bowl with sage up and down.

"How does the sage work?" he finally asked.

Selina shrugged. "I'm not really certain."

"Then how do you know it works?"

She stopped and looked over at him. "Some things you must believe in without proof."

"Ah, faith."

"Yes."

He shook his head. "I'm finding the idea that burning sage will get rid of the negative feelings in this house a little odd."

Selina tightened the grip on her bowl. She placed it on

a bureau before turning back to him. "Then why are you allowing this? And why are you even following me around the house?"

"I honestly don't know," he admitted and then walked away slowly.

Selina spent the afternoon finishing the third level. Once she was done, she decided to spend the evening with Kate. Not that she was hiding from Colin. That night, she returned to her bedroom on the third floor, knowing she'd never sleep in the room next to his.

The next two days followed the same pattern. She spent as much time as possible with Kate. When she knew Colin was occupied in his study or out riding, she'd worked on the second floor. Now finished with the east wing, she moved toward the west wing . . . and his bedchamber.

She waited until she noticed him leave the room before heading inside. She hadn't been in this room since the first morning she'd met him. Today, the curtains were already open and sunlight filtered through the diamond-shaped panes. There was nothing feminine about this room. Dark wood paneled the walls and deep red carpets covered the floors. The large bed looked like mahogany to her, along with the bureau and small desk in the corner. The bedcoverings were the only lighter thing in the room and Selina still thought them to be too deep a shade of gold for her tastes.

Not that any of that mattered. This was his room, certainly not hers. He could decorate his bedchamber in black if he wished it. She must get back to work before he returned from his ride. She'd spent so much time procrastinating, he might even come back now.

She picked up her bowl and walked the room. She refused to think about how she slowed to a stop and stared at his bed. Telling herself not to wonder which side of the bed he slept on, she turned away. She crossed the room and held up her bowl until she heard the door squeak open.

"I didn't expect you to be here," he said in a strangled tone.

"You did tell me to cleanse the house . . . that includes your bedchamber."

He leaned his tall body against the door, effectively blocking her only escape from the handsome brooding man. "I suppose I did say that."

The man was driving her mad. Could he possibly have no idea that she heard every breath, felt every movement he made? Didn't he realize how much she desired him?

"Well?" she demanded. What did the man want from her now? Was she supposed to stop cleansing his room?

She looked over at his blue eyes and stopped fidgeting. It was as if the room suddenly became smaller until the only thing that mattered was him. She wanted to kiss him again. Feel his lips against hers. Feel the sensation of his velvety tongue swiping across hers.

"Selina?" he said in a hoarse voice.

"Yes?"

"Remember how I said I would never ask your permission to kiss you?"

She frowned slightly. "Yes?"

"Good." He closed the distance between them and suddenly his lips were on hers. He moved them backward until he had her against the door . . . a very closed door, cloaking them in privacy.

Chapter 14

Colin twisted her in his arms until she was pinned against the closed door. He deepened the kiss as she opened to him. He wanted to lay her down on that bed and make love to her all afternoon. But already his desire for her was growing too fast. He couldn't do this. Making love to her would be madness when he would be leaving the estate soon.

Slowly, he pulled away from her tempting lips. She stared at him as her witchy green eyes filled with disappointment.

Disappointment?

Did she not want him to stop?

"I'm sorry," he whispered. But as he attempted to move away from her, she held on to the lapels of his black jacket.

"I'm not," she said softly.

Before he could withdraw from her, she stood on her tiptoes and kissed him. He pulled her against his body and explored her mouth. Insatiable hunger urged his advances as his hand moved to her muslin-covered breast. A deep moan from her throat sounded like a siren's call to him.

She arched her back, filling his hand with her rounded breast. Rubbing his thumb over her tight little nipple was his undoing. He wanted her against the door, on the bed . . . anywhere.

He should stop but seemed unable to think of anything but delving into her softness. It had been far too long since he'd been with a woman. His heart pounded against his chest as her tongue swept across his in a heated match.

She trembled in his arms and a feeling of power crashed over him. He made her quiver with desire. He made her moan with pleasure. There was only one thing he wanted more . . . to hear her cry out with passion as she reached her climax. He wanted that far more than he should.

He trailed his lips down her soft neck until he reached the bodice of her dress. He lifted his head and stared down at the wonder in her eyes. "Stop me now, Selina. I don't have the strength."

Her pink tongue moistened her full lips. "No," she whispered.

No? As in no, he shouldn't continue? Or no, as in don't stop? He couldn't get this wrong. "What do you want, Selina? Tell me."

She reached for the buttons on the front of her bodice and slowly undid each one. And he had his answer. He pushed her fingers away and slid the dress down her body with his shaking hands. He turned her around to untie her stays. Unlike a few nights ago when he did the same thing, this afternoon he would see all of her. He kissed the nape of her neck. She trembled against him.

"Is it supposed to feel this exciting?" she whispered.

Oh, dear God. She was as innocent as he'd thought. The idea of being the first man inside her surged his passion higher. "This is only the beginning."

"Oh."

Finished unlacing her stays, he let them drop to the floor with her dress. He turned her back to face him. Her rosy nipples protruded from her shift. His cock throbbed in anticipation for her. He needed to think of other things.

Cold things.

But the heat of her body beckoned him more than any siren's call ever could.

"Come to the bed," he said, pulling her hand as he walked toward the massive bed. He needed to be inside her now. To feel the soft wetness of her. To feel her inner muscles clench against him as she found her release.

His desire was quickly spiraling out of control.

He yanked off his boots and then his jacket. He desperately wanted to feel her naked body against his. Desire clawed at him, urging him to take her slim hips in his hands and thrust into her silky depths.

Already, he could feel himself far too close to the edge.

Selina took a step closer to Colin and then quickly untied his cravat before her courage deserted her. She could not believe she was standing before him in just her shift. Her hands shook as she reached for the buttons on his linen shirt. After divesting him of his shirt, she reached for the buttons on his trousers.

Hard fingers held hers tightly. "I'll do that."

"I want to see you," she whispered. She looked up into his blue eyes and gasped at the passion she saw. He wanted her as much as she wanted him. A sense of power enveloped her. She pushed his hands away and unbuttoned his trousers.

Before she could get any further, he pulled her down onto the bed with him. He landed on top of her. His body sliding over hers. Moisture pooled between her thighs.

"Colin," she said softly.

"Hmm?" He nibbled on the side of her neck as his hands lifted the hem of her shift.

"I feel like I'm drowning."

"Good," he whispered.

Good? She should feel like her breathing was out of control? As if every breath might be her last?

He pulled the garment off her until she was naked, save her stockings. When had she lost her shoes? As his mouth covered her breast, she realized it didn't matter.

Selina arched against him and moaned softly. Gooseflesh rippled along her skin. Her body ached for something unattainable, something she didn't even know existed before now.

His hand skimmed across her stomach, delving lower until he split her folds. She let out a slight gasp as his hard fingers touched her so intimately. His thumb found her tight nub and rubbed until she couldn't think, much less breathe.

"Colin," she moaned.

"God, Selina, you're so moist and warm for me."

"Please," she begged for relief.

"Yes," he whispered against her breast. He moved quickly away from her to remove his trousers.

While she'd seen men without clothing, she'd never seen a man's cock like this before. It was long and hard, and she wanted to touch him. He pulled her closer to the edge of the bed until she thought she might fall off.

Then he was there, probing her entrance. With agonizing slowness, he entered her until he reached her maidenhead.

"Oh God, I wasn't positive you were a virgin," he said with a groan. "This might hurt." He withdrew slightly before pushing deep inside her.

"Oh," she cried out.

"God, no," he shouted. He thrust inside her one more time. "No." He collapsed on top of her. "I'm sorry," he mumbled. He quickly pulled out of her and dressed. Staring down at her, he said it again. "I'm sorry."

And then he left.

Selina stared at the closed door. Anger, frustration, and emptiness filled her. Why had he left her so quickly? Perhaps her inexperience had annoyed him. Slowly, she dressed and left the room, wondering if that was really all there was to making love. She knew it wasn't. Mia had told her about the pleasures a man's body could bring to a woman.

Maybe she wasn't as good at this as his late wife. The pain of that thought sliced through her like a knife. She couldn't compete with a dead woman.

Colin stormed into his study and locked the door behind him. He'd never embarrassed himself as he did with her. He poured a large glass of brandy and gulped it down. She must think him some kind of adolescent who'd never been with a woman. He didn't think he'd been this horrible at making love since his first time. Now he'd ruined her first time.

He could not imagine facing her again.

In fact, he wouldn't. She would only stay the night and then be back at Hartsfield Hall. As soon as Kate felt ready to leave, he would depart too. And he'd never return.

He poured another glass of brandy and shook his head. He would have to apologize to her again. His conscience would never allow him to leave without an explanation. But the idea of talking to her about what just happened only made his anger grow. He hurled the glass at the fireplace in frustration.

He sank into a chair and closed his eyes. Why hadn't he just left her alone? Because from the moment he met her, he'd desired her. His guilt had increased when he realized days ago that he wanted her more than he'd ever wanted Mary. He had wanted Selina's wildness. Her passion.

And instead of showing her the wonders of making love, he'd selfishly pleasured only himself. He'd left her unsatisfied. When he should have departed only after he knew she would never want another man other than him.

He walked back to the decanter of brandy and poured

himself another glass, wanting nothing except to forget he ever met Selina.

Selina peered inside Kate's room. After leaving the bedroom, she'd had no idea where to go. She couldn't stay in that adjoining room. And she couldn't risk him finding her in the room where she'd been hiding for days.

"Would you like some company?" Selina asked.

Her patient smiled over at her. "Please, I'm dreadfully tired of my mother's companionship."

Selina looked around the bedchamber. "Where is your mother?"

Kate laughed. "I asked her to retrieve a book for me from Colin's library. It should take her at least an hour to find the book since I doubt my brother has it in his stacks."

"Devious, Kate."

"She's driving me mad! She won't stop talking about the miscarriage when all I want to do is forget it."

Selina sat in the chair nearest the bed. "Will you be able to do that?"

Kate shrugged. "I don't know for certain. But sitting here thinking about it all day isn't helping me. I want to get out of this bed."

"If you're up to it, then go ahead and get out of bed."

"Are you sure? My mother insists I stay in bed for a fortnight."

"Kate, you are the best judge of whether or not you should be up. That is where physicians get things all wrong. Your body will tell you what it can and can't do. You just need to listen."

Kate nodded. "I will get up later. Now you must tell me what's wrong."

Selina frowned slightly. How did Colin's sister know something was wrong? "Whatever do you mean?"

Kate rolled her eyes and shook her head. "You've been crying. Did my brother do something to upset you again?"

"Of course not," she exclaimed quickly. Watching Kate's disbelieving expression, Selina knew she would have to tell her something. "It's nothing your brother did."

"Then what is troubling you?" Kate shifted to her side, allowing her to stare at Selina.

She couldn't tell Kate the exact truth about what was bothering her. But maybe if she handled her questions just right, she might get the answers she desperately needed. "I have been thinking about something lately."

"Oh?"

"I am expected to have a child. More specifically, a daughter to carry on the wise woman tradition."

Kate reached for her teacup on the nightstand. "I'm not sure I understand. Are you thinking of marriage?"

"Not exactly," Selina whispered. "There is no man interested in marrying me, but there is one I might consider. . . ."

Kate's blue eyes widened. "A lover?"

Selina nodded as her checks heated with embarrassment. She could not believe she was about to ask a woman five years younger than she about sex. "What is it like?"

"Oh, you want to know about that." Kate laughed softly.

"Yes."

Kate leaned closer to her. "We did it three times. The first time wasn't that wonderful. It hurt but John tried to make me feel good."

Which was more than her brother had done. "What about the other times?"

"It was the most incredible feeling ever. I felt like I was flying out of my body." Kate giggled. "But one of my friends told me her new husband was awful in the bedchamber when they first were married. He couldn't do more than enter her before he was done."

"What caused that to happen?"

"Inexperience. Once they started to make love on a regular basis, everything worked out perfectly."

But Selina doubted inexperience was Colin's issue. After all, he and Mary had been married for over a year before her death. They had plenty of time for the marriage bed. Plus he had a reputation as a rake in town. Feeling as frustrated as when she walked into the room, she only said, "Thank you, Kate."

"I don't believe I helped you with your decision."

Selina shrugged. "Perhaps I should wait a while before making this decision."

"Who is the man?"

Her cheeks burned. "No one you know. Just a man from the village."

Selina finally changed the subject to Kate's betrothed and they talked for a few hours. Selina enjoyed Kate's company. She missed having a friend to talk to like this. While she had Mia and sometimes Tia, they were much farther away so they rarely got together more than once a month.

"I believe I shall join you for dinner downstairs," Kate announced.

A little sigh of relief escaped Selina. At least now she wouldn't be alone with Colin. "I think that is a fabulous idea."

"You must go change into a better dress. With Mother joining us, she will expect us to dress for dinner."

Selina glanced down at her pale green muslin. There was nothing wrong with this dress. But if the duchess expected a fancier dress, then Selina would have to figure out something.

"I shall meet you back here at half past six. Then we can go downstairs together." Selina walked back up to her room and glanced at her meager selection of dresses. Her best dress was a dark blue muslin, so that would have to do for dinner.

She rang for help from one of the lady's maids. Betsy

helped her dress and put up her hair. Selina looked in the mirror and again wondered why the ladies insisted their hair be put up. It only made her look older.

"You look beautiful, Selina," Betsy said, clapping her hands together like a child.

"Thank you, Betsy." Selina glanced at the clock and decided to walk down to Kate's bedchamber.

She knocked and was told to come into the room. Selina strolled inside and stopped dead. Kate's expression said it all . . . gaped mouth and wide eyes.

"Selina, that dress will never do," she gasped. "It's muslin."

"It is the best dress I have." As she examined Kate's dress, Selina noticed the differences—silk for one. Handcrafted ivory silk with real pearl buttons down the back and seeded pearls at the waist. She could never afford a dress as beautiful as the one her friend wore.

Kate shook her head. "No, I must have something that will work for you."

"I cannot wear one of your gowns." Although, the idea of wearing a gown such as that made her ache with envy. She wanted a dress of silk, even if it meant wearing her hair up in some tight, uncomfortable style. It would be worth the pain.

"I know just the thing. I was thinking about giving it to my maid since she is smaller than I am. It never fit just right. Madam Duvall's apprentice made it instead of the expert." Kate giggled. "Instead, I shall bestow it upon you."

Kate pulled out the most beautiful moss-colored silk dress. She held it up to her and Selina immediately noticed that it was too small for her friend's taller frame. It might be a bit long on Selina but right then she didn't care if it dragged on the floor. She wanted to wear that dress even if it was only one time.

"Come along, then. Try it on,"

Selina nodded. Only a few minutes later, she looked in the mirror and gaped at her reflection. The color was perfect for her skin tone and eye color. And the sensation of silk on her skin was like sin. Tempting her to think thoughts about Colin that she shouldn't, such as what he would do when he saw her in this gown. Would he want to strip her naked slowly . . . languidly? Undoing one button at a time, kissing her skin as it was bared by his adept hands?

"It's perfect," Kate exclaimed, drawing Selina out of her erotic musing.

"I don't even recognize myself."

"Good. Then perhaps my brother won't either."

Selina glanced over at the devious look on Kate's face. "What do you mean by that?"

"My brother is far overdue to realize there are other women in the world than his late wife. While Mary was a lovely person, it's past time for him to desire another woman. Maybe even marry again."

Desire. Selina assumed that's all they had between them. After being intimate with him, she knew he definitely desired women again, no matter what his sister thought.

"That may be but I doubt I am the woman he would do either with." Especially the marriage part. That was never a thought that had entered Selina's head.

"At least he shall notice you in this gown."

Perhaps he would. But perhaps he shouldn't.

Chapter 15

Colin paused in the salon by the small table where the decanters stood like soldiers waiting to die. He'd already killed one half-empty soldier of brandy this afternoon. Perhaps he should retire to his room so as not to embarrass himself again today. Once was definitely enough.

But he turned his head, all thoughts of leaving the room drained from his mind. The only way he wanted to depart the salon was with Selina in his arms. She looked like one of the women he would see at any London party . . . only more beautiful. The green of the dress matched her eyes as if it had been made specifically for her, which was beyond mad since he knew she couldn't afford such a dress. Where the bloody hell had she gotten that silk dress? Seeing the look of pleasure on his sister's face, he understood exactly what she was up to this evening.

The low-cut gown emphasized her perfectly rounded breasts and the long length of her neck. He wanted to shower her graceful neck with kisses until he reached those peach nipples. Feeling his penis react to her presence, he squelched his degenerate thoughts.

"Good evening, ladies," he said with a quick bow to them.

"Where is Mother?" Kate asked as she sat on the gold velvet divan.

"Her maid said she had a headache and wouldn't be joining us. But I am especially pleased to see you up and about tonight." He walked over and kissed her cheek.

"Thank you."

"And you, Miss White," he said stiffly. He was not about to let his rampant desires get the best of him again. That could never happen where Selina was involved. Although, as he stared at her in that seductive green dress, he wondered why he couldn't have her one more time. Not one logical reason came to him.

"Thank you, Your Grace," she said in a more demure tone than he'd ever heard her utter.

"Sherry?" he asked as he glanced back at his sister.

"Yes. And one for Selina."

Or maybe more than one for Selina so she might forget the utter mess he'd made of this afternoon. "Very well."

He poured the glasses as his hand shook with desire and longing and the need to have his wise woman once more. That would cure him, he decided. After handing one glass to Selina and one to Kate, he turned toward his sister. "Have you decided what you shall do about the wedding?"

"I wrote to John this morning. I told him we should postpone until his mourning time is over. I also told him I might just stay the summer here."

"Stay the summer?" he asked incredulously. He'd assumed she'd want to leave as quickly as she could to be with her betrothed.

"Yes. John is a rather private person. He will need to be alone with his grief before he's ready to talk about it." Kate sipped her sherry and then stared down at the reddish liquid in her glass.

"Did you tell him about the baby?" he asked softly.

"I told him there was no need to rush the wedding. And

that I hadn't been feeling well lately. I couldn't take the chance that someone else might read the note."

"I'm sure he will understand your meaning," Selina commented before sipping her own drink. "With you deciding to stay for the summer he will understand what happened."

Kate nodded and blinked quickly. "I can only hope that the added distress over the loss of our baby won't upset him in his grief."

Colin turned away from the women and glanced outside. "Was he pleased when he found out you were with child?"

"Yes. Once we both overcame our initial shock, John was very excited about becoming a father. He told me he didn't care if it was a boy or a girl."

He turned back toward the women just as Kate wiped a tear from her cheek. "I'm sorry, Kate."

She nodded. "Mother told me we received an invitation to Mrs. Littleton's ball. I believe we should attend. It will get our minds off current events."

"If you wish to go, we shall," he replied before looking over at Selina who appeared uncomfortable. He wondered if she had ever been taught to dance and immediately realized how stupid a thought that was. A woman like Selina did not dance or go to balls. But he wished she could attend, wearing that dress.

He would love to see the flickering candlelight dance off the silk of her dress. Or the catch of light from a diamond necklace around her slender neck. She should go to a ball.

Roberts cleared his throat at the doorway and then announced dinner. Kate rose from her seat and quickly walked toward the dining room, leaving Colin and Selina alone.

Colin held out his arm for her. "Shall we?"

"Yes," she replied in a shaky tone.

He had no idea what to say to her as they walked to the dining room. Bringing up the topic of this afternoon's misstep was not an option. He didn't know how he'd ever be able to speak of what happened . . . although he knew he must. "Lovely weather today."

"Yes."

Well those few choice words did get him ten steps closer to the dining room. "My sister looks quite well. Thank you again for all your assistance with her."

"It is what I do," she murmured.

"Yes," he replied for a lack of anything better to say. Thankfully, they reached the dining room. Three place settings were arranged near the end of the table for a more intimate conversation space. Kate had a smug little grin on her face as they entered the room. Obviously, her quick departure from the salon had been planned.

He held out a chair on one side for Selina who sat down and flashed a knowing smile for his sister. Then Colin assisted Kate with her chair before taking his own seat. A footman immediately brought a plate filled with roasted lamb. Guilt seemed to kill his appetite. He had to make things right with Selina, even if that meant telling her the truth.

And he intended to do that just as soon as Kate retired for the evening.

"Kate, do not tire yourself out tonight. I want you to get to sleep early," he said in a gentle tone.

His sister rolled her eyes at him. "I am quite well thanks to Selina. I do believe I might be able to stay up for some card games or maybe even chess."

"I think it might even be good for you," Selina commented. "You have been stuck in your room for days. An evening with some light entertainment will do you wonders."

Kate smiled over at him. "There, you see? Even Selina agrees."

As dinner progressed, Colin found himself watching the two women intently. They seemed to have formed a tight bond of friendship in a very short time. He knew it was good for his sister to have a companion while here.

"It's such a shame you cannot accompany us to Mrs. Littleton's ball. You would love the music and the dancing," Kate said enthusiastically.

"I don't dance," Selina said, staring down at her food. She pushed the peas around on her plate.

"Oh but you could learn," Kate replied. "The steps are not difficult to learn or half the ladies in the *ton* wouldn't dance."

Selina smiled. "It is not my place to go to a ball."

Colin felt Selina's embarrassment from across the table. He stared at his sister, trying to make her understand without words that she needed to end this conversation.

"You would love a ball," Kate continued without even a glance at him. "The women are dressed in their finery and the men," she paused with a wistful sigh, "they are glorious in their dress clothes. I can just imagine the crush of men who would want to dance with you."

"I doubt that," Selina mumbled.

"Kate," Colin spoke up to end this embarrassing conversation. "I believe we need to discuss the refurbishing of the house."

His sister turned her head toward him. "Now? There is no hurry to complete the work. John and I cannot marry until his mourning time ends in three months. If we then rush to the altar, it will only cause talk. I'm quite certain he would agree that a six-month wait is more appropriate."

"But that will be the dead of winter," Selina commented. "Surely, you wouldn't wish to have your guests travel here in bad weather."

Kate fell silent for a long moment. "I hadn't thought about that. Oh, how I wish John was here to help with this decision."

Selina nodded in sympathy. Perhaps with a little more prodding on her part she might change Kate's mind about marrying here. "If you wait until spring, very few people will want to travel all this way for a wedding. Maybe a wedding in town would be better."

And then she wouldn't have to see Colin again. He would leave the estate for good. That thought should have made her feel better but a bitter taste filled her mouth. She sipped her wine only to have it taste like vinegar. She slipped a quick glance at him. His lovely lips were turned down as if he, too, found either his food or this topic of conversation distasteful.

"I cannot wait an entire year to marry, Selina," Kate finally said. "What am I to do?"

"Why not have a small wedding in town after Easter?" Colin suggested.

He also seemed to want the wedding in London and not here. From a practical standpoint, she could see his reason. Why waste money refurbishing a house that no one will live in and no wedding will take place in?

Selina looked over at her friend as guilt sliced through her. She truly enjoyed Kate's company and didn't want to see her friend in anguish after what she'd just been through with the miscarriage. "Why not have a small wedding here right before Christmas?"

Had she really just said that? The entire point was to push the wedding to London, not have it here in the middle of winter. She needed a certain man out of her life, not returning in a few months . . . or worse, not leaving at all. She must have control over her life again. And that could never happen as long as he remained here refusing to allow her to live in her cottage.

"That could be rather pretty if we have snow," Kate said slowly. "We could transform the ballroom so it looks like a snowy day. If we have it here, we could invite the neighboring families and I'm sure some people from farther away would attempt to come if the weather holds."

Selina wanted to bang her head against the table. Instead

of getting the man out of her life, she'd managed to make sure he returned in a few months. Plus he would still have to refurbish the house so he would remain here longer. There had to be a way to dissuade her.

"But won't it be more difficult to get people to attend the wedding at that time?"

Both Kate and Colin stared at her. Colin's dark brow raised in question.

"Didn't you just suggest this idea?" he asked with a smirk.

"Yes, but your sister needs to think through all the details. Planning a wedding is a tremendous ordeal."

"Not terribly," Kate said, again contradicting Selina's plans. "It's far less difficult than planning a ball. The wedding would be mostly family with a few friends. Probably no more than a hundred people."

That sounded like a huge undertaking to Selina. If a wedding of one hundred people was only a small party, how many people were invited to a ball? She shook her head in confusion. The life these people led was so different from her simple existence out here.

"I do believe this is settled," Kate announced. "John and I shall marry before the new year."

"Don't you think John should have some say in the matter?" Colin asked. "After all, he is the groom."

Kate's smile lit the room. "We are in love. He will want to marry me as quickly as possible." She pushed her plate away and rose. "In fact, I believe I shall write to him this very moment. After that, I will check in on Mother and go to bed. Good night."

Selina felt panic rush through her veins. She could not be alone in the same room as Colin after their disastrous day. Already as Kate reached the threshold, Selina could feel the room closing in on her . . . and him. Without Kate as a buffer, Selina feared what she might say or do. There had to be some reasonable excuse she could use to leave.

"Shall we retire to the salon?" Colin asked as he scraped his chair back.

"I believe I will just retire for the evening. Thank you."

"Before you do, might I have a word in private?"

What did he mean by that? She could only think of one thing that required privacy and that would not happen again. "Is that necessary?"

"Yes," he replied stiffly. "In my study."

"Very well." She walked down the long corridor to the study. After entering the room, she took a seat by the window and glanced out into the dark night. She started, hearing the door click shut.

"I . . . I . . ." he muttered, then walked to the brandy. He poured two snifters and brought one to her.

"What did you want to say, Colin?" She took the glass and sipped the heady drink. Warmth spread throughout her body. Was it the drink or his nearness that caused such a reaction? She prayed it was the brandy.

He took a mouthful and swallowed. "I wanted to apologize for my behavior this afternoon. I . . ." He walked away from her. "The truth is, I haven't been with a woman in many years and I embarrassed myself and should have taken more time with you and made sure you enjoyed yourself."

He hadn't been with a woman in years? How was that possible with all the stories she'd heard about him. "I don't understand," she whispered. "I've heard what people say about you and it is far from pleasant."

A tinge of color crossed his cheeks. "Everything you might have heard about me and other women was fabricated to ruin my reputation."

"Who would do such a thing?"

"Me."

Oh, dear God, it all made sense. He didn't want another woman after his wife died so the stories of his conquests were just that . . . stories. Her heart went out to him. She could only imagine how difficult that had been for him to say aloud. "Thank you," she said softly.

"For what?" He turned around and stared at her.

"Being truthful with me." Slowly, she stood and walked toward him. She reached out and caressed his cheek. "Was I the first since Mary?"

Red colored his cheeks. "Yes."

Selina's heart pounded in her chest. "Why me?" she whispered. "After all this time. Why me?"

"You are the first I have truly desired since her."

Chapter 16

What in God's name had made him say that to her? The next he knew he'd blurt out that he loved her. And he certainly didn't love the willful woman. He desired her unlike any woman but passion and love were completely separate things. If a man were lucky enough to have both, then his life would be perfect. But Colin understood there was no such thing as perfect in his life.

"Thank you for what you said, Colin," Selina said in a soft tone. "I should retire now."

Just thinking about her lying in the bed only a room away made his shaft thicken. "I shall escort you to your room."

"There is no need," she said in a rush. "I know the way."

"I insist." He held out his arm for her.

She pressed her lips together, then looped her arm with his. He felt a slight quiver from her as they walked down the hall. Perhaps she was not so unaffected by him. But could she ever want him again after how he treated her?

They walked through the corridor in silence. He'd never felt so unsure of himself with a woman before now. Not that he'd been any type of rake before he married Mary, but he'd had a few willing women.

"I will return to Lord Hartsfield's estate tomorrow," she commented as they paused by the door to his room.

"Oh? What if my sister needs you? I believe Hart's estate is too far."

She stared at the door. "Your sister is fine now. Far better than most women who recently suffered a miscarriage. I expect her youth is the reason. But it matters not. I cannot stay here in your house when you have asked me to leave."

Colin clasped her shoulders and turned her to face him. For a long moment, he just stared into her emerald eyes unable to say the words that he wanted to speak. Finally, he whispered, "Now I'm asking you to stay."

She went completely still for a long moment. Her eyes told him what she could not. He had no doubt that she was debating with herself. But as he watched her breasts rise and fall, her eyes dilate with passion, she would soon say what they both wanted to hear.

"No," she whispered.

And that was not what he wanted to hear. "No?"

"That is what I said."

"Why?"

"Are you mad?"

"Quite possibly. Come inside and talk to me in private."

"That would be improper."

Colin raised a brow at her. "Indeed? When have you ever been proper?"

She gave a brief nod. "Very well."

He opened the door to his room and walked inside. He waited for her to enter and close the door before continuing, "Do you have any idea how much I want you? How long I've waited to feel this way again? I've been dead inside for the past eight years until I returned here and found you."

He walked toward the window and stared outside as the long shadows of dusk darkened the skies. "I've never felt this way about a woman." He looked back at her. *"Any woman."*

A slow, seductive smile lit her face as she tentatively walked to him. "Any woman?"

"Yes."

"Why me?"

"Oh dear God, the questions women ask," he muttered. "I honestly don't know. You should be the last woman I'm attracted to . . . and yet, I can't keep my eyes off you. You enter a room and I know it before I turn and see you. You drive me mad on so many different levels."

She stepped closer. "And that is why you want me?"

He laughed softly. "I suppose it is."

"Hmm," she said as she reached his position by the window. "Perhaps that is a good enough answer."

Before she could utter another word, he kissed her. Hard at first, as if to punish her for making him admit so much to her. But as she slowly opened to him, he softened the kiss and let his tongue warm the recesses of her mouth. He wrapped his arms around her, bringing her tightly against his body. He wanted her now.

But this time, he would go slowly. She would learn exactly what it meant to be seduced, made love to, and ravished. She moaned softly as his tongue played with hers. He wanted her to be as crazed with desire as he was right now.

Colin worked at the buttons on her dress, eager to see her naked again. Finally, he had the last small button through its hole. He skimmed his arms up her back and broke the tight grip she had on him.

Selina backed a step away and stared at him. His admission that he wanted her more than his late wife had softened her heart to him. She wanted to feel him shower kisses all over her body. To teach her how to please him. To help her learn how to please her.

"I'll do it," she whispered. She watched his eyes darken as

she slipped her dress over her shoulders and down her waist until it pooled between them. "Now, I get to remove an article of your clothing."

He groaned as she slid her hands up his chest, under his jacket until she reached his shoulders. She glided the jacket off his broad shoulders, enjoying the sensation of his muscles tightening as she caressed his arms.

"Do you have any idea how much I want you right now?" he asked.

She smiled at the tight tone of his voice. "I think I do."

"Oh no," he said as he brought her roughly up against his hard cock. "You have no idea."

"Show me," she said. "Show me how to pleasure you."

"That is not going to happen tonight."

Selina glanced up at him. "Oh?"

"Tonight is all about you." He smiled slightly. "Turn around."

She did as he demanded. Immediately she felt his finger working the knot of her stays and then the gentle tug of the string through the loops. Her stays suddenly dropped to the floor. Her breath quickened as heat crossed her cheeks. She still wore her chemise but that was only thin cotton.

His arms wrapped around her from behind. His thumbs brushed her aching nipples. Her head fell back against his shoulder as desire weakened her muscles. He moved his hands up the top of her shift and then quickly pulled the garment down her body.

He spun her in his arms and pressed her against his chest. Unable to move or speak, she stared at the dark look of passion in his blue eyes. His lips caught hers in a crushing kiss. As his tongue played with her, her folds moistened in preparation for him. Slowly, he eased away and bent over her, catching her nipple in his mouth.

"Oh dear," Selina muttered.

He smiled against her breast and then moved down her

stomach. He knelt beside her and played with the curly hair between her thighs. Selina's knees went weak when he split the folds and touched her gently.

Need spiraled through her. She wanted him inside her now, sating this wanton longing she had been feeling since their previous encounter. Instead, he moved his mouth closer and kissed her thighs. Shivers ran up her body.

Surely, this wasn't proper. Then again, that's what she was known for. His lips moved upward until he reached the apex of her thighs. Before she could utter a word of denial, he brushed his tongue between her legs.

"This is wrong," she uttered.

"No," he rasped against her folds. His tongue delved deeper until she felt him pushing into her as his finger rubbed her clit.

Desire weakened her, pulling her along until she closed her eyes and the release washed over her. She'd never felt anything like this before. Her heart pounded against her chest as she attempted to catch her breath.

Colin rested against the downy hair between her legs. He was rock hard with desire but he had at least made her see that women could take their pleasure too. Slowly, he stood and kissed her flushed face. He found her lips and let her taste herself as he had her.

This slip of a woman was becoming far too important to him.

He felt her fingers on the button of his shirt. He smiled as he realized that she was no more done for the night than he. After pushing her fingers away, he yanked the shirt over his head.

Her fingers slid over his chest and brushed across his flat nipples. He reached for the buttons on his trousers eager to let her fingernails skim up his hard length. As he reached to remove them, she brushed his hands away and took over.

"It's your turn for pleasure," she whispered. She pulled the trousers over his hips and then giggled as his cock sprang forth.

She divested him of his shoes and clothes before looking back down at his cock. "May I?"

"You can touch me." *Dear God, please touch me.*

Her fingers ran up the long length of him until she found the top. Circling her palm around him almost did him in. He closed his eyes, reveling in the moment and trying to find some self-control so he didn't come in her hand.

Warm moisture enclosed him. He opened his eyes and fought for control. She was on her knees in front of him, sliding her mouth up and down the length of him. Desire clawed at him. There was no waiting.

He reached down and pulled her to her feet.

Blinking she looked up at him. "Didn't you like that?"

Colin laughed softly. "Far too much, Selina. If you'd kept that up, the evening would be over now."

She frowned slightly and then as if understanding his meaning, a slow smile lit her face. "Oh."

He clasped her hand and tugged her toward the bed. "Come on, we aren't done yet."

She giggled and walked to the bed. He picked her up and brought her down on the soft mattress. "What else do you mean to do?"

This time, he chuckled. "Let me show you." He sucked her nipple until she squirmed under him. Her hips grazed against his shaft, tempting him to hurry. He tickled a finger down her belly until he reached her moist folds. Feeling how damp she was, he shifted until his cock prodded her entrance.

He moved slowly, letting her stretch to his size. Feeling her tense, he slid his mouth back to her breast. A soft moan erupted from her as he inched forward into her tightness. With no barrier, he finally reached the hilt. Moist heat encircled him, pulling him closer to the brink.

But not this time.

She would reach her climax before he came deep inside her. As he slid out and then back in, she moved her hips in the rhythm. Her moans increased as he quickened the pace.

"Colin," she moaned.

He felt her tighten around him as she reached her peak. Unable to stop, he followed her over the precipice as waves of pleasure racked his body.

Finally, he collapsed on top of her. Neither could slow their breathing down as they attempted to recover their senses. He inhaled the heady scent of her before rolling off to lie on the bed.

A part of him felt guilty for his actions. Not because he was betraying Mary, but because he took Selina's innocence. She wasn't the type of woman a duke married. She was the type a man kept as a mistress.

He turned on his side and watched as she dozed, naked and sated. Her blond hair spread across the coverlet like the rays of the sun. His thoughts turned dark as he remembered how Mary always insisted on keeping her shift on as they made love. He had thought it endearing that after a year of marriage she still felt embarrassed to have him stare at her.

Selina never seemed shy about her body with him. She had stood in front of him as he pleasured her with his tongue. Something Mary had never allowed. Selina was a free spirit who understood that what happened between a man and a woman was a natural act.

A frantic knock on the door interrupted his thoughts. "Yes?" he whispered so as not to awaken her.

"Your Grace, I need to speak with you," Mr. Roberts said in a rush. "If you do not mind, I would prefer not to do it through the door."

"I'll be there in a moment."

Gingerly he moved off the bed and found his disheveled clothing. After dressing quickly, he went to the door and walked into the hall. If Roberts thought it strange not to be invited into the duke's bedchamber, he never said a word.

"What is the matter, Roberts?"

"It's Miss White, sir. I cannot find her anywhere. I searched her room and checked with your sister. No one has seen her since dinner."

"Perhaps she had to check on someone outside of the house," he said as he slid a glance toward his door.

"She would have told one of the footmen."

Damn her for being conscientious to the servants. "Why is she needed now?"

"Davie Patterson was climbing a tree and fell out. His mother thinks he broke his shoulder."

A child was hurt. Colin would have to wake her or face her wrath. But he also knew she would be dreadfully embarrassed if discovered in his room. He had to come up with some excuse so he could wake her without Roberts discovering the truth. "Let me change and I will go out looking for her."

"Thank you, Your Grace. I would feel much better knowing you were searching for her. I sent Randall out looking but . . ."

Roberts didn't need to say another word. Everyone knew Randall's abilities were limited at best. The poor man would more than likely get lost on the estate as darkness fell. "Have a horse saddled for me, Roberts."

"Yes, Your Grace."

Now he just had to explain what happened to Selina without her getting upset. Although he doubted that would be possible. As Roberts walked down the corridor, Colin turned toward his room.

Approaching Selina quietly, he worried about her reaction. Somehow, they would have to find a way for her to escape the house without notice. He sat down next to her and kissed her bare shoulder. A slight moan escaped her lips.

"Selina," he whispered.

"Hmmm?"

"You need to wake up. Someone needs you."

She popped up into a sitting position. He barely had time to get out of the way. "What? Who's sick?"

He quickly explained what happened as she dressed.

"Damn fool," she muttered as she grabbed her stays. "Can you help me with these?"

"Of course." It took far longer to loop the stays through the holes than it did to loosen them. "There."

She grabbed the dress and held it out at arms' length. "I can't wear this to attend to a patient."

"Don't you have your day dress in the room next door?"

She slid a glance at the connecting door. "Certainly," she said quickly. "Why don't you go downstairs and tell Mr. Roberts that you will go look for me outside?"

Why did she suddenly seem in a rush to get rid of him? "Won't you need help with your dress?"

"No, it buttons up the front."

"You will need help getting downstairs without being seen."

She shook her head. "I can run down the servants' steps. If anyone sees me, I'll . . . tell them they must have just missed me after I was visiting Kate's room."

"Very well." He pulled his Hessians on and then walked over to her. He pulled her up against his chest and kissed her firmly. "Don't get caught," he said with a laugh and then strolled out the door.

He highly doubted her plan would work but kept his thoughts to himself. Perhaps she would be lucky enough not to be caught by the staff. Then again, he wasn't sure why it mattered. She had told him that the tenants want her to have a child whether within the bounds of matrimony or not.

The idea of Selina carrying his child stopped him at the top of the stairs. He'd been so carried away by desire, he never thought of the possibility. She could be with child at this very moment.

His child.

He grabbed the rail as emotions flooded him. He'd told himself he would never get another woman with child. The thought of losing another wife and child left him cold. He could not go through that again.

He would not go through that again.

Chapter 17

Selina watched as Colin reached the stairs. "Go down the steps," she whispered.

Why wasn't he moving? She had to get him out of the corridor so she could run upstairs to the room where her dresses were. He grabbed the railing and she was certain he was about to depart. Instead, his legs didn't move.

"Go," she whispered again.

Finally, he started down the steps. Releasing a long breath, she raced out of his room and up the back staircase. She reached her room and closed the door behind her. She pulled out a dress from the linen press and quickly dressed. She had no idea what had actually happened to Davie Patterson's shoulder, but his mother would be worried sick.

She pulled her small valise out from under the bed. After putting on her short boots and tying her hair back, she ran back down the servants' steps. Thankfully, no one saw her and she was outside in only a few seconds.

Following the path with light from the full moon, she walked toward the Pattersons' house. A branch snapped behind her. Selina stopped to peer back toward the house.

"Is there a reason you didn't wait for me?"

She let out a sigh. "I had no idea you would want to accompany me."

Colin caught up with her. "You shouldn't be out here alone."

"How do you think I deliver babies? They rarely seem to arrive during the daylight."

"You should have a servant to go with you."

Selina laughed and shook her head. "You wealthy lords have no idea how anyone else lives, do you?"

He stopped. "Of course I do."

"No, you do not. I barely afford the rent here. Many times, it's only because the tenants all pitch in when I'm short. I can't afford a servant or a horse."

"But I can," he said slowly.

"Do not even think it," she scolded him. "I am not your mistress and will not take charity from you."

He nodded. "I understand."

She doubted he had any idea of what she went through every month. The tenants did their best to pay her but most had little to their own name. She sold her poultices and dried herbs at the market but the money rarely was enough for the rent.

Not that she would have to worry about it this month. She'd be damned if she paid him a farthing while she hid out in his house.

"How much farther is it to the house?" he asked.

"Haven't you called on Mrs. Patterson since your return?"

He turned his head away. It was far too dark to notice if he had the good sense to look embarrassed.

"You haven't called on your tenants, have you?"

"I don't know them any longer," he said softly. "I only know the names from the ledger my steward sends me every month."

"It's time you paid a call on every one of them. And you shall start tomorrow afternoon."

"Selina," he said, then paused for a long moment. "They hate me."

"They don't hate you." Perhaps extreme dislike in some cases but not all. "If you give them a chance to get to know you, they will come to appreciate all that you do."

"And what exactly do I do for them?"

He would have to ask such a difficult question. "You provide them with a home. They have excellent farmland. You give them a generous stipend for their crops."

"I don't make an appearance on this land for eight years. I don't make necessary repairs on their homes or my own."

Hearing the guilt in his voice, she had to help him. "They will forgive you if you only give them a chance. They all know why you haven't returned for so long. Let them into your life and you will find absolution and friendship."

"I don't know how much longer I will be here, Selina."

Her step faltered. Even knowing a relationship with a duke was out of the question, she'd become used to seeing him every day. Talking with him. Making love with him . . . even if it was only twice.

She didn't want him to leave.

And yet, she knew it would be best if he left.

Then she could resume her old life. With no one to speak with except the neighbor's cat who came to visit. She would miss the cur if he returned to London.

"You've become very quiet," he said in a soft tone.

She glanced up to see the Pattersons' house coming into view. She couldn't admit to him that she would miss him. Besides, their relationship was wrong in so many ways. It would be far better if he left. "We're almost there."

At least now, she could focus on Davie's injuries and not the idea of losing the man she might just be falling for.

Falling for?

That could never happen. She couldn't let it.

She pushed the disturbing thought out of her head and knocked on the door.

Mrs. Patterson pulled open the door. "Selina, thank God you're here. . . ." Her voice trailed off as she noticed Colin. "Yer . . . Your Grace," she stuttered. "Welcome to my home."

"I hope you don't mind, Mrs. Patterson. Miss White had been at my home looking after my sister. I didn't feel comfortable letting her walk here alone after dark."

"Of course." She waved them inside. "Davie is in his bedroom, Selina. He's in terrible pain. I think it's broken."

"I'll take a look. He most likely broke his arm in the fall and the pain is radiating to his shoulder." She turned to Colin. "Your Grace, I might need your assistance."

Colin looked slightly taken aback. "You might?"

She took his arm and led him away from Davie's mother. "If the arm is broken, I might need you to hold him down while I set it."

"Can't his father assist you?"

She smiled at his squeamish tone. "No, his father died last year."

Colin closed his eyes and nodded. "Very well, then. Of course, I will help you. It can't be much worse than assisting in a foaling."

"Mrs. Patterson, is Davie's room the first door on the right?" she asked, turning toward the woman.

"Yes, do you want me to come with you?"

"No, you stay down here. The duke will assist me tonight."

Mrs. Patterson's mouth gaped and then she recovered. "Call me if you need me. I'll be putting Mary to bed."

Selina glanced about the room until she noticed the three-year-old sitting in a chair in the corner, sucking her thumb. "Good evening, Mary."

The little girl's eyes grew large. She withdrew her thumb and said, "Hello, Miss Selina."

Mrs. Patterson came up beside Selina. "She's still a little

shaken from what happened. She was throwing her doll up in the air when it got stuck in the tree. Davie went up to fetch it for her."

"Will he be all right?" she asked softly.

"Let me go look at him, sweetling." Selina walked up the steps and Colin followed behind her. "I hope it's not too serious."

Colin inhaled deeply and continued up the stairs. Nausea roiled in his belly. This was mad. He was no physician. And neither was she. "Do you think we should call for the doctor?"

She stopped in front of a door. "No, I do not. I've seen that man do more harm than good."

She opened the door to Davie's room with a smile. "Well, Davie, I hear you're quite the hero tonight."

He groaned. "No, Miss Selina. I was just trying to help my baby sister."

"Like any good hero would," Colin added.

"Who's he?" Davie asked.

"If you weren't already in pain, I'd punch you," his older sister said. "That's His Grace."

Davie's eyes widened. "Sorry, Yer Grace. I never met you before."

"Meg, go down and help your mother get Mary to bed," Selina ordered.

"Yes, ma'am." The girl ran from the room after a quick curtsy to Colin.

He remained at the foot of the bed as Selina sat down next to Davie. He watched as she examined the boy's arm and shoulder. Davie's shoulder looked swollen.

"Davie, were you hanging from the tree before you fell?" Selina asked and then moved to her bag.

"Yes, ma'am."

"Your Grace, I will definitely need your assistance. It looks like Davie didn't break his arm after all."

"Then why do you need me?"

"He dislocated his shoulder." She turned back and looked at him. "I will need you to hold him while I put it back in place."

"Is it going to hurt?" Davie whispered.

She walked over to the pitcher and poured some water into a glass. She mixed some powder into the water. "I'll give you a little something to help the pain. Once it's back in place, you'll feel so much better. And you will get to wear a sling for a week or two. You shall be able to brag about your heroic deed to all your friends."

Davie smiled as he took the glass from her. He scrunched up his face as he sipped it.

Colin walked over to the bed and said, "My nurse always told me it was better to drink the bitter medicine down quickly."

"Exactly," Selina remarked. "And then you get a lemon drop." She waited until Davie had swallowed all the water before handing him the treat.

"Thank you."

"Are you ready?" she asked Colin.

No. He'd heard tales of how painful this was and he would never be ready to watch an eight-year-old go through it. He looked over at Davie who was starting to yawn. "Yes, I'm ready."

"I need you to hold him down. Even though I gave him the laudanum he still might fight you."

Colin nodded and then moved over to hold Davie in place. The door opened behind him and he heard Mrs. Patterson gasp. Selina never took her eyes off Davie. With a deep breath in, she rotated his shoulder until it popped back into place. Davie screamed and Colin held him tight.

He glanced back to see Mrs. Patterson hold a fist to her mouth, tears streamed down her cheeks. "It's all right now, Davie," he crooned. "The worst is over."

He wiped away the tears from the boy's cheek. "Shh, no one but us will know you cried."

Davie nodded. "Thank you."

Selina went back to her bag and pulled out a sheet of cotton. She folded it into a triangle and then moved to the bed. "Help him sit up."

Colin reached behind Davie and pushed him up to a sitting position. "Now you get that sling."

Selina arranged the sling in place and then started to pack up her valise. She pulled out a small bag and gave it to Mrs. Patterson. "Give this to him every four hours for the pain. I'll come back and check on him tomorrow afternoon. I want him resting for at least a week."

Colin snorted. "Good luck. No eight-year-old boy is going to rest in bed for a week."

Selina glared back at him and then smiled at Mrs. Patterson. "At least try."

"You did a great job tonight, Davie," he said, squeezing the boy's hand.

"No, I didn't," he mumbled.

"What do you mean?"

"I couldn't reach Mary's doll. I tried to jump for it and that's when I fell."

Colin saw the disappointment on Davie's face and knew what he had to do. "I'll be right back."

"C-Your Grace, where are you going?" Selina asked.

"I shall return in a moment." He ran downstairs and grabbed the lantern from the table. He walked outside and held the light up toward the tree in front of the house. Smiling, he climbed up the tree and reached for the cloth doll stuck on a limb.

With the doll in hand, he returned to Davie's bedchamber. He held the doll behind his back. "Do you think the patient can get up for just a short moment?"

Selina frowned. "I don't . . ." Her voice trailed off as he

turned just enough that she could see what he held. "I think he can get up for a moment."

"Why?" Davie mumbled.

"The laudanum is making him sleepy," Selina commented. "You need to hurry."

"Come on, boy," Colin said, gently helping Davie out of the bed. "You must return the maiden's doll."

"What?"

"Your sister's doll," he said, holding out the toy.

"You got it!"

"Yes, but your sister doesn't have to know that. You can tell her you were able to get it."

Colin walked with Davie across the hall to his sisters' bedroom. Meg let them in and smiled when she saw what they held.

"She'll be so happy! She's been crying ever since Mama put her in here."

Davie went over to his sister and sat on the bed. Mary looked up at him and cried harder.

"Mary, it's all right. Look at what I have for you."

Mary's wet eyes grew large when she saw her doll. "You got Molly!"

"Yes, His Grace helped me," Davie said and then smiled back at Colin.

Colin's heart filled with joy. It had been years since he thought about children. He'd always wanted a large family, at least he had until Mary died, then his dreams of children died too. But now, he wasn't certain. Still, the idea of losing another woman he loved still haunted him.

He focused his attention back on Davie. "Come on, boy. Miss White will have my head if I don't get you back into bed."

Davie kissed his sister's forehead and then grabbed Colin's hand. His heart squeezed as firmly as his hand on the lad's. He wanted this.

He wanted a child of his own.

Chapter 18

Selina awoke the next morning and knew she had to force Colin to get out and meet his tenants. After watching him last night with Davie, she'd seen a side of him she never expected. Never would she have thought that the duke would climb a tree to get a child's doll.

Colin had insisted she stay in the room next to his again last night. But she had decided that after they met with the tenants, she would make certain he knew she was not staying there any longer. She would insist he let her move back into her cottage.

She needed to put some distance between them. Her heart was weakening and she knew falling in love with a duke was foolhardy. No good would come of that and the sooner she put a stop to their relationship, the less pain she would feel when he ended things. And if he ever found out the lies he'd been told by both her and her mother, he would despise her.

She dressed quickly and went in search of him. She found Colin dining alone in the breakfast room. "Good morning."

"Good morning to you."

She sat down and a footman promptly filled her cup with tea. "Thank you."

"I shall bring you a plate, Miss White."

"I trust you slept well?" Colin asked and then sipped his tea.

"Yes." When they had returned from Davie's home, he had tried to get her to sleep with him. But after almost being discovered that evening by Mr. Roberts she declined. She would be terribly embarrassed if anyone found out they had been lovers.

"Your Grace," Selina started and then paused as the footman placed a plate of eggs and ham in front of her.

"Yes, Miss White?" His lips twitched as if he found the idea of them being so formal amusing.

"I need to check on Davie and some of the other tenants this morning. Would you like to accompany me?"

He stared down at his almost empty plate before finally saying, "Yes. I would enjoy that. It would give me the chance to greet the tenants."

"Wonderful. Shall we leave at ten?"

"Perfect." He rose from his seat. "Please excuse me but I need to get some work done before we leave."

She nodded. She couldn't help but watch him as he left the room. He cut a fine figure in his buff trousers and brown jacket. Or maybe it was just the way those trousers stretched across his derrière.

Spending more time with him was not a smart idea. She should be moving herself back to the third floor. But she had to force him to get to know his tenants again. They needed repairs on their homes as much as his house needed them.

"Good morning, Selina."

Selina looked up from her half-eaten breakfast to see Kate and the duchess entering the room. "Good morning, Kate, Your Grace."

"Good morning, Miss White," Kate's mother replied formally. "You look quite pensive this morning. Is everything all right?"

Selina shrugged. "I was just thinking that I must leave.

Kate no longer needs me here. I believe I shall return to Mrs. Featherstone's cottage."

Kate and her mother shared a long look. A footman broke their silent conversation as he placed a teacup in front of Kate.

"Perhaps that would be for the best," the duchess said softly.

Kate openly glared at her mother. "I was actually hoping Selina might join us at Mrs. Littleton's ball. We can say she is my paid companion."

Her mother tilted her head in thought. A footman placed a small plate of toast and jam in front of her. "Perhaps she could. But don't you think some people might recognize her?"

"I really have no desire to go to a ball," Selina commented. Well, she did have the desire to attend but knew it was out of the question. "I don't even know how to dance and the ball is late next week. Besides, I have nothing suitable to wear to a ball."

Kate waved a hand at her. "That is not an issue. My maid is a fabulous seamstress and can alter one of my dresses. As far as the dancing, you would only need to learn one or two dances."

Selina laughed softly as she nodded her head. Who would even ask her to dance? Perhaps Colin out of pity, but he would be the only one.

"I do believe it would be a good experience for her," the duchess said. "We shall start the dress fitting this afternoon at three, followed by a dance lesson."

Selina could only stare at the mad women across the table from her. "I cannot pass as a paid companion."

"Of course you can," Kate replied. "You might not have all the social skills needed but you are intelligent and beautiful. The men only notice your beauty, but the women will note your wisdom."

"I really must decline."

Kate leaned in closer and said, "No, or my brother will discover who has been living on the third floor."

Selina felt slightly faint. Her new friend was threatening her. Why? What possible good could come out of her attending a ball? She didn't fit in with these people. But she couldn't let Colin discover her hiding place either. "Very well," she bit out. "I will attend the ball with you."

"Of course you will," Kate said with a catlike grin.

"Excuse me, I must get ready," Selina said as she scraped back her chair.

"Where are you off to?" the duchess asked.

"I have to see to a few of the tenants."

"Perhaps you should take the duke with you," the duchess said softly. "He needs to reacquaint himself with his tenants."

Kate nodded. "That would be a good idea."

"He is planning to escort me," Selina replied as she reached the threshold.

"Excellent," the duchess said under her breath.

Kate waited until she was certain Selina had departed. Then she giggled softly. "Did you see her reaction? She was positively irate that I would force her to go to a ball."

Her mother laughed too as she placed her teacup down. "You had better be right about those two."

"Mother, this is the first time in years I've seen Colin smile, really smile. Not that fake one he gives people to be sociable. I even heard him laugh. He loves her whether he realizes it or not yet. But he will."

"I have to admit, he does seem different."

"And getting Selina out to a small ball in the country will help her see that she can do this. She might never want to attend the Season but over time she will gain some confidence."

Her mother nodded. "True, but your brother needs to make

an effort to get her into Society. If we paint her as the daughter of a country squire, she will slowly be accepted. But under no circumstances can anyone discover her true background."

"Do you think anyone would know her?"

"The only two I can think of would be Hartsfield and Middleton."

Kate sipped her tea. "Yes, but they are his friends. I believe they would support him when he marries her."

"*If* he marries her. He may still let convention decide his life," her mother replied.

"I know he loves her. I have seen the way they look at each other when they think no one is watching."

"True but that might just be lust."

Kate shook her head. "It's love."

Her mother released a long breath. "I do hope you're right. That boy needs to love again."

Colin waited for Selina outside by the horses. He couldn't help but feel a bit nervous. After all, he'd been home for a month and still hadn't greeted his tenants. One more thing for them to hold against him.

His lips turned upward as she walked across the grass. Her slender hips swayed under the yellow muslin dress. His smile turned into a large grin as he noticed her beautiful blond hair was put up into a loose chignon. Tendrils blew across her heart-shaped face. His heartbeat increased the nearer she came.

"Are you ready?" she asked once she'd reached him.

"Not really," he admitted.

"They will be pleased to meet you."

He assisted her onto the mare and then climbed on his horse. "If you say so. I am not quite certain they shall all be happy to see me again."

They started at a slow trot. "You might be surprised. The

key to getting to know your tenants is listening. Put away your fears and just hear what they are saying. Most of their issues are with the upkeep of their homes."

If their homes were anything like his own, he could understand their irritation with him. He would have to talk to his steward and get the needed repairs done on the tenants' homes to appease them.

They arrived at the Pattersons' home first. Colin looked up at the house in the daylight and could see the repairs needed on the thatched roof. After he helped Selina down, they walked toward the house. Little Mary opened the door before they reached it and ran toward him. She launched herself into his arms.

"Thank you," she said as her chubby arms latched around his neck.

Surprised at the warmth suffusing him, he held the little girl tight against his chest. "What is this about?"

Mary pulled back and looked at him. "Davie said you saved Miss Molly."

"Miss Molly?"

"My doll," she said with a giggle.

"Mary, you are getting to be such a big girl," Selina said. "It's almost your birthday, isn't it?"

Mary's brown eyes sparkled. She lifted her hand and put up four fingers. "Four."

"Very good," Colin remarked. Slowly, he put her down and instantly missed her.

"Is Davie at home?" Selina asked.

Mary nodded. "He's in bed. Mama told him not to move."

Colin could only imagine the pain that caused the boy. Nothing would stop him from getting outside when he was a lad. Mary took his hand and led him inside.

"Mama, he's here."

"Who is here—" Mrs. Patterson stopped and curtsied. "Your Grace."

"Mrs. Patterson," he said with a nod. "How is Davie this morning?"

"He's mad that I won't let him out of bed."

"I'll go take a look at him," Selina said and then left the room.

"Can I get you some tea, Your Grace?"

Even though he didn't want tea, he didn't wish to insult the woman. "Yes, that would be lovely."

"Please sit down," Mrs. Patterson said as she put the kettle on to boil.

As soon as he sat, Mary clamored up on his lap. She stuck her thumb in her mouth and rested her head against his chest. He smiled down at the little cherub, again wondering what it would feel like to have his own child sitting on his lap.

"Looks like you made a new friend, Your Grace."

"She told me Davie admitted the truth."

Mrs. Patterson pulled out teacups as she nodded. "She knew Davie didn't get the doll when he fell out. She's a right smart girl. She knew he couldn't get it with his arm in a sling."

"Mrs. Patterson, what do you need around here?"

She glanced back at him as she poured the hot water. "What do you mean, Your Grace?"

"I know your husband died. I'm just wondering what type of help you need around the house. Is the roof leaking? Do you need a footman to come by and help you with any repairs?"

She blinked furiously. "My roof started leaking this spring after a windstorm."

"I shall get a man to come by and fix it."

She placed a teacup in front of him. "Bless you, Your Grace."

"What else do you need?"

"Nothing," she replied, staring into her cup.

"Why, Mrs. Patterson, I do believe you are holding something back."

She wiped away a tear. "Your Grace, I love it here. My children are so happy . . ."

"But . . . ?"

"I have to leave. The little bit I earn from sewing won't pay for what I need. I have a brother in Suffolk who will take us in."

Colin could tell from the quivering tone of her voice that there was more going on than just her leaving. He wished Selina would return. She would be able to get Mrs. Patterson to talk about it. Or perhaps, he could try.

"Why don't you want to live with your brother?"

"He's a terrible man, Your Grace. I fear he may do . . . unnatural things to my babies." She continued to stare into her tea.

Colin closed his eyes for a long moment. There was no chance he would let this woman take her children to her brother's home. "Mrs. Patterson, would you consider working up at the manor house for me?"

She looked up. "What do you mean?"

He laughed softly. "My home is in disrepair. Most of my servants are twice your age. I need to start bringing in some younger servants so the older ones may think about retiring."

"You want me to go into service?"

"Yes, but you would be able to keep your house here and come home every night."

"I can cook, sir."

Colin smiled. "Then I will speak with Mrs. Roberts."

"I know she would appreciate the help, Your Grace," Selina said from the bottom step. "Her legs are bothering her more and more every day."

"Will you think about it, Mrs. Patterson?" Colin asked as Mary stirred on his lap.

The woman smiled. "There is nothing to think about,

Your Grace. I would be honored to go into service in your household."

"Excellent." He took one last sip of tea. "I might need some help with this," he said, nodding to the little girl on his lap.

Selina laughed and walked over to Mary. Slowly, she picked up the girl and handed her to Mrs. Patterson. "Davie is doing just fine other than his petulance. Give him another day in bed and then let him slowly get up and do things. But not too much at first."

"Thank you, Selina."

"We must go now. We have a few more tenants to visit." Selina kissed Mary's forehead.

"Of course," Mrs. Patterson replied and then walked them to the door. "When would you like me to start at the house?"

"Next Monday would be fine," Colin replied. Now he just had to hope he hadn't stepped on Mrs. Roberts's toes. She might have wanted to speak with Mrs. Patterson first to make sure they would work well together.

"I will be there."

He and Selina walked to their horses. After he helped her up, she stared down at him with admiration in her green eyes.

"That was the most thoughtful thing you could have done for her."

He shrugged, knowing if he hadn't been absent for eight years, he might have known of Mrs. Patterson's troubles immediately. He had duty to come here and take care of his tenants. There would be no more wallowing in self-pity. Selina had shown him that life goes on . . . and he could too.

Chapter 19

Selina walked from the stables tired after a long morning of tenant visits with Colin. Every day for the past week they had been greeting the tenants together. Then every afternoon she had spent learning new dance steps with Kate. Selina wanted nothing more than to lie down and take a nap. But now she had to be fitted for a gown for a ball that she had no business attending.

No one would take her for Kate's paid companion. For some reason, Kate wanted her there but Selina doubted it was just as a companion. She wondered briefly if Kate was trying to help her find a husband as a way of thanking her after the miscarriage. Or even more unthinkable, Kate might believe Colin would be a perfect husband for her.

That was a mad idea, indeed.

Kate would know that Selina wasn't fit to become a duchess. It was laughable to think Colin would even want her to be his wife. She didn't think he had changed his mind about marriage and children at this point.

Even if he did look more handsome than she had ever seen when he had Mary on his lap last week. There was something about a man holding a child that touched her heart completely.

Colin cleared his throat and then clasped her elbow. "Come with me for a moment."

He led her to the reflecting pond. They both sat on the edge. She looked over at his windblown hair and was tempted to push the black hairs out of his face.

"Thank you," he said softly and then kissed her hand.

"For what?"

"Showing me what I needed to do with my tenants. I feel horrible about how they've been neglected for the past eight years."

She smiled. "Good. I'm glad you have seen what needs to be done. Now, will you act upon it?"

He nodded and kissed her hand again. "I plan on speaking with my steward tomorrow. I want money allocated to fix the cottages. If the tenants need something, I want them to go to Mr. Hughes and understand that he will act immediately."

"Thank you," she whispered, touched by his words. She never expected he would react this way. All she'd wanted him to do was meet the people who lived and worked his land. "I need to go now."

"Where are you off to?"

"Your sister wants to speak with me." She had no idea why she didn't mention the ball. Perhaps it was because she didn't want to see his reaction. He would probably ridicule her for going.

"Very well, I will see you at dinner then." He rose and held out a hand to her.

"I do believe it's time I returned to Mrs. Featherstone's home. I have spent an extra week here only to please Kate. And she no longer needs me."

"No," he said quickly. "Stay here."

"I do not belong." And staying would mean returning to his bed again. While she wanted that desperately, she knew making love with him was only an illusion. One she must stop. She'd been able to avoid him the past few days by staying close to Kate. But she could sense his frustration rising. He wanted her again . . . and she was weakening.

"We will discuss this later."

She nodded. "If you wish."

She walked back to the house and up to her room on the third floor. She had thirty minutes before she was supposed to meet with Kate. She fell to the bed and stared at the white ceiling.

Being with Colin the last week had left an impact on her that she'd never expected. He touched her heart when he let little Mary on his lap and when he offered Mrs. Patterson a position. There were several times during the day that she would catch him staring at her. And what she saw in his eyes frightened her—admiration, desire, and quite possibly love.

Could the Duke of Northrop be in love with her?

Could she be in love with him?

The second question was far too easy to answer. Yes. Somehow, the arrogant man had gotten under her skin and deep into her heart. And he could never find out that she loved him.

Today she had realized the truth about him. The man was far more softhearted than she'd thought. She wasn't sure why it surprised her. This was the same man who hadn't been with another woman for eight years. He had loved his first wife so deeply that he'd never imagined wanting to be with another.

But he had been with Selina.

He'd told her he desired her even more than his late wife. And that led her back to her first question. Could he be in love with her? She was starting to believe it true.

If that was the case, she had to leave. He would hate her if he ever discovered the truth. No matter how he felt about her, the secret she had kept from him would destroy any chance of love for them.

The ball was in a few days. As soon as it was over, she would leave. Or at least pretend to return to Mrs. Featherstone's. Then once he left, she could go back to her cottage and try to forget him. She wondered if that would ever be possible. As long as she lived on the estate, she would be reminded of him.

She brushed a tear off her cheek.

She glanced over at the clock and then quickly changed into her lavender dress. The first fitting for her gown was in five minutes. Perhaps Kate would give some indication why she felt it necessary for Selina to attend this ball. If not, then she would corner her later and demand the truth.

After checking her appearance in the mirror, she paused. Neither Kate nor her mother had told her where to meet them. She shrugged and decided to try Kate's room first.

She raced down the servants' staircase to the second floor. She rapped on Kate's door.

"Come in," Kate's voice called from inside the room.

Selina opened the door and then smiled. Kate stood on a small stool as her maid finished a few touches on the beautiful gold gown.

"Kate, you look so beautiful."

"Thank you. In another minute, you will be next." She giggled. "I found the most perfect gown for you."

The door to the bedchamber opened and the duchess walked inside. She nodded her approval. "That is beautiful." She strolled closer. "Although, I dare say a bit immodest. Perhaps a bit of fichu at the bosom."

"I am almost a married woman, Mother."

"You should have already been married," the duchess muttered.

"I will be married in no time at all. I might as well enjoy a ball or two before that happens," Kate retorted.

"Very well, where is the dress for Selina?"

Kate pointed to the linen press. "The sage-colored one. It will match her eyes."

Selina sat in the tapestry chair by the window feeling more uncomfortable by the minute. Perhaps she could make some excuse. She started to force a cough just as the duchess turned with the most beautiful gown Selina had ever seen. That masterpiece could not be for her to wear.

The duchess held it up. "What do you think, Selina?"

The green silk dress had silver thread shot through it, which made it catch the rays of sunlight filtering inside. With candlelight, the gown would shimmer. The bodice had cap sleeves hemmed with ivory lace. "It's more beautiful than anything I've ever seen," she whispered.

"Excellent," Kate said. "Go try it on. I'm done now."

Even knowing she shouldn't, Selina couldn't help herself from trying on the dress. She went behind the screen and a maid assisted her with her clothing. The silk dress caressed her skin as the maid buttoned up the back.

"All set," she said.

Selina walked around the screen and both women gasped. She turned and stared at her reflection in the mirror. "I look like . . ."

"A duchess," said Kate with a grin.

"It is so beautiful." Selina held out the skirt and then twirled.

"Now let Sally check the fitting." Kate helped Selina up on the stool.

For the first time, Selina looked at the gown in a critical manner. It fit her almost perfectly. As if it had been made for her. But that wasn't possible.

Sally checked the fitting and nodded. "Perfect. I just need to hem it."

"I am a bit taller than she is, Sally," Kate commented.

Hardly a bit, Selina thought. Kate was several inches taller and this dress only needed to be an inch or two shorter. Not to mention the most obvious difference, Kate was larger in the bosom than Selina. These two ladies were definitely up to something. Instead of confronting them now, she would wait until she could get Kate alone.

Of course, that was an impossibility. As soon as they had finished the fitting, the two ladies whisked her off for dancing lessons. They had even brought in a dance instructor from town today.

Mr. Bryant taught her several country dances and even the scandalous waltz, although the duchess frowned the entire time he danced with Selina. She was certain she would never remember them all.

"I shall be back tomorrow at four," he said as he packed up his music. "We will review the dances we learned today and maybe have time for a few more."

"More?"

"A lady must know all the current dances," the duchess interjected.

"Yes, a ball will have many different sets. You must be prepared to dance them all." Mr. Bryant added.

That would never happen. Already her feet ached and it had only been two hours. While Mr. Bryant departed, she glanced around. It was time to get Kate alone . . . except she had already left while Selina had been talking with Mr. Bryant.

"Your Grace, do you know where Kate went?"

"To get ready for dinner. You must go now too. A lady always dresses for dinner and after an exertion like dancing for two hours, you must wash."

"Of course," Selina mumbled. Even the duchess was acting oddly. Calling her a lady. Dressing for dinner. Oh dear God! They couldn't possibly believe she and Colin were in love. But as she walked to her room, certain comments came back to her.

Kate had said Selina looked like a duchess when she tried on the ball gown.

The duchess has said a lady must know all the current dances. And had said something similar about dressing for dinner.

No, no *no!* She was not about to let them continue that line of thought. She quickly washed and dressed in her yellow muslin for dinner. Then she raced down the servants' stairs to find Kate before it was time to eat.

She rapped forcefully on Kate's door. "Kate, let me in this instant."

The door creaked open but it was Sally who stood on the other side. "Lady Katherine has gone to the main salon for sherry before dinner."

Frustration rolled in her. Maybe she could catch Kate before Colin and the duchess joined them. But just as she reached the last step, she heard Colin's voice upstairs.

"Selina, let me escort you." He hurried down the stairs.

"Good evening, Your Grace."

A dark brow rose. "So formal."

"Yes, we are about to have dinner. Your sister and step-mother will be there too so formality is to be expected."

His full lips quirked. "Indeed."

They walked into the salon and Kate's eyes widened. Oh, she was up to something. But now Selina would have to wait to discover what Kate plotted.

"Good evening, Kate," Colin said, then kissed his sister on the cheek. "What have you been doing today?"

"Mother brought in a dance instructor to teach us some new dances."

"New dances?" he asked as he took a seat on the sofa. "The Season only ended a few weeks ago. How could there be any new dances?"

Randall brought glasses of sherry to all of them. Selina

remained standing near a window. Randall gave her a wink as he handed a glass to her.

"Actually," Kate continued with her lie, "there are a couple of new dances and I finally received permission to waltz so I needed to learn that dance."

Selina shook her head as she sipped her sherry. The lies kept piling on. Kate danced the waltz like an expert. Why was Kate refusing to tell Colin that the teacher was here for her?

The duchess arrived just as Randall announced dinner. They all retired to the dining room.

"Good evening, everyone," she said as she took her seat.

"I heard quite the tale of you helping one of the tenant boys last week," Kate said as she glanced between Selina and Colin.

"I could never have helped Davie without the duke's assistance," Selina replied as heat filled her cheeks.

The duchess stared at Selina for a long moment. "Tell me, dear, how exactly did the duke decide to join you?"

Oh dear, the woman was prying. "The servants could not find me so they asked the duke if he had seen me. He decided to help them look for me. Once I heard what had happened, I went outside and the duke insisted on accompanying me."

The older woman pursed her lips before nodding. "I see."

"It was good fortune that he did," Selina continued. "Davie's shoulder was dislocated and I needed someone strong to help hold him down while I set it."

"Good fortune, indeed," the duchess remarked with a sharp look at Colin.

"Leave it be, Georgina," Colin said sharply.

"Leave what be, Colin?"

"You are trying to determine if one of us is lying. Though why, I should like to know."

The duchess laughed softly. "Oh my dear boy, you are imagining things. Why would either of you be lying?"

"Why indeed, Mother?" Kate interrupted. "Selina did nothing but attend to one of our tenants."

"And walked alone in the dark with the duke. It's highly suspicious. If a woman did that in town, she would be scandalized."

Colin's fork landed with a clink on his plate. "This is not London, Georgina. Would it have been better to let Miss White go alone?"

"Of course not, but a servant could have assisted her. There was no need for you to do so." She picked up her cup and sipped her tea.

"Excuse me," Selina said, scraping back her chair. "I have lost my appetite."

"Sclina, wait," Kate called after her.

Selina didn't stop. She walked back upstairs and to the bedchamber where she'd slept last night. How could a man walking with a woman be so scandalous? She would never understand Society's rules.

And why would the duchess remark on it? Selina could have sworn the woman was involved in the scheme to get her to the ball. Perhaps good sense had finally overcome the duchess's delight in seeing Selina in a beautiful gown and dancing.

She plopped on the bed and curled up. She had to leave. Her feelings were too conflicted when she was so near Colin. She'd fallen in love with a man who was so completely out of her reach that any relationship, save mistress, was out of the question.

Although not one of the tenants, nor her friends, would condemn her for such a liaison with him, she couldn't continue it. Her heart was far too involved now.

But where would she go? The first place he would look for her was the cottage. Kate knew about her hiding place on the third floor. Mia really didn't have room at her mother's home.

Tia's house on Middleton's land was just too far away to reach Colin's tenants should they need her.

She supposed there was only one option left. She would have to find another room upstairs. Kate would assume Selina had moved back into her room on the third floor but she would instead move to the west wing. Kate wouldn't look for her there since it was so far from the servants' staircase.

The family wouldn't stay much longer at the estate and once they left, things would return to normal. Then she could go back to her cottage.

A knock interrupted her musing. "Who is it?"

"It's Colin. I need to speak with you."

She wasn't sure she could see him right now. While she had made her decision her heart weakened every time she was alone with him.

"Selina," he called again from the hall.

"Go away, Your Grace."

"Like hell I will," he said as he opened the door. "If I remember correctly, this is my house."

She swallowed back the instant desire that flowed with seeing him standing against the closed door. His black hair looked tousled as if he'd been raking his hands through it. It had been neat when he had sat down to eat.

"You should not be in here," she commented. "It's almost as scandalous as walking in the dark with me."

He laughed softly. "Oh, this is far more scandalous." He stepped closer to her. "I've always taken great pride in behaving properly with a lady."

"But I'm not a lady, just some woman who lives off your land."

He tilted his head. "You are far more a lady than most of the women of the *ton*. They would love to get me in a bedchamber alone. Or better yet, to have been discovered walking in the dark night alone with me. That would garner a proposal for certain."

And yet, sleeping with her didn't convince him to propose. God, what was she thinking? Even if by some odd chance he did ask her to marry him, she could never accept.

She looked up into his blue eyes and was lost. She might not be able to marry him but she did want him. And she had to stop that nonsense too.

"Why are you here, Colin?"

"I wanted to apologize for my stepmother."

"There is no need," she replied stiffly. "She was only stating the obvious. If anyone but your family discovered you were out with me, people would talk. Or worse, demand you marry me."

"Would that really be worse?"

"Of course," she said, getting up from the large bed. She needed no reminders of beds and him. "We are completely different people from vastly different social standings."

"And that matters?"

She turned and stared at him. "Of course it does."

"It should not," he whispered and then stepped closer. His breath heated her cheek.

Fight it, she told herself. No good could come from being with him again. But as he pressed featherlight kisses on her forehead, she remembered the last time she was with him. She wanted that again. The sensation of his bare skin rasping against hers. The taste of his heated kisses. His mouth and tongue teasing her nipples until she thought she might faint from the pleasure of it.

Without another thought, she brought her arms around his neck and pressed her lips to his. This was a fool's passion and she was the biggest fool ever. And at that moment, she didn't care.

Chapter 20

Colin's control slipped as she responded with such passion to his kisses. He had only come here to apologize for his stepmother's remarks. Now, he had to have her. Desire had taken over his good sense. He wanted her up against the door, or on the chair, or the bed, anywhere as long as it was now.

"Colin," she moaned as his lips traced her jaw.

"I want you so desperately."

"Yes, now," she whispered. "Please now."

He laid her on the bed with her legs dangling off it and then pushed up her layers of skirts. Her eyes widened as she realized his intent. A sensual little smile curved her lips.

He pulled down his trousers and in one swift move, pulled her legs up against his chest and entered her tight wetness. "God," he groaned.

"Colin," she said breathless. "Please now, I need you moving inside me."

He replied to her whispered demand and slid out quickly and back inside. Her legs curled around his back, drawing him in even farther. He could feel her pulse against his shaft and knew she was already close to the edge. He increased his rhythm, faster and faster until she clenched his cock and shook with her climax.

"Colin," she screamed.

Hearing her call out his name as she reached her orgasm brought him over the edge. "Selina," he moaned repeatedly as he spilled his seed into her.

He looked down at the beautiful woman and was lost. This slip of a woman, who had no idea of Society or propriety or any of the harsh rules he had grown up with, had taken his heart. How had she done that? He had been so certain no one could fill the void left by Mary. But Selina had not only filled that void but had opened him to an even stronger feeling of love.

She had shown him the importance of his ancestors' lands and the value of the tenants. The look on tenants' faces after she'd been at their homes was something he wanted to see more often. He wanted to show her and them that he could do better than he had. He wanted to be a better person for her.

He wanted to marry her.

She blinked open her eyes and smiled up at him before quickly masking the raw emotion on her face. That was the first time he'd ever seen her do such a thing. Normally, she was so easy to read.

"Are you all right?" Perhaps he had been too rough with her. Although, she had certainly acted as though she'd enjoyed herself.

"I'm fine, but you should go," she said, pushing at his shoulders to move him off her.

"Why?"

"Someone might discover you here," she said with a light tone to her voice that didn't match the pain on her face.

"That didn't seem to bother you the last time. Did my stepmother speak to you?"

She shook her head. "Ever since I took care of Kate, the duchess has treated me very well."

Colin slipped a handkerchief between them as he pulled out of her. He dragged his trousers back up and buttoned them. She straightened out her skirts and rose from the bed.

Watching her every movement, he knew something was bothering her.

"Selina, I'm not leaving until you tell me what is wrong."

She pressed her lips into a tight line. "I have to leave."

"What do you mean?"

"I don't belong here. I only stayed because Kate needed me. Well, she is healthy enough that I can return to Mia's house now."

Oh, dear God, he couldn't let her leave yet . . . ever. But he also sensed telling her that he loved her would not be well received at the moment. "Please stay," he whispered, staring into her emerald eyes.

"I cannot."

"At least tell me why."

"This"—she motioned between them—"is . . . was wonderful. But it's not real. It was only a fantasy and I can't continue living in a fantasy. My life is here on this estate as the wise woman. Taking care of the tenants and the servants. That is my lot in life."

"It doesn't have to be," he whispered.

"Yes, it does."

Hearing the firm tone of her voice, he knew she would never change her mind tonight. Something or someone had forced her to make this decision and he was bound to find out who. In the meantime, there was only one way to keep her on the estate. "Then move back into your cottage."

Her full lips gaped open. "Are you serious?"

"Yes. Move back to your home."

Her lips trembled as she blinked furiously. "Thank you."

He nodded, unable to say what he really wanted to tell her. Perhaps a little distance between them would help him make the decision. "I suppose I should go now."

"Yes."

He headed for the door with a heavy heart. He reached

for the handle and then turned. "Are you visiting tenants tomorrow?"

"Yes, I have a few people I need to check on."

"May I accompany you? Then we can get your things from Hart and return them to the cottage."

She closed her eyes. He waited for a rejection. Slowly she nodded. "Yes. You should greet all the tenants and they seem to accept you better when you're with me."

"They do," he admitted.

"Good night, Colin."

"Good night, Selina. I shall be ready by ten tomorrow." He opened the door and then headed for his study. God, he wanted a drink. He wanted more than that right now. He wanted to forget the look on her face when she told him she needed to leave.

Once in the study, he poured a large snifter of brandy and sat in the velvet chair by the empty fireplace. He looked up at the large portrait of Mary over the mantel and wondered what she would think of him at this moment. While she had been raised a proper lady, a perfect woman to become duchess, would she think this crazed idea of loving Selina was madness?

He knew in his heart that Mary would think it was insane. Her mother had taught her that only women of quality become duchesses. A simple countrywoman could never be accepted in Society. And how would Kate and his stepmother react?

Seeing Georgina at dinner, he knew she would be appalled by the idea. Kate had befriended Selina and most likely owed the wise woman her life. She would be far more accepting of Selina.

But the rest of Society would shun her.

Could he really do that to such a gentle woman?

She might hate him forever. She had already told him how she would dislike London, even though she had never been there. She needed the wide open spaces of the estate to keep her happy. And he had no choice but to go to town at times. He took his position in Parliament very seriously.

"What are you doing down here?"

Colin turned toward the door where his sister stood in the threshold wearing her dressing gown. "This is my study."

"Yes . . . but I thought you had, er, retired for the evening." She walked into the room.

"I couldn't sleep."

"Me either." She poured a glass of brandy and sat down across from him. "I thought I would pilfer some of your fine brandy."

He lifted his glass in salute. "Great minds and all that."

"Cheers." She sipped her brandy and then stared over at him. "So why couldn't you sleep?"

"No reason."

"Of course."

He heard the sarcasm in her voice. "Selina told me she was leaving."

"What do you mean?"

"She insisted on leaving here."

Kate sat upright. "You told her she couldn't, right?"

"How am I supposed to do that? She was only here because of . . ."

"My miscarriage. If I can say it, you should be able to at this point. But Selina can't leave."

He drained his glass and frowned. "Why not, if that is what she desires?"

"That is not what she desires," Kate muttered in an angry tone.

"What do you mean?" He rose and poured another glass for himself, wishing this day would end already. Kate held up her snifter for him to add more. Apparently, he wasn't the only one having a difficult day, or evening, as it were.

"She's just scared," Kate finally replied.

"Of what?"

His sister shook her head and waved her hand around the room. "This. You. Us. Society. All of it."

"You mean your mother."

"Of course not. Selina and Mother were getting along fine."

Colin sat back down. "Are you mad? Weren't you at dinner tonight?"

Kate smiled. "Ah, I understand now. Mother brought up those things for your benefit."

"What!"

"She mentioned the walking in the dark as a reminder to you that you were behaving improperly. She thought it might make you realize how you have treated Selina so you would do the right thing."

"The right thing?"

"Marry her."

"Georgina wants me to marry Selina? The woman is no one. The *ton* will eat her alive."

"Not with Mother and me by her side. We are both very influential and have many friends who do not want to get us angry."

This was the last conversation he'd expected to have with Kate tonight. It still made no sense that the duchess would accept Selina. "Why would your mother want me to marry her?"

Kate smiled and shook her head. "You really don't know?"

"Of course not, that is why I asked you!"

"The same reason she has pushed women at you every Season. She wants you to fall in love and find happiness." Kate sipped her brandy. "We can both see how you feel about Selina. The way your eyes follow her when she enters a room. The slight smile that you sometimes try to hide when she's near. And quite honestly, I believe you have been intimate with her. I don't want a niece or nephew born on the wrong side of the blanket."

"Did she tell you we had been lovers?"

"No. But Mother and I both noticed how you put her in your adjoining bedroom when there are many other rooms she could have slept in, including the one she'd been hiding in for more than a week before I found her."

Colin frowned again. "What room are you talking about? She hadn't been hiding in the house."

Kate laughed and then finished her brandy. "Right under your nose."

"How is that possible? I would have heard her, seen her." *Sensed her.* Then he remembered the apparition he'd thought he'd seen in the third-floor bedchamber. She had been the ghost. "Why?"

"Because you removed her from her cottage. The servants were not about to let that happen so they helped her by hiding her upstairs."

His own servants had gone behind his back. In hindsight, he knew they would have done anything to keep her here. Even risk their positions. They hadn't cared because they owed him no allegiance after how he'd treated them, the tenants, and the estate.

"So how will you stop her from leaving?" Kate asked quietly. "You can't let her return to Hart's lands."

He rested his head back against the chair. "I told her she could leave."

"But now you have to stop her. You love her!"

"True, but she might not love me."

"Of course she does." Kate banged her glass on the table. "Everyone can see how she looks at you. She's the one who insisted you greet the tenants. She wants them to love you too."

"Perhaps," he drawled. "But she may not be ready to admit her love to anyone, including me."

"And letting her leave will only make it harder for her to see what a wonderful person you are."

He smiled. "Thank you, Kate. I do realize I want her near. She refused to stay in the house. So I did the only thing I could think of."

"And that is?"

"I told her she could move back into the cottage."

Kate giggled. "Well done, brother. But she is still too far away. How will you court her if she's not here?"

"Oh, I don't plan on being far from her at all. In fact, since it is my cottage, I do believe I might move in with her."

Chapter 21

The next morning Selina awoke groggy and out of sorts. Drat that man for keeping her up most of the night. She had gotten what she'd wanted for the past month. She should be ecstatic that he'd given his permission for her to move back to her cottage.

So why wasn't she?

She dressed slowly and then sat on the bed. Because she knew in her heart that she would miss him terribly. In one short month, he had come to mean everything to her. Not only did he smile more, she did too. Returning to her cottage meant very little time alone with Colin.

And while her mind tried to convince her that it was for the best, her heart disagreed.

Unable to face him and his family yet, she rang for breakfast in her room. While she waited, she walked to the window and glanced at the vastness of his estate. She loved the view from this room. She could see the reflecting pond and the rolling hills. If she moved to the other window, she could see the horses being led out of the stables.

As much as she didn't belong here, she hated to leave this beautiful home.

She turned at the sound of a knock on the door. "Yes, come in."

Randall opened the door. "Mr. Baker asked you to see them as soon as you can. His father is not doing well. He thinks it might be his time."

"I'll get my bag," she said, even though she doubted there was anything she could do. At eighty-five, the elder Mr. Baker had lost most of his mind. He'd been bedridden for the past six months.

When Randall turned to leave, she remembered Colin was supposed to go with her today. "Is the duke awake yet?"

"Yes, he went for a ride this morning."

"Please let him know where I went. He wanted to greet more of the tenants with me today."

"Yes, miss."

She gathered her things and departed without breakfast. She passed a footman carrying her tray and picked up a piece of toast on her way down the stairs. "I'm sorry but I must leave," she said to him.

"I understand, miss."

She walked quickly to the Bakers' home and Miss Baker let her in.

"He's not well at all, Selina."

"I shall check on him. Where is your brother?"

"Edward is with him now."

Selina headed to the small bedroom on the main floor. Inside, the room was darkened and stunk of bodily waste. "Good morning, Mr. Baker."

She walked directly to the windows and opened the curtains. "Why is this room so dark?"

Mr. Baker rose from his seat near the bed and shrugged. "Ain't that what you're supposed to do?"

Selina wanted to shake the man. "No. Get this room cleaned up right now. All chamber pots emptied and I want fresh linens on this bed."

"Now, Miss White," Mr. Baker strolled closer. "The man's going to die so why does it matter 'bout the linens? It's just more for Bertha to wash."

The rancid smell of his breath almost made her vomit. There were very few tenants she truly disliked but this man was one. Being near him always made her skin crawl. "Do as I say, now, or I leave."

He took a step even closer. "Go ahead and leave. Bertha's the one who called for you, not me. He can die anytime. One less mouth to try and feed. Now you," he said as he reached for her unbound hair, "I wouldn't mind watching you eat . . . me that is."

A sliver of fear wove through her. Mr. Baker had never been this overt in his intentions. "Bertha, can you come here for a moment."

"Don't you come in here, Bertha," Mr. Baker shouted. "This is between her and me."

"Indeed," said a menacing voice from the threshold. "Somehow I think I might have a say in this."

Selina breathed again. "Your Grace, can you please escort Mr. Baker out of this room?"

She glanced over to see a gleam of anger in Colin's eyes.

"With pleasure, Miss White."

"Your Grace?" Mr. Baker said with a gulp.

"Mr. Baker, you and I need to have a little conversation outside." Colin strode toward him and grabbed his arm. He dragged him out of the room.

Once they left, Bertha entered the room. "I'm sorry, Selina."

"I know, Bertha. I've tended your bruises before." She went to the bed and examined Bertha's father. "He is severely dehydrated. When did he stop drinking water?"

"I don't know. Edward wouldn't let me tend to him. That's why I called for you."

The man was trying to kill his own father. "All right. Try

to get him to drink. And clean up this room. The windows should be open to get some fresh air in here. I'll come back tomorrow to check on him but he might not make it."

Bertha nodded. "I know."

Selina gathered her things and walked out to find Colin. Leaving the house, she saw Colin leaning against a tree with a very self-satisfied look upon his face. Mr. Baker ambled toward her, holding his stomach.

"I owe you an apology, Sel . . . Miss White."

"Apology accepted." She glanced over his shoulder to see Colin give a quick nod. "But you are not to tend to your father. From now on only Bertha will look after him."

"All right." He walked away from her with a quick look back at Colin.

"What an odious man," Colin said as they started walking to the next tenant's home.

"You have no idea."

They walked along in silence for a short while until Selina put a hand on his arm to stop him. She looked up into his blue eyes and never wanted to look away. "Thank you."

"It was not any great deed. Bertha was in the next room. I'm quite sure she would have assisted you."

Selina averted her eyes and shook her head. "No, she would not have. She is terrified of her brother. She has come to me several times with bruises and scrapes that I know he caused."

"Dammit," he yelled. He turned around and strode back in the direction they had come from. "I should have known about him. I'm the goddamn duke!"

"Colin, where are you going?"

"To get that man off my land."

Selina trotted to catch up with him. "Well then, wait for me."

He slowed down and smiled back at her. "You don't seem too angry that I'm forcing him to leave."

"Not at all. That man is dreadful. I honestly don't know what might have happened today if you hadn't shown up."

They arrived back at the cottage to hear pottery being smashed and shouting inside. Colin burst into the house and dragged Mr. Baker outside. "Get in and see to Miss Baker, she's hurt."

Selina raced inside to find Bertha cowering in the corner of the room. Shards of pottery were strewn on the floor around her and blood dripped down her face. "Oh, Bertha, I'm so sorry."

Slowly, Bertha rose to her feet. Her skinny arms trembled. "Not your fault, Selina."

"I should have told the duke sooner. I forget that he doesn't know as much about his tenants as I do." Gently, she wiped away the blood and examined the cuts on her face. "These should heal in no time. They aren't deep."

"Thank you, Selina. If you hadn't forced the duke to return, I don't know what might have happened."

She searched her bag for willow bark. "I didn't force him, Bertha. As soon as he heard what has been happening to you, he turned around and came back. His Grace will not tolerate that kind of behavior on his lands."

Bertha looked up at her with big brown eyes. "His Grace is forcing Edward to leave?"

"Yes."

"But where will I go?"

Selina put the small bag of herbs on the table. Without Mr. Baker's support, Bertha would have nowhere to live. "I don't know," she admitted. Unlike Mrs. Patterson, Bertha couldn't work at the manor house while trying to care for her father.

"You will stay right here," Colin said as he came back in. "Once your father is well . . ." He left the "or dead" unspoken. "I will find you a position."

"Thank you, Your Grace. But what's going to happen to Edward?"

"I told him I want him off my land immediately and to never set foot on it again."

Bertha nodded and a look of relief washed over her. "Thank you again, Your Grace."

"If he gives you any trouble, just let me know," Colin said. "Good morning, Miss Baker."

Once they left the house, Selina giggled. "You rather enjoyed that, didn't you?"

"Enjoyed what?"

"Taking that man to task."

"I will not stand having a man on my land who hurts women and children."

Selina nodded. "Or the elderly."

"Exactly." He lowered his head and kissed her softly. "I protect what's mine."

Her heart pounded in her chest. Was he implying that she was his?

"Come along, Selina. We have more tenants to visit."

After they had finished their visits, they made their way back to her cottage. Colin had told her that he'd had the servants pack up her things from Hart's property as well as the few she kept at the duke's home. By the time they had arrived, everything was back at the cottage.

Colin hadn't told her about the surprise. He'd made the footman remove the bed from the room she'd been sleeping in on the third floor and bring it here. It was time she discovered he knew her secret.

Selina walked inside and smiled broadly. "Thank you again, Colin. You have no idea how much this means to me."

She brought her bag into her bedroom and stopped at the doorway. "What is that doing in here?"

"Is there a problem, Selina?"

She turned around and glared at him. "Where is my bed?"

"Whatever do you mean? Isn't that the bed you've been sleeping in for the past few weeks?"

Her face paled in the waning light. "You knew about that?"

"I learned of it just last night."

She stared away from him as if attempting to process what she'd learned. "Who told you?"

"Does it matter?"

"Yes."

"Kate."

She squeezed her eyes tight. "Thank God," she said quietly.

"Why are you thanking God that my sister told me?" He folded his arms over his chest.

"The servants had nothing to do with it."

He laughed harshly. "They had everything to do with it." He slowly realized why she'd wanted it to be his sister who had told him. "You don't think I would blame the servants for what they did, do you?"

She blew out a long breath and shook her head. "At first when you came back, yes, I would have believed it of you. But not any longer." She turned to face him. "Something in you has changed. For the better, I might add."

"I have you to thank for that," he whispered. "I was so angry with everyone when I came here."

"And now?"

"Now, I wish I had returned sooner. I wish I had returned from this living hell I'd let myself drown in for years." He stared out the window and could see his home from here.

Warmth enveloped him as her arms wrapped around him. Her head rested on his back. "Grief is a horrible thing. I once watched as my mother tried to heal a young woman. She died several weeks later and the only cause my mother could think of was that she'd been so heartbroken over the loss of her betrothed that she had lost the will to live."

Hearing her talk about her mother made his muscles tense.

He hadn't thought about what she'd done to Mary and their son in a couple of weeks. He knew it wasn't Selina's fault. So he inhaled deeply and released the anger.

"Are you all right?" She gently rubbed his back muscles.

Remain in the moment, he told himself. Selina was important, not her lying mother. "Yes."

He twisted in her arms and brought her against his chest. Holding her like this always sent desire straight to his loins. "Do you like my gift?"

"It was very sweet but I cann—"

He cut her off with a hot kiss. "Yes, you can accept it."

"But I—"

Again, he kissed her in order to stop her from refusing the gift. But as her arms wrapped around his neck, he knew she would be happy to have that bed in a minute.

"What are you doing?" she asked breathlessly.

"Kissing you."

"Yes, but why do you keep cutting off my—"

Her arguments made no impression on him when she was kissing him back so sweetly. He wanted to move her to the bedroom now. As he took a step back, she lifted her head.

"Is this the reason for the bed?"

He pressed his lips against the pulse hammering her neck. "Your former bed was much too small for the both of us."

"True but I hadn't intended on sharing."

He moved to her ear and swept his tongue around her lobe. "Now that is dreadfully selfish, sweetheart." He felt her smile against his cheek.

"Well you know how terribly selfish I am."

He reached for the button on her dress. The last time was far too fast. Today, he wanted to linger. Shower her body with his mouth and watch her come several times. "Oh, I want you to be extremely selfish right now."

"So I suppose you want to test my new bed."

"As duke, I should definitely make sure my gift to you is

perfect." He walked her backward into her bedchamber until he felt the post of the bed.

"I have slept in this bed before," she said as he slipped her dress off her shoulders. "I remember it being quite comfortable."

"Noted." He quickly unlaced her stays and let them drop to the floor. Leaning in close, he whispered, "But have you slept in this bed with another man?"

She gave him a seductive smile that almost sent him over the edge. "I suppose I must make certain the bed will be comfortable with another person in it."

"Always a good idea," he said, then laid her back against the pillows.

Selina succumbed to the magic of his kisses. His tongue playfully caressed hers as his fingers reached for the buttons on the back of her dress. She tried not to laugh as he fought the restraints.

"Goddamn buttons," he exclaimed as he lifted his swollen lips off her own.

"Let me help you." She nudged him so he would get off her and then she rolled over onto her stomach. "Better?"

"Much."

Once the buttons were undone, he worked on her stays. She felt them loosen but he remained on top of her. When she attempted to roll back, he pinned her shoulders. Soft kisses landed on her shoulders and then his lips moved downward. She shivered as his tongue blazed a path across her back, following the line of her chemise.

He pushed the short sleeves of her dress off her shoulders and down her arms. Selina wiggled to free her arms of their confines. Next, her stays and chemise were removed in much the same manner.

"Wouldn't it be easier if I turned around?" she asked with a giggle.

"Perhaps," he said as he pushed her softly back down on the bed. He kissed her spine from the top all the way . . .

"What are you doing?"

"What do you want me to do?"

As his tongue touched the cleavage of her derrière, she had no idea what to say. "Anything you want," she whispered.

He groaned and laid his cheek against her bottom. Excitement and anticipation raced through her veins. He reached for her stockings and untied each garter before continuing to kiss his way across her backside. She trembled as his lips gently kissed her thighs and the back of her knee.

This was right where she wanted to be no matter how wrong it might be. She loved the feel of his hard muscles against her body and the intensity of his kisses. Maybe she was just a plaything to him. Or maybe she was his salvation from his despair. But right now, it didn't matter because he was making love to her. This was not a quick rutting for his satisfaction. He was showing her what this should truly be like with him . . . always.

His hands kneaded her bottom and each time his thumbs spread her open slightly, Selina trembled as her fold moistened in preparation for him. He grazed one hand down her crack until he reached her clit.

"Colin," she exclaimed as he rubbed her. She closed her eyes and let desire take her wherever it could. She moaned as his mouth replaced his finger. "Oh, God."

She writhed against the bed as his tongue played with her. One finger pressed into her softness, followed by another. She couldn't stop climbing higher as he slid his fingers in and out of her. Giving into the passion, she cried out his name as her release washed over her.

He slowed the movement of his hands while she recovered from the tumultuous sensations running through her. His staggered breath heated her bottom as she fought to control her own. Just as her heartbeat slowed, he rose and turned her over.

"Now for the front," he said with a devious smile.

"The front?" she squeaked.

His blue eyes sparked with desire for her. "Oh, yes. The front."

Her eyes widened as he quickly removed his clothes. He stretched out across her body and warmed her to her soul. She wanted this moment to go on forever even though she knew it could not. At some point sanity would return. But for now, she would savor the sensation of his lips traveling the length of her body and pretend that in another world they could find happiness together.

As his mouth found her taut nipple, she gasped from the sheer joy and agony his mouth gave her body. She trembled as need rose in her again. How was it possible that she would so quickly want him after that last climax? But want him she did, possibly even more than just a few moments ago. In this position, she could feel his hard length against her thigh and desperately wanted him deep inside her.

Instead, his mouth traveled lower again to kiss her sex.

"Colin," she moaned. "No more. I want you."

He smiled against her thigh and pressed a finger into her wetness. "I believe I noticed that."

"Now."

"No."

"Why?"

He laughed softly. "I'm not ready yet."

She groaned. "You felt ready."

"Soon." He nipped her leg with his teeth.

"Please," she begged as his finger worked its magic deep inside her.

"Perhaps."

"You're horrible," she whispered and then all words

stopped as another earth-shattering climax rolled through her body. "Not fair."

"Very fair."

"Now?" she whispered, still desperate with need for him.

He rose up above her and smiled down at her in such a manner that her heart started pounding in her chest. The look bordered on love. How was that possible?

"Now."

With one swift movement, he was deep inside her, filling her completely. Before she could fully recover from her last orgasm, she was quickly climbing toward another. Each fierce stroke brought her closer to the edge. His moans of pleasure urged her on. Unable to stop it, she arched her back and succumbed to the pleasure of his body.

He froze over her and groaned as his peak hit. Opening her eyes, she watched as pleasure overrode all other things. When he finally relaxed on top of her, she knew she was in too deep with Colin.

She loved him.

Chapter 22

Selina rested her head against Colin's bare chest and wondered how exactly she had ended up in bed with him again. The whole point of moving out was to get some distance from the distracting man. Instead, she'd just spent the most incredible hour in bed with him ever.

She closed her eyes and shivered. She'd had no idea a woman could climax that many times.

With his strong arms around her, she felt sated and safe. She suddenly couldn't remember why she wanted to get away from him. Then it came back—the reality that this was nothing but a fantasy. That he was a duke and she was . . . nobody.

"Selina? Are you here?"

Her eyes opened wide. What was Mia doing here today? She lifted her head and stared into twinkling sapphire blue eyes. Pressing her finger to his lips, she put her lips against his ear. "Do not say a word."

He nodded with a smile.

"Mia, stay out there. I'm just changing and then I'll be out. Start the fire for me so we can have tea." That would keep her busy and hopefully making enough noise so that she wouldn't hear them.

"All right."

Selina jumped out of bed and gathered her things. "Help me," she whispered.

Colin laughed softly. "Come here."

He helped her with her stays and buttons while she attempted to put her hair up. He slapped her bottom. "All set. Should I get dressed and come out?"

"Don't you dare!" She picked up his clothing and threw it at him. "Get dressed."

"How am I supposed to leave if you both are out there?"

"Climb out the window!"

"Someone might see me," he remarked. "And that would be scandalous, indeed."

He was trying to make her insane. He was getting perverse amusement out of this situation. "Just leave."

She walked out of the room and closed the door, praying he would leave them in peace. "Mia!"

Her dearest friend gave her a big hug. "I heard the news and had to come see you. Why did he change his mind?"

She shrugged nonchalantly. "The man is quite mad. I'm only hoping he doesn't change his mind again."

Mia looked her over critically with a frown. "Selina," she drawled.

"What is it?" Hopefully, no more questions about the man in her bedroom.

"How exactly did you change your clothing?"

"What do you mean?"

"You seldom wear that dress because it's one of the few you own that buttons up the back."

Panic raced through her. She hated lying and it was worse to lie to someone you loved. "I was changing my boots, not my gown. Kate's maid helped me dress today. My boots were muddied from visiting the tenants today."

"And it took you that long to put your other boots on?" she asked with suspicion. "What is really going on, Selina?"

"Nothing," she squeaked. God, she was a terrible liar. Her voice always rose an octave or two.

Mia glanced at the closed door. "Did you have a man in there with you?"

"What?"

"Did you finally decide to take that offer from the tutor in town? What was his name? Neil, Nathan . . ."

"Nigel Bateman, and no, he is not in my bedroom."

"Well, shall we find out who is?" Mia raced to the door and opened it wide.

Selina chased after her. "Mia, don't!"

Mia stared into the empty room. Finally, she recovered, "Where did that come from?" She pointed to the bed.

There was no way of making this sound good. "It was a gift."

"From?"

"The duke. For saving Kate's life," she added quickly. "I had commented on how comfortable the bed was and he thought I should have it."

Mia dragged her to the table. "Sit down."

"What is wrong?"

She grabbed the tea and water and poured. While it steeped, she just stared at Selina until Selina squirmed in her seat. Mia handed a cup to her and then sat down across from her. "Are you mad?"

"What are you talking about?" Selina asked and then blew on her tea.

"When did you start sleeping with the duke?"

"I am not . . ." Her shoulders sagged under the weight of another lie. "How did you know?"

"No man gives a woman a bed like that without a good reason. Saving his sister is not a good reason." Mia picked up her cup and then put it back down. "Selina, this is madness. You cannot be the duke's mistress."

She hadn't thought about it before now but taking that bed

made her his mistress, not just a lover. She covered her mouth and stared at her friend. "Oh Mia, I accepted the bed. That makes me a whore."

Mia patted her friend. "You are not a whore. Do you love him?"

She closed her eyes and nodded. "I shouldn't but I do."

"Oh, Selina."

"I know." Slowly over tea, she told Mia everything, from how she'd hated him in the beginning to how he had changed and she came to love him.

"What are you going to do?" Mia asked.

"Nothing," she admitted. "There is nothing I can do. While he is here, I will enjoy his company. When he leaves, he will take my heart with him."

"What are you doing here?"

Colin turned and greeted his sister as she entered the salon. "Where else would I be?"

"With Selina. You told me you were moving in with her."

"One step at a time, Kate." He poured another glass of sherry and handed it to her. "How do you think she would react if I told her I wasn't leaving her house on her first day back? She'd be furious with me."

Kate acknowledged his answer with a nod. "True."

"Plus there was a little issue of Miss Featherstone paying a visit this afternoon."

"Dreadfully inconsiderate of her."

"Exactly."

"Well, that at least explains why she didn't show up for—" She stopped abruptly.

"For what?"

Kate eased into a chair. "I might as well tell you. While Mother had brought the dance instructor in, we thought Selina should learn some of the dances too."

"Why is that?"

"Just in case you should decide to ask her to dance sometime."

Colin shook his head. There wasn't much chance of that happening out in the country.

"How did she like her gift?"

He chuckled. "You heard about that?"

"The entire household is talking about it. Quite scandalous, you know. And yet, most just felt you were being generous. I did tell people that it was for saving my life."

"And I thank you for that." He gave her a quick salute with his glass. "I heard a letter arrived for you today."

A dreamy look came over her. "It was from John. He is still grieving but wants to see me again. Mother and I thought we might go to Suffolk in a fortnight. John is there and I can see him. He wants us to set a date."

"Excellent. He is a good man, Kate."

"He is," she said. "And Selina is far too good a woman to let go because of Society. So you have a fortnight to get things settled because I'm not leaving until I know you are betrothed."

He frowned. "I cannot guarantee this will be settled by then."

"Why haven't you told her you love her?"

"I will."

Kate shook her head. "Tomorrow."

"As you wish, sister dear."

The next day Colin spent much like the prior days. He and Selina visited with tenants. He watched her tend to the people with so much love that it made him proud. She would make a wonderful wife and duchess. She might not be the conventional type Society preferred, but with a little help from his sister and stepmother, she would be accepted.

After another afternoon of making love to her, he decided he would talk to her about all of this tomorrow. They had no tenants to call on so he planned to have a picnic luncheon at a small pond on the outskirts of his estate.

But tonight, he had to escort Kate and the duchess to this damned ball. He knew what it meant for him. An evening fending off the mamas determined to throw their unmarried daughters at him. Marriage would be a blessing. Then he would only have to discourage the married women looking to become a duke's mistress.

He waited at the foot of the stairs for the ladies to join him. Finally, Kate floated down the stairs in a gold silk and lace creation that made her look like an angel. He knew that she was far more devil than angel. "You look lovely tonight, Kate."

"Thank you. And you look devilishly handsome. You had best have a care or the young ladies will fall prostrate at your feet begging to be your duchess."

He laughed. "I will listen to your wise words. Where is your mother?"

"She begged off. Something about a dreadful headache."

So he would be stuck watching his sister. He supposed it was a good excuse not to dance with the unmarried women. "Very well, then." He held out his arm for her. "Shall we be off?"

Selina finally turned and faced the mirror. After almost two hours of getting ready for this ball, her transformation was complete. She barely recognized the reflection staring back at her.

The duchess had insisted that her personal maid dress Selina's hair. And the effect was magical. Anna had piled Selina's blond hair into a simple chignon and then had artfully cut tendrils to frame her face. She had then clipped a few silver butterflies into the design to catch the silver threads in the gown.

"Oh, my," she whispered.

"You look beautiful, my dear. We must leave now."

"Where is Kate?"

"She went ahead with the duke."

Selina frowned slightly. "How will it look if her companion does not show up with her?"

"My dear, you will be arriving with the Duchess of Northrop. No one will care that you didn't arrive with Kate."

"Oh."

By the time they arrived, there were carriages lining the drive. Selina had never seen so many finely dressed people getting out of carriages. As they waited for their turn to disembark, the duchess gave her a few more lessons in propriety. "You do not speak to a man to whom you have not been properly introduced. Only then may you converse or dance should he ask."

Selina almost laughed. No one would ask to dance this evening. Even with her finery, she was still just a nobody to these people. "Yes, ma'am."

The duchess droned on about not dancing more than twice with any man and a few more dull topics. Selina listened but turned her attention to the beautiful women giggling as they walked into the house. She felt completely out of place here.

"Your Grace, perhaps I should return to the estate."

"Why would you think such a thing?"

She glanced down at the silvery gloves covering her hands and arms. "I don't belong here. With them."

"Nonsense, dear girl. What do they have that you do not?"

"A name, wealth, position, beauty."

The older woman laughed. "You have a name, quite a lovely name. You have position, perhaps not in Society but certainly at the estate. You have a wealth of love from the people on that estate. And you most definitely have beauty."

Selina continued to stare at her gloves. The duchess had only said those words to make her feel better. And it did help. Not that she felt confident, but the duchess had made her feel as if there was no reason she could not attend. "Thank you."

The duchess patted Selina's hand. "Don't ever let them see your fear. They will eat you alive."

The carriage rolled to a stop and a liveried footman opened the door and assisted them down. As soon as her foot touched the ground, Selina felt transformed, like Cinderella at the prince's ball. She had just better not lose her slipper tonight.

The sound of music filled the air and became gradually louder as they entered the house. The duchess linked her arm with Selina's.

"Courage," the duchess whispered.

Together they walked down the corridor. A nervous quiver washed over Selina the closer they came to the ballroom. At the entrance to the room, a butler stood to announce the names of the guests. The duchess leaned in and whispered something in the butler's ear.

The man announced them. "Her Grace, the Duchess of Northrop. Miss Selina White."

Several heads turned at the announcement. Selina knew they only looked over to see the duchess; still it made her heart pound. One set of sapphire eyes caught hers. She couldn't look away from Colin's startled gaze. A slow smile lifted his lips as he watched her.

"Come along, dear girl. There are several people you should meet."

Selina looked away from Colin's intent stare. Once they started to move across the room, she lost him in the crush. The duchess brought them to a crowd of slightly older women. They appeared to be mostly in their late forties.

The duchess introduced her to all the women. Several held titles that Selina couldn't keep track of with all the names.

"And how are you acquainted with Her Grace?"

Before she could answer, the duchess replied, "She is a dear friend of Kate's. I was running late so Selina decided to wait and arrive with me."

Several of the women looked at her critically but one or two gave her a quick smile. Selina had never felt so uncomfortable in her life. "Your Grace, I see Lady Katherine by the refreshment table. If you don't mind, I shall go speak with her."

"Of course you should be with your friend. But remember you are not acquainted with many people here so proper introductions must be made before any dancing."

Selina smiled at her. "Of course, Your Grace." She bowed slightly. "Lovely to meet you ladies."

With a sigh of relief, she walked toward the refreshment table where Kate stood talking with another young lady. When Kate saw her coming, she smiled.

"Selina, I'm so glad you decided to come." Kate hugged her. "You must meet a friend of mine. Lady Miranda Richmond, Miss Selina White."

Lady Miranda smiled. "So good to meet you. Kate has been chattering all evening about you."

Selina gave Kate a quizzical look. "Lovely to meet you, Lady Miranda."

The musicians finished a country dance. Both Kate and Lady Miranda glanced about the room. Men made their way to dance with the ladies. A tall, handsome man bowed in front of Lady Miranda and asked for the next dance. She quickly agreed. Another man came up to ask Kate the same thing.

Kate bit her lower lip and slid a glance at Selina. "Perhaps the next dance, Mr. Easton."

Selina leaned closer to Kate. "Go dance and have fun. I shall be fine here with a little lemonade."

"Are you certain?"

"Yes, go."

"Very well." Kate linked her arm with Mr. Easton's and walked toward the dance floor.

"That was very kind of you but now you are alone."

Selina smiled before she turned to the seductive voice behind her. "I could tell your sister wanted to dance. Soon she will be married so she should enjoy herself."

"Will you give me the pleasure of this dance?" he asked with his arm held out as if there was no chance she would reject him. And he was right.

"If you don't mind trampled toes, I would love to dance with you."

"I will take that chance. I'd heard you had a lesson."

"A few but I'm not sure how well that will do."

He smiled over at her. "Just follow my lead." He looked her over from head to toe. "You look beautiful tonight."

"Thank you."

"I do believe I am about to make every other man in the room envious."

Heat swept across her cheeks. "I highly doubt that."

He brought her into his arms. "No, I am definitely dancing with the most beautiful woman in the room."

Chapter 23

"Why are you here?" Colin asked as they danced. He could not believe he was dancing with Selina at a ball. And she danced as if she'd been doing it for years.

"Your sister and mother insisted I come along. They said I could tell people I was a companion for your sister while out in the country."

"I see." He had no doubt this was Kate's way of showing him that Selina could manage quite capably in Society. Not that there was much Society here. But he supposed it was a good way to start.

"I forgot to tell you that Bertha Baker paid a call on me and told me her father is much improved." Selina smiled up at him causing his heart to pound.

"And her worthless brother?"

"Has not been seen since the day you removed him from your land."

"Excellent. At least that's one problem solved."

She giggled. "Only one? How many more problems do you have?"

He was looking at the biggest one of all. "Only small issues with the estate and getting the tenants' houses back in order."

"As well as your own."

"Yes."

Before he knew it, the dance had ended. Unable to find Kate, he escorted Selina to his mother for safekeeping. He needed a drink and some air. After picking up a glass of brandy, he headed out on the terrace. The warm night air had made many couples escape the heated room for a chance to kiss in the moonlight.

Perhaps he should have brought Selina out here with him. Then he could have stolen a kiss from her.

"Well, what an interesting evening this has turned out to be."

Colin turned and smiled at his friends. "Hart, I can understand that you felt obligated to come to this party, but Middleton? What in the world brings you to a country ball?"

Both men laughed.

"It's the social event of the summer," Middleton quipped. "How could I possibly stay home?"

"True," Colin said with a smirk. "Not quite up to the standards of a Season ball."

"Hardly," Middleton commented. "Do you see any loose married women around?" He shook his head. "Disgusting. These married ladies all seem to love their husbands."

"And why exactly is Miss White here?" Hart asked.

"The duchess and my sister thought she should attend. After my sister was ill a few weeks ago, Sel—Miss White and Kate became fast friends."

"Selina, is it?" Middleton noted. "How interesting."

"Just a slip, Middleton. Nothing more."

"Of course." He glanced back into the ballroom and smiled. "I do see someone I know is not a happily wedded woman. Adieu, gentlemen." He sipped his brandy and walked away to find some entertainment for the evening.

Hart leaned against the terrace balustrade. "So why is Miss White here again?"

"I told you."

"So why did you dance with her?"

"My stepmother insisted." Colin wondered why his friend had decided to interrogate him.

"She is quite beautiful," Hart added. "Perhaps I shall ask her to dance tonight."

Colin's fists clenched around his glass of brandy. "That would not be a good idea, Hart."

"Oh?" Hart grinned at him. "I don't think you have to worry. I did notice the looks she gave you while you were dancing together."

"What looks?"

"The one a woman in love gives to her man."

"I do hope you're right, Hart."

"She is a good woman, Northrop. Far too good for a dullard like you."

"You're probably right about that."

"Now, I'm off to find a dance partner to fill the time."

Colin decided to stay out here longer. If he went back into the room, he would want to dance with her again. He glanced about until he found a bench that faced the ballroom. He looked up to see Mr. Bainbridge escort Selina to the floor. Colin's fingers tightened around his glass as jealousy raced within him. He couldn't ever remember feeling this way when Mary had danced with other men. Why would he with Selina?

He loved her.

He had loved Mary too.

But with Selina, the feelings were different. Stronger. Deeper. With Mary, he had never felt the overpowering lust he felt with Selina. He had loved Mary in a much calmer manner. It was odd actually.

They were very different people and yet he loved them both.

Staring into the ballroom, he knew what he had to do

tonight. The idea of watching any other men dance with her while she was not legally his was driving him mad.

He would tell her he loved her.

And he would propose.

Watching her dance, he realized just the way to ask her. Every woman in the *ton* knew that three dances in one night was as good as a proposal. But he doubted Selina knew that little fact. Not that he was trying to embarrass her. By dancing with her three times, everyone in that room would understand what she meant to him. And no one wanted to upset a duke.

There was no time like the present to set this plan in motion.

Selina stood by the duchess as Mr. Bainbridge bowed over her hand. The dance had been enjoyable but the company less so. The man did nothing but speak of his hounds. Of course, when a man had ten dogs, what else was there to talk about with a woman?

"I would love to call on you tomorrow," he said as he let go of her hand.

Selina slid a glance to the duchess, begging for assistance.

"I'm terribly sorry, Bainbridge," the duchess replied, "but we will not be at home tomorrow. We have several calls to make and then shopping to do."

"Of course, I shall stop by another day, then." After a quick nod, he walked away.

"And was it dreadful?" the duchess asked with a smirk.

"Nothing but dogs."

"I had heard he does love those hounds." The duchess gave a little shiver. "Dreadful things." She leaned in closer. "Some say they ate his late wife."

Selina giggled. "That is a terrible rumor to spread."

"I didn't start the rumor."

Selina looked around as another dance started. She had already decided to sit this one out. It was far too warm in this room. She wondered how the gentle-bred ladies of the *ton* managed without breaking into a sweat or worse, fainting.

"Are you enjoying yourself?" a deep voice asked from behind her.

She glanced back to see Colin holding two glasses of lemonade. "I am."

He handed one to her and one to his stepmother. "Would you care to dance again?"

"Thank you but I need a moment to rest."

"Of course," he said with a quick nod.

"Northrop," the duchess said, "Thank you for dancing the first dance with Miss White. It was very kind of you to make certain she didn't feel left out."

"It was my pleasure, Your Grace."

Several of the women surrounding the duchess started whispering to each other. Selina wondered what they could be saying so quickly.

"Would you care for a turn about the room?" Colin asked.

"I would enjoy that if it is all right with the duchess."

The older woman nodded her consent. "Just stay in the confines of this room so I can see you."

Colin's lips twitched. "Of course. And where is Kate?"

The duchess's eyes grew large. "She . . . she was here just a moment ago."

"That was a terrible thing to do to her," Selina said as they walked away.

"Hardly. It was nothing but a gentle reminder that her own daughter should be watched with just as much concern as you."

As they walked, Colin would stop and introduce her to people he knew. She would never remember all their names. Not that she had to worry about that. This would be her first and last ball.

"I do believe another dance is set to begin," Colin said with a smile. "If I don't take you on the dance floor now, another gentleman will whisk you away from me."

"Very well, we must dance then." Selina smiled from the sheer enjoyment of the evening. If she had been home tonight, she would have read and then gone to bed, unless she had a tenant to look in on. This was far more pleasant.

As the musician started, she had a dreadful thought. She tugged on Colin's sleeve to stop him.

"Is there a problem?" he asked.

"I don't believe I know the steps to this dance." Heat flooded her cheeks. "Perhaps you should find another partner."

He tilted his head closer to hers. "There is no other woman I want to dance with tonight."

She blinked quickly. "Thank you."

"I mean it." He tugged her. "Come along. It's not much different than the other country dances."

Reluctantly, she agreed and let him lead her to the dance floor. Not really knowing the steps, she had no chance to speak with him as he told her the steps just before she had to do them. By the time the dance was finished, she was exhausted.

He led her away chuckling softly. "You didn't seem to enjoy that as much as the first dance."

"No," she admitted. "It was far too complicated."

As he led her back to his stepmother, she noticed several gentlemen milling about the older woman.

"Damn," Colin muttered under his breath.

"What's wrong?"

"By dancing with you, I have shown that you are a very eligible young lady. Now they will pester you for dances all evening."

"Is that bad?" Wasn't dancing the whole idea for having a ball?

"No," he said but anger laced his voice.

She glanced over at him and wondered if he could possibly be jealous of the attention. The thought made her feel warm and wonderful all at once. "Would you take me outside for a breath of air?"

"Why, Miss White, that might be considered quite scandalous."

"True, but if I return to your stepmother, I will be forced to dance with those men."

He held out his arm. "Follow me."

She smothered a giggle. Seeing the dark look on his face, she had no doubt that he was jealous. And that made her quite happy.

"There are enough people on the terrace that your reputation will be safe," he said.

This time she did giggle. "My reputation? I didn't know I even had one."

He gave a quelling look. "All women have a reputation. It's best to keep it as sterling as possible."

"Yes, Your Grace."

The slight breeze felt wonderful on her face. She took a seat on a bench overlooking the gardens. She had such an urge to take off her slippers and run in the dewy grass. That would not help her reputation.

"Don't even think about it," he warned.

"What are you talking about?"

"Walking in the grass barefoot."

She looked up at him with her mouth gaping. "How did you know I was thinking about that?"

He reached out and skimmed the back of his hand down her jaw. "I do believe I know quite a bit about you, Miss White."

"As do I you."

"Yes, you do."

Far too quickly, they returned to the ballroom and the

duchess insisted she dance with several other young men. Even as she danced with them, she wanted to be back in Colin's arms. Jealousy streaked through her when she noticed him take a lady out on the dance floor. Was that how he'd felt when she danced with other men?

She didn't like the sensation at all. But she knew she couldn't dance with him any more tonight. The duchess had warned her against accepting more than two dances with the same gentleman. Even two dances might be encouraging a suitor.

And yet, she had danced twice with Colin.

After her last dance, she returned to the refreshment table and picked up a glass of wine. Kate made her way through the crush toward her. She plucked a glass of rapidly warming lemonade and sipped it slowly.

"This is awful," Kate said, placing the glass back on the table.

"The wine is much better."

"Mother has told me never to drink spirits at a ball. She's afraid I will cause a scandal."

"I am far more likely to cause a scandal than you," Selina replied with a laugh. "You at least understand all the inane rules of Society."

Kate dismissed her comment with a wave of her hand. "You will have no problem learning them too."

Selina slowly turned toward her friend. "Why would I need to? While this has been wonderful, this is my first and last ball."

"The gentlemen in the room can't take their eyes off you. They will be paying calls on you as soon as they can. The house will be loaded with flowers and gifts for you."

She clutched Kate's arm. "I do not want any of that. Is that why you brought me here? To gain a fashionable husband?"

"Of course not," Kate said with a laugh.

"Then why?"

"To make my brother jealous."

"What are you talking about?"

Kate shook her head and then sipped her lemonade again. "It is apparent to everyone that he is in love with you. Mother and I thought he should see that you are his equal. No one in the room has dismissed you or given you the cut direct."

Selina's world was tilting. Did Colin love her? It was far too mad an idea to consider.

Before she could think about it further, she caught sight of him walking toward them. "May I have this dance?"

He was asking her a third time? The man had definitely lost his mind. "It's not appropriate to dance with you again, Your Grace."

"Of course it is," he said with a pointed look at his sister. "Kate, didn't you tell her that the two dance rule was only for acquaintances? For family and dear friends, that rule is invalid."

Kate's eyes widened as she considered his words. "That is true. I suppose Mother forgot to tell you that."

"Yes, she did forget to tell me." She stared at Kate. "Are you certain it won't cause talk?"

"Of course not," Kate replied.

The strains of a waltz started. "A waltz! It is my favorite dance." Selina clutched Colin's arm. "Come along."

Once they reached the dance floor, the room started to buzz with excitement. Selina glanced around and noticed everyone talking. "What is going on?"

"I believe they think there will be a betrothal announcement tonight."

"Oh, how wonderful," she said as they twirled about. "I wonder who it might be."

He gave her a wicked smile. "Yours."

"My what?" Selina sputtered. How could they believe such a thing?

"Your engagement."

She had shown no special interest to anyone . . . except Colin. "You lied to me, didn't you?"

"Oh? About what?"

"This dance!"

"Shh, you're causing a scene." His lips twitched as if he found this matter quite humorous.

Humor was the last thing she thought of in regard to this mess. "Why?"

"Isn't it obvious? My stepmother and sister seemed to think we should marry. Hart believes something in me has changed. And the only person responsible for my abrupt change is you."

The room was spinning faster than they were. She closed her eyes to find some sense of normalcy. But he had changed her life just by taking a third turn on the dance floor. "I think I feel sick," she mumbled.

"Stay with me, Selina. The dance will be over soon and we can discuss this in private."

They danced closer to the terrace where a slight breeze moved the curtains.

"Bloody hell." Colin turned them so quickly she almost lost her footing.

"What—" The rest of her sentence was cut off by the sound of a pistol firing.

Then Colin went limp in her arms. "Oh my God!" she screamed as they fell to the floor. As her head hit the floor, her world went dark.

Chapter 24

Selina awoke in a strange bedchamber. The haze of the evening slowly washed away and she remembered what happened. She sat up quickly and then inhaled deeply as a wave of dizziness overwhelmed her.

"She's awake."

She blinked and focused on the sound of Kate's voice. "Where am I?"

Kate walked over to her and clutched her hand. "You're in one of the guest rooms of Mrs. Littleton's house."

"Where's Colin?"

"Mrs. and Miss Featherstone are here looking after him."

"Where is Mia? I must speak with her now." Selina closed her eyes, praying the dizziness would soon pass.

"I shall get her for you."

Kate walked away while Selina continued to breathe in deeply to calm her nerves. She had to find out what had happened to Colin. She could hardly remember anything except hearing a loud sound and then falling to the ground.

"So you decided to wake up, did you?" Mia walked into the room with a smile. "I would wager you don't remember much at all."

"No," Selina said, suddenly wondering why her shoulder hurt. Did she land on it after they fell?

"Do you remember being shot?"

"What are you talking about?" She had not been shot. That is something a person would remember.

"Yes you were, but you were only grazed. His Grace probably saved your life by turning you away from the gunman."

"Where is Colin?"

"The duke is well. He is still sleeping off the effects of the laudanum Mother gave him."

"Why did she give him laudanum?" God, she wished this awful taste in her mouth would go away and her head would clear. She felt as if a piece of her mind was gone.

"For the same reason I gave you some," Mia said with a smile. "Just not as much. Your wound needed just three stitches."

"Stitches?" she mumbled. "You sewed me?"

"Of course, Mother was busy with His Grace."

"What happened to him?" Mia had said Colin had turned her away. He'd protected her from the shooting. So how could he have been hurt? It must have been the fall. Probably his bad ankle again. "How is Colin?"

"Selina, sit back and let me tell you what happened while you were sleeping."

Selina resisted the urge to get up and see Colin. She doubted she could even stand much less walk to wherever he was at the moment. She knew he was in good hands with Mia's mother watching him.

"Lady Katherine told me she saw the entire thing. A man was standing at the terrace doorway. As you and the duke danced closer, the man raised his pistol and shot at the duke. She said His Grace must have noticed the man because he turned you quickly so you wouldn't be hurt."

Selina put a hand to her head. "Wait, how did I get shot if he turned me?"

"The bullet went clean through him and then grazed your shoulder."

"He was shot!" She rose to her feet only to start to falter.

Mia grabbed her arm and forced her to sit back down. "Yes, His Grace was shot but he is all right. The bullet went straight through."

"He saved my life," she said softly. Colin had put himself in harm's way to save her. Her heart swelled with love for him. "Can I see him now?"

Mia looked up and waited for her mother to nod before she spoke. "Yes, but I believe he is still unconscious."

"I don't care. I have to be there when he wakes."

"Of course you do." Mia helped Selina to her feet.

Another wave of dizziness swept over her. "Don't ever give me laudanum again."

Mia laughed. "I shall do my best not to. Just don't get shot again. You scared me to death."

As they walked toward the bed, Selina asked, "How did you get here?"

"Lord Hartsfield sent for us. He wanted no one to attend to his dearest friend but us."

Selina smiled and wondered if Mia would ever realize that Hart was in love with her. She approached the bed and blinked away tears. He looked so pale.

"Sit down, dear girl," the duchess commanded.

Kate rose from the chair closest to Colin so Selina could sit next to him. She sat and then clutched Colin's warm hand in hers.

"How is he, Mrs. Featherstone?"

Mrs. Featherstone put her hand on Selina's good shoulder. "The shot went straight through. I think I got all the clothing fibers out of the wound but you can never be certain. You know what happens next."

Wait and see if a fever sets in. Selina always hated that

part. It could take days for a fever and then there was no guarantee that he would recover. "And me?"

"You shall be fine. When the bullet grazed you, it was where your shoulder was bare. Mia cleaned it out but she didn't see any fibers in there."

"Thank you both for coming tonight."

Mrs. Featherstone squeezed Selina's shoulder. "Of course we could come for you and the duke. Just as you would if we needed you. It's part of being a wise woman."

Selina stared at Colin's pale face. She had never imagined she could love someone as much as she did him. It was all her fault that he'd been shot. He'd been trying to protect her.

She wondered how upset he'd be when he discovered a wise woman tended his wounds instead of a surgeon. Perhaps he had learned that a male physician wasn't always needed.

"Selina," Mrs. Featherstone said. "I will leave you everything you need for the evening. If you aren't up to the task of watching him, Mia can stay with you."

"Thank you, Mrs. Featherstone. I shall be fine once the laudanum wears off." She smiled at Mia. "And don't ever let your daughter give me that dreadful stuff again."

"Would you rather have felt me sew you up like a dress?" Mia asked with a laugh.

"No, I suppose not. Thank you both again."

"We shall return tomorrow to see both our patients. Give him more laudanum when he awakes. It will ease his pain." Mrs. Featherstone put a vial of laudanum and another of willow bark on the table by his bed. "Send for me if he starts a fever."

"Of course."

The room settled down in a silent watch. The duchess and Kate let Selina stay closest to Colin's bed as they took chairs by the window. The only sound in the room was the ticking of a clock on the fireplace mantel.

Selina continued to stare at Colin's face. As the night wore on, the stubble on his face grew darker. She liked the look on him. He groaned once or twice but otherwise slept peacefully.

"Selina," Kate whispered. "I am going to get Mother to bed. We are in the room one down on the left. I shall return after she is asleep."

"You don't need to return. I will let you know if he awakens."

"I can't let you sit here alone with an unmarried man. It would damage your reputation," Kate explained logically.

The duchess stood up slowly and yawned. "They are as good as engaged and you know it, Kate. He danced three times with her."

Kate shot her mother an angry glance. "It still isn't right."

"As soon as he wakes, they will be properly betrothed," the duchess insisted.

"Come along, Mother." Kate shook her head as she led her mother out of the room.

Engaged.

Selina returned her gaze to the man she loved. Until tonight, she had never thought it possible that he might love her. Or that she might fit into his world. But tonight had been magical.

Several men had asked her to dance and wanted to court her. Of course, they might not have if they knew her true background. But it didn't matter. The duchess had told her that just being seen with her and Colin gave her the appearance of respectability.

Marriage to him would force her to go to London and into Society. Surely, someone would discover her background. Rumors were certain to follow. Colin would tell her that what people said didn't matter. But it might reflect poorly on Kate and the duchess. Selina would hate to ruin Kate's life.

Besides, none of it mattered.

Once he discovered the truth, he would hate her forever.

* * *

Colin blinked his eyes open. He had no idea where he was, except he was certain the dimly lit room was not his. His shoulder hurt like blazes. He turned his head slightly and smiled. Selina sat in the wingback chair next to the bed with her head tilted against the corner. Her eyes were shut and her breathing even.

What had happened?

He racked his brain for a clue. The last thing he remembered was dancing a waltz with Selina as she realized what a third dance with him meant. Her face had been flushed and her eyes bright with dismay.

Then something happened.

But what?

Colin moved his head in the other direction and noticed that Kate had fallen asleep on a small sofa. He closed his eyes and tried to think about what happened. Everything was blank after dancing with Selina.

He attempted to turn on his side and pain radiated from his shoulder. He couldn't suppress a groan. Damn, he didn't want to wake her. He felt his right shoulder and touched a linen bandage.

What the bloody hell had happened?

He needed answers but wasn't willing to wake either woman yet. Instead, he lay back against the pillows and shut his eyes. Perhaps if he rested, the pieces of the puzzle would fall into place.

Except his eyes wouldn't remain closed. He stared at Selina and then noticed that she, too, had a bandage on her shoulder. Frustration surged in him. He'd never felt so helpless in his life.

He couldn't take this any longer. "Selina," he whispered.

Her full lips lifted into a slight smile but her eyes didn't open.

"Selina," he said slightly louder but hopefully not loud enough to wake Kate.

She groaned slightly and rubbed her eyes. Finally, she opened her eyes. "You're awake!"

"Yes, what the bloody hell happened to us? And where are we? Why is my sister sleeping on the sofa? Where is the duchess?"

"Slow down," she said with a hushed laugh. "How did you wake with so many questions? When I woke, I was completely fuzzy-brained."

"When you woke?" he asked, confused by her statement. "Didn't you just now awaken?"

"No, earlier when you were still sleeping. After the laudanum wore off. Dreadful stuff. I only use it because it works so well."

"Darling, you are rambling and my patience is wearing thin. What the hell happened?"

"You don't remember anything?" She leaned forward and touched his forehead.

"The last thing I remember is dancing with you. After that it's all a blank."

"You were shot while we were dancing." She slowly explained what occurred.

"Why would someone shoot me?" Even as he spoke, he thought of how he'd treated the servants and tenants on the estate. Any one of them might have been angry enough to shoot at him.

Selina stared down at their joined hands. The look on her face told him there was much more to this story.

"What is wrong, Selina?"

"I don't think they were aiming at you."

"What are you talking about? Whom else would they have been aiming for?"

"Me," she whispered so quietly he almost didn't hear her.

"You?" Was she mad? "Why would anyone try to shoot you? Everyone on the estate loves you." Then he remembered Mr. Baker. He might blame her for being banned from the estate. God, why didn't he realize what could happen before he'd told the man to leave.

"Not everyone loves me."

"Did you see the man who shot me?"

She nodded slowly. "At first when I woke, I didn't remember seeing him. But just now when I was napping it all came back to me. I saw the man. It just didn't register in my mind as it happened."

"I'm going to kill Baker."

"Baker?"

"Bertha's brother. The man I banned from the estate after he was rude to you and hurt Miss Baker." He squeezed her hand. "I'm so sorry, darling. I didn't think that the man might blame you."

She frowned and shook her head. "It wasn't Mr. Baker, Colin."

Colin searched his brain for one other person who might hold some resentment toward her. Maybe someone had found out about them and thought it wrong. "Who was it, Selina?"

"Before I tell you, I need you to promise me something," she said softly.

"What do you want me to promise?"

"That you will do nothing to hurt this man or his family. The man is still hurting and I am positive he wasn't in his right mind last night."

How the hell could he promise her that? Right now, he wanted to throttle the man who did this to them both. "Very well, I promise. Now tell me who tried to hurt you."

"I tried to see her again a few days ago. I just had to make sure she was feeling better. I was hoping she would tell me that she and her husband would try to have children again soon." Selina blinked back tears.

"What happened?"

"He was there again. He told me to leave his property and never attempt to see her again." Selina sniffled. "I just wanted to help her."

Colin closed his eyes in thought. "It was Mr. Wells, wasn't it?"

"Yes," Selina wiped away a tear.

He clenched his fists and bit his tongue to keep from forbidding her from her healing. He knew that she would never give up her passion. But it took every bit of willpower he had to not speak up. He only wanted to protect her.

"Colin, I know he might have killed you."

"Killed me! He might have killed you."

"He is not himself. They haven't given each other time to heal from the death of their child. You should understand that more than any man."

He gritted his teeth. "I do understand that better than anyone. And as much as I wanted your mother dead, I never attempted to kill her."

Selina's face went pallid. Her green eyes gleamed with tears.

"Oh, hell, I'm sorry," he whispered as guilt rushed through him for hurting her. God, he was an imbecile.

"I have to leave now." She rushed out of the room before he could even attempt to sit up.

"Dammit, Selina. Come back."

Chapter 25

Colin struggled against the nausea as he stood. Damn those women for stripping him down to his undergarments. Now he had to find his clothing. The room was too dimly lit to see much of anything away from the candle on the nightstand. He lifted the candle and searched for his trousers.

"What the devil are you doing out of bed?" Kate said sharply as she sat up. "You should be lying down and resting."

"I need to find Selina."

"She was in the chair watching you. She probably just needed to relieve herself." Slowly Kate rose and stretched.

"She was here talking to me. I said something completely inane and hurt her feelings."

"Oh damn you stupid men. You always speak without thinking." She walked over to him.

Colin grabbed the chair as a wave of dizziness swept over him. Kate clasped his arm and led him back to the bed. "I need to find her, Kate."

"It's four thirty in the morning. How far could she have gone?"

He inhaled deeply, realizing his sister was right. He doubted Selina would even know the way home from here. She rarely left the estate.

"You're right," he admitted sheepishly. "Besides, she wouldn't have left her patient. Did you watch as she stitched me up?"

Kate frowned. "She didn't care for you. That was Mrs. Featherstone's work. Hart rode back to his home and picked them up. He didn't want anyone else to care for you."

Selina didn't tend him. "I don't understand. Was Selina too upset by the shooting?"

Kate sat in the chair next to him. "Didn't she tell you?"

"Tell me what?"

"The bullet went through you completely and grazed her shoulder. Miss Featherstone cared for Selina while Mrs. Featherstone tended you."

She'd been shot. He closed his eyes and remembered the small bandage on her shoulder. And he had let her walk out of the room. "I have to find her."

He attempted to sit up only to have his sister force him back down. Damn he was weak.

"You will go nowhere. She most likely went to our room. I will go find her and bring her back."

"Thank you, Kate."

She smiled down at him in a teasing way. "Just don't get shot again. You about killed me."

"As you wish. Now go find my betrothed."

Kate searched her room and a few of the empty rooms on the floor but Selina was nowhere to be found. She couldn't have left the house. Kate walked down the steps and searched in the salon, library, and study. Finally, she heard movement toward the back of the house and was certain she'd found her missing friend.

Entering the kitchen, she said, "Excuse me, have you seen Miss White?"

An older woman with a large apron walked toward her. "Out of my kitchen, my lady. This is no place for you."

"Yes, but have you seen Miss White?" Kate quickly described her.

"All the fancy ladies are abed, which is where you should be, my lady. Now off with you."

Kate stomped her foot but then turned on her heels and continued her search. After two hours, the sun had come up and there was no sign of Selina. Feeling completely inadequate, she returned to her brother's room. He was going to be so angry.

As soon as she opened the door, he sat up in bed. "Did you find her?"

Kate closed the door and leaned against it. "I searched everywhere for her, Colin. No one has seen her."

"Why would she have left?"

"I can't imagine. She hadn't left your side from the moment she awoke from the laudanum."

He understood why she would have been upset with him. After all, he'd said he wanted to kill her mother. But that was in the past. "I want my carriage readied. She went back to her cottage."

Where she feels safe. He should have known if she was upset that would be the first place she'd go. Nothing, not even a gunshot wound, would stop him from finding her and apologizing. He had to make her understand that while he had loved Mary, he was over her now. Mary would have been furious with him for grieving this long.

And she would have liked Selina.

"Colin, you are not ready to leave yet."

"Either you help me or get out of my way. But I will find her today."

"Your Grace, you are going nowhere."

Colin looked toward the door where Mrs. Featherstone stood in the threshold with Miss Featherstone behind her. "Good morning, Mrs. Featherstone. While I appreciate you tending to me last night, I am perfectly well."

She walked into the room and pursed her lips. "Indeed. Since I am quite certain you have no book or practical knowledge in healing, I will be the judge of your health. Now sit down."

Something about the tone of her voice made Colin falter. She reminded him of his own late mother.

"Where is Selina?" Mia asked in bewilderment. "While her wound was superficial, she still shouldn't be doing too much today."

"That is why I am leaving. I need to find her." Colin reached for his shirt and suppressed a groan. Just that little movement had sent shooting pain from his shoulder down his back.

"Your Grace, I will ask you once more to sit down," Mrs. Featherstone demanded. "Mia, go find Selina and make sure she is all right. Once you find her, send word to His Grace. In the meantime, I will keep the duke in bed where he belongs." She gave him a hard stare until he sat down.

He only obeyed her command because he knew her advice was sound. He really was in no condition to go riding across the countryside trying to find Selina. But he needed someone to go after Mr. Wells. "Miss Featherstone, while you are looking for Miss White, can you ride to Lord Hartsfield's home and tell him I must speak with him immediately?"

She tilted her head and smiled at him. "That shouldn't be a problem." She opened the door and motioned to someone in the hall. "His Grace needs to speak with you."

"Thank you," Hart said as he walked past her. "I didn't think a little thing like a pistol wound would keep you down."

Colin knew his friend only teased to rile him. "I'd like to see you try it sometime. Then you'll have this bossy termagant commanding your every move."

"Now, now, Your Grace," Mrs. Featherstone said with a smile. "You just do as I say and I won't be so harsh."

"Yes, ma'am."

Hart sank into a chair by the window. "So how bad is it?"

"The wound? I will survive—"

"I meant the reason you need to see me at eight in the morning." Hart crossed his arms over his chest. "You know who shot you, don't you?"

"Yes, but they were aiming at Miss White, not me."

Mrs. Featherstone gasped as she lifted the linen off the wound.

"Am I all right?" Colin asked, suddenly concerned.

"I apologize, Your Grace. I heard what you said just as I lifted the bandage. Why would anyone try to hurt Selina? The tenants love her."

Colin told them both about Mrs. Wells. "Selina said she did notice him just before he shot us."

"You have to find her, my lord," Mrs. Featherstone said to Hart.

"No," Hart said, staring at Colin. "I have to find Mr. Wells."

Colin nodded. "Exactly."

Selina finally reached her cottage and wiped away the vestiges of her tears. Her feet ached from walking in her dancing slippers. She wanted nothing more than to soak in a tub of hot water for an hour. But she couldn't.

She could not remain here. As much as her heart ached, she had to leave him . . . and the tenants and the servants. The long walk had cleared her mind. He would never understand what happened that night. Nor would he ever forgive her either.

There was only one option left to her.

Unable to reach the buttons on her silk gown, she grabbed a knife and sliced it down the front. She would not cry over a ruined gown. Even if it was the most beautiful thing she had ever worn.

She divested herself of her stays in the same manner. Who

creates clothing that requires another person to help its wearer in and out? It was insane.

Once she returned to her worn cotton dress, she pulled out her valise and packed only a few dresses and the things most important to her. She would ask Mia to bring her other items once she was settled.

She closed the door behind her and as much as she didn't want to, she headed on the long walk to Tia's house. Her friend wanted to chase Middleton's younger brother to London. Now was her chance. Selina doubted Middleton would concern himself with the wise women on his estate. He usually spent more time in London than out in the country, anyway.

As she walked away, she refused to turn back and look at the estate she loved so much.

"Where else could she be?" Kate asked as they slowly returned to the Littletons' home.

Mia was never one to cry but she blinked back the tears as she jumped off the horse. They had searched everywhere. "I honestly don't know. I can only hope Lord Hartsfield found her."

"Or at least found Mr. Wells," Kate added.

"That is still no guarantee that she is safe." Fear gripped her. Mia had to be missing something.

"We have to tell Colin," Kate said.

"I know."

Mia followed Kate up the steps of the grand house. Where could Selina have gone? While she'd never been to London, Selina had told her she had no desire to go there.

Kate opened the door to the duke's bedchamber only to find him pacing the room. "Why are you out of bed?"

"Did you find her?" he demanded as he halted his stride.

Kate shook her head. "We searched everywhere we could think of, Colin."

Mia cleared her throat. "If I may, Your Grace?"

"There is no need for formalities. Say what is on your mind."

"We searched her cottage and interviewed the tenants and servants. No one has seen her, but I did notice the remains of the gown she had been wearing and some of her things were gone. We then rode to my mother's home and checked there. It didn't appear that she had been there."

"Then where the bloody hell is she?"

Mia excused the coarse language when she noticed the pained look in his eyes. This was not just about one of his tenants missing. He loved her. She pressed her lips together to keep from crying. "I don't know, Your Grace. We then went to my sister's house and she hadn't seen her either."

"Would she lie to protect her?"

Mia bit down on her lip. "I don't believe she would, Your Grace. I told her that you were terribly worried about Selina's safety."

"Thank you both."

"Colin," Kate implored, "you really shouldn't be out of bed."

"I am fine. Mrs. Featherstone told me I could get up but to be careful not to pull my stitches."

Kate gave Mia a beseeching glance. "Your Grace, even though my mother told you getting up was all right, you must have a care. You did lose a lot of blood last night. It can take a few days to fully recover from that alone."

"I realize that, Miss Featherstone." He must have heard how harsh he sounded. "I apologize."

"I understand, Your Grace. You are worried."

Her mother walked back into the room with a tray of soup. "Back in bed, Your Grace. I have a light supper for you. And do not think about telling me you can't eat. You will eat or I will spoon it down your throat myself."

Mia almost laughed aloud at her mother's attitude and the duke's reaction.

"Very well," he conceded. "But I will not lie down. I will sit at the table."

"As you wish," her mother replied.

Kate glanced about the room. "Where is my mother?"

"She is resting." Mrs. Featherstone placed the tray on the table. "She feels terribly guilty about what happened so I gave her a little something to help her sleep."

"Why would she feel guilty?" Mia asked. It wasn't as if she had paid Mr. Wells to shoot at them.

"Selina didn't want to attend the ball. My mother and I insisted. I . . ." Kate's gaze remained on the rug. "I coerced her into coming."

"And how did you do that?" he asked.

"I might have told her that I would tell you about where she'd been living after she left her cottage."

Heavy footsteps approached the room. The door hurled open and Hart pushed a man and a woman into the room. It was one of the first times Mia had ever seen him so forceful. Her heart increased its beat against her chest.

"Mr. and Mrs. Wells, Your Grace," Hart said with a bow.

"Your Grace," Mrs. Wells started, "I had no idea what my man was about last night. I never would have tried to hurt you."

Mia shrank back into the corner as the duke rose slowly from his seat. "Hurt me? Do you think I give a damn about myself? You and your husband attempted to kill Miss White. And for that I will see you both hang."

Mrs. Wells fainted into a lump on the floor. Mia knew she should do something but was unable to move. Sudden fear of the two men overwhelmed her. Thankfully, her mother checked on the younger woman and found hartshorn to waft under her nose.

Mrs. Wells awoke with a jerk. "What happened?"

"We were trying to determine why you and your husband would attempt to kill Miss White," the duke said in a menacing tone.

"It wasn't me," she insisted. She pointed at her husband. "It was all him."

"Your Grace," Mr. Wells said, "I didn't mean to hurt you or Miss White."

"Oh?" The duke raised a dark brow at him. "Then what was your intention?"

The man had the grace to flush and then stumbled over his words. "We, I just wanted to scare her. I, we just wanted her to know the pain we have suffered. I was hoping this would make her want to leave the estate."

The duke glared at the man and then grabbed him by the lapels. "Do you think she didn't feel any pain when your wife lost that child? I found her outside of my house that night, crying in the rain because she was so upset about what had happened."

"I had no idea, Your Grace. I wasn't aiming for her or you, Your Grace. I aimed high but the sight is off on my pistol. I would never try to hurt you."

The duke pulled the man closer. "Where is she?"

The man frowned. "Who? Miss White?"

"Of course, Miss White. She left here this morning and hasn't been seen again. Did you hurt her?"

"No, Your Grace," Mr. Wells said quickly. "I ain't seen her since last night at the ball."

"Get him out of here, Hart," the duke said, pushing Mr. Wells away.

"What do you want me to do with them?" Hart asked as he grabbed them both by the arm.

"Escort them off my property." The duke stared at them both. "And do not ever return."

They both nodded and as they left Mia finally stepped forward again. "Your Grace, in order to help find her, we might need to know what exactly caused her to leave so suddenly."

The duke sat back down and stared at his cooling soup. "When she was telling me what had happened with Mrs. Wells, I made a comment about her mother."

Mia looked at her mother and frowned. "What did you say?"

"I told her that what had happened to Mrs. Wells was no reason to shoot a person. And that I had wanted to kill her mother after I lost my wife and son but had never acted on that thought."

"Oh, dear God," Mia said and then slapped a hand over her mouth.

Chapter 26

Selina woke the next morning after a fitful night on Tia's small sofa. Tia had been so happy to see her last evening and had started packing for London immediately. She would leave on the next post this afternoon.

"You're awake," Tia said, fumbling with the kettle. "I was just putting on some tea."

"That sounds lovely."

"Once you've had breakfast, I'll show you where everything is. Do you want me to introduce you to the tenants?"

Selina rose and folded the blanket. "No. I would prefer to keep my presence here quiet for a short time."

Tia shrugged. "Very well. Do you want some toast or eggs?"

"I can't eat this morning." Her stomach was in knots. She had lain awake half the night wondering if Colin was all right. Then berating herself for caring about a man who could be so cruel.

"I have no appetite either. I can't believe I'm going to London to find Jonathon."

Selina took a seat at the small, scratched table. "Do you really think this is a wise idea?"

"Of course it is. That dratted Middleton forced Jonathon

to go to town to get away from me. He thinks I'm going to seduce his brother."

"Isn't that exactly your plan?"

Tia rolled her eyes. "Not exactly. I hope to ring a proposal out of him first. Then I shall seduce him."

"Good luck."

"Thank you!" Tia fluttered around the fireplace and read- ied the tea. "I just wish you had made this decision a fortnight ago. It may take me some time to find Jonathon in town."

"You don't know where to find him?"

Tia laughed. "He is either at the viscount's town home or at the Albany. Where else would he be?"

Selina rubbed her forehead. Her friend needed to be stopped but she was more stubborn than Mia when she made up her mind. Nothing was going to stop her from going to London. "Do you have a place to stay?"

"Yes, I wrote to one of the former tenants' daughters. She has a small place with her husband. She will let me stay there until Jonathon proposes."

That was one saving grace, Selina thought. She sipped her tea and worried again about Colin. It was a little too early to have started a fever. She shook her head, angry with herself for caring.

"So why did you leave, Selina?" Tia blew at her tea and then sipped it.

Selina stared at the steam rising from her cup. Slowly, she told her friend everything that had happened.

"Selina, he was devastated by the loss but it's been eight years. You said he had changed over the past two months. You have to tell him."

"I cannot," she cried. "I can't look into his eyes and tell him the truth. He shall hate me forever."

"But you can't live a lie either. He deserves to know."

She'd never felt like such a coward in her life. "I know. I just need a few days to think about the best way to tell him."

"There is no best way," Tia said softly. "Just tell him. If he loves you like I believe he does, he will forgive you."

"He should have been told eight years ago."

"Your mother was protecting you."

If her mother had really wanted to protect her, she shouldn't have been too drunk to deliver a baby that night.

Colin rose from his bed determined to return to his home and start his search for Selina. Mrs. Featherstone had given her blessing as long as he remained feverless. Other than his shoulder still giving him pain, he felt fine.

Kate opened the door to his room. "The coach is ready, Colin."

"Excellent. Any word?"

"Nothing. Mr. Roberts sent Randall over this morning to say there was still no sign of her at the house or her cottage."

He nodded sharply. "Did you think of any place she might have gone?"

"No, I asked Miss Featherstone again last evening before she left. Did she seem particularly upset by what you'd said? I thought it odd that she appeared so pale after you told her about the exchange between you and Selina."

"I agree. I will go to Hart's today and speak with her. I do believe she is withholding information."

The entire ride home, he stared out the window, praying he would see her walking along the road. But he arrived home with no sign of her. Even though Mia had already checked her cottage, that was the first place he went. Entering the cottage, he found the remnants of that beautiful green gown she'd worn. He picked up a piece and stuffed it into his jacket pocket.

He returned to his house and checked every room. With a house this size, he knew she could be hiding here again. After turning up nothing, he sat down in his study and poured a brandy.

"Did you find anything?" his stepmother asked, walking into the room.

"No, I have no idea where else to look."

"I am so sorry, Colin." She walked to the small table and poured herself a glass of brandy.

He had never seen his stepmother drink anything but a glass of wine or sherry. And never at three in the afternoon. "It is not your fault or Kate's. I know what you were doing. It was the right thing to do. Bringing her to a small country ball would give her the confidence she needed to see that she could marry me."

"That is what I thought." The duchess sat down across from him. "She is a lovely young woman, Colin. And I only want to see you happy. Eight years is too long."

"I know that now, Mother." It was the first time he had ever called her that. He had been nine and defiant when his father had married her. Colin had refused to call her anything but the duchess or Georgina.

She wiped away a tear. "You will find her, son. I know you will."

He finished his brandy. "I will find her. I'm heading to Hart's to speak with Miss Featherstone. I believe she is hiding something from me."

"Good luck. If she makes an appearance here we shall send word."

More determined than ever to find her, he headed in the direction of the Featherstones' cottage. Again, he scanned the woods as he rode hoping for a sign of Selina. He reined in at the cottage and carefully dismounted. His shoulder was still aching.

"Your Grace," Mrs. Featherstone said, opening the door. "What brings you here? Is your wound bothering you?"

"Only a little. I came to speak with your daughter. Is she at home?"

"She went to help one of the servants."

"Thank you. I shall ride up to the house, then. Thank you again for caring for me."

"Of course, Your Grace."

Colin rode up to the main house. After giving his horse to a stableboy, he was welcomed inside.

"Good afternoon, Your Grace," the butler said with a bow. "I shall tell his lordship that you are here to see him."

"Actually, I came to speak with Miss Featherstone. Her mother told me I would find her here."

"I'm sorry, Your Grace, but she left about ten minutes ago. She said she had a few more visits to make."

Damn. He didn't feel like returning to Mrs. Featherstone's cottage to wait for her. That older woman had a stare that would frighten any man.

"Shall I tell his lordship you are here?"

"Yes." Perhaps a bit of brandy with Hart would ease his frustration.

The butler sent a footman to search out Hart while Colin waited in his study. He poured two snifters of brandy and set one on a table for his friend. Then he walked to the window and stared out at the overcast day.

He prayed she was all right. The more time that passed, the more he worried some harm may have befallen her. He'd never forgive himself if that were true because of some foolish words he'd spoken in front of her.

"Any word?"

Colin shook his head. "No. I actually came to speak with Miss Featherstone."

"She left only a few minutes ago."

"I know."

Colin sipped his brandy and let the heady liquid wash over

his tongue. Maybe getting completely sodden would ease his mind. He doubted even that would help.

"Where the hell is she, Hart?"

"I wish I knew." Hart sat down and drained his glass in one large gulp. "Is there any possibility she went to London?"

"She once told me she had no desire to leave the countryside for the ills she would see in town. I just can't imagine she'd run there." Even still, he would contact a Bow Street runner tomorrow to start searching.

Hart placed his glass back on the table. "I asked Miss Featherstone about Selina's family and she told me Selina had never met her father's family. Mrs. Featherstone admitted the man married down. He was the second son of a squire in Suffolk."

"How can I find her when I have no way of knowing where she might be?"

"You might not be able to, North. She might be out of your life forever."

Colin clenched his fists. He would not stop searching for her until he found her. As the evening wore on, the men continued to drink until they were so deep in their cups, Colin knew he would be spending the night.

Mia awoke the next morning feeling sick to her stomach. It just wasn't like Selina to leave without a note to her. She slowly sipped her tea while her mother paid a visit to a sick tenant.

A knock scraped the door. "Come in."

One of Middleton's tenants opened the door. "Good morning, Miss Featherstone. I have a message from Miss Tia for your mother."

"Thank you," she said and reached for the message. "Would you like some tea?"

"Thank you, no. I am off to the village." He bobbed his head. "Good day."

Mia glanced at the missive and decided to open it in case Tia needed assistance with a delivery. Scanning the note, she muttered, "Stupid girl."

Then she read more and raced out of the house. She lifted up her skirts and ran up the hill toward Hart's stables. She had to get to the duke's home as fast as possible. The earl wouldn't mind if she took one of his fastest horses to deliver this message.

"What are you about this morning, Miss Featherstone?"

She slowed down and breathed in deeply. She shouldn't be surprised to see him at the stables. He was always an early riser. "My lord, I need to borrow your mare."

"Is there a problem with your horse?"

"She's too slow. I know where Selina went. The duke needs to hear about this."

Hart's face relaxed and his molded lips lifted. "Then there is no need for a horse. He is in my house probably still abed."

"He's here?"

"Yes. Most likely with a raging headache like I have this morning." He laughed gruffly.

"I will give you something for it." She followed his quick stride, barely able to keep up without breaking into a run. Obviously, his headache was not as bad as he stated.

Hart ran ahead and into the house. Just as she arrived, she heard him tell a footman to wake the duke immediately. "Come with me. We shall wait for him in the library."

Mia walked down the marble-floored corridor to the library. She had only been in here a few times but loved the pale blue walls and shelves filled with books.

"So where is she?" he asked after the tea arrived for all of them.

"She went to my sister's house. I must have arrived before

Selina did so Tia hadn't seen her at that point." She stared down at the letter in her hands and fought back tears.

"What is wrong, Miss Featherstone?"

"She's gone," she whispered.

"Miss White is gone?"

She shook her head. "No, Tia. She decided to chase after the viscount's brother. She went to London. I don't know if I'll ever see her again."

"I'm sorry, Mia," he whispered.

"What is going on?" the duke asked as he entered the room. "Why the hell am I up at his hour?"

Mia smiled at the grumpy man. "Your Grace, we have found her."

"What? Where?"

"She is at my sister's house."

"Thank God," he said and raced from the room without even saying good-bye.

Selina spent her morning in her new home organizing the shelf near the fireplace so she could find what she needed. She then checked Tia's herbs and found her supply lacking many basic items. She created a list of things she either would need to buy or forage for in the woods.

But none of the busy work kept her from thinking about Colin. She still worried that a fever may have set in. Perhaps he was lying in bed right now . . . dying. Oh, God, she couldn't think like that. She had to stop before she went mad.

Tia was right. At some point, she would have to face him and tell him the truth.

The front door suddenly hurled open and Colin filled the doorway. Her heart pounded as he stared at her with a mix of anger and relief in his eyes. He slammed the door shut.

"Where the hell have you been?" he demanded. He advanced on her position by the cabinet that held Tia's herbs.

"Do you have any idea what you have put me through the past two days?"

His anger emanated from him like the heat from a fireplace. And yet, he had never looked so handsome. His face was unshaved and dark with stubble. His clothes looked rumpled as if he'd slept in them, and judging by the smell of stale brandy permeating the air around him, he probably had slept in his clothes.

He slammed both of his hands on either side of her shoulders, trapping her against the cabinet. "Have you nothing to say?"

"Me?" She finally found her voice. "You tell me you wanted to kill my mother and then wonder why I ran off!"

"I was trying to make a point."

"Well you did a very poor job of it."

He closed his eyes and breathed in deeply. "Perhaps I did. But it was no reason to run off and tell no one where you were going. Do you have any idea how worried everyone is?"

She hadn't really thought about anyone else for the past two days. Normally, all she did was think of other people's feelings. "I'm sorry. I will apologize to everyone. But right now, I'd like you to leave."

"I am not going anywhere until you tell what really made you run off."

She should tell him everything and be done with it. Once she told him, he would never want to see her again. But she didn't want him to leave just yet. She had to find a way to stall. "How is your wound?"

"I am fine."

She sensed he was nearing the end of his patience. "Are you certain?" She placed her hand on his forehead to feel for a fever. "You are nice and cool."

"Selina," he growled.

"I cannot tell you," she admitted. "If I do you will hate

me forever." Tears flooded her eyes, blinding her to his handsome face.

"I could never hate you, darling."

"Oh, you could. You have no idea."

"Selina," he said again, closer to her face. "If you don't tell me now . . . hell, I don't know what I shall do."

"Do you hate my mother?" She had to know.

"I do not like what happened."

"Do you hate my mother?" she pressed again.

His jaw clenched. "I did for many years. But I am working through those feelings, thanks in part to you."

Tears streamed down her cheeks. "My mother was not at fault that night."

"I know. You have told me that several times."

"It wasn't her fault," she cried. "It was mine."

He reached out and caressed her cheek. "Darling, you weren't even there. The servants told me it was just your mother upstairs."

"They lied to protect me. Everyone lied to protect me from you that night."

His brows furrowed. "What are you talking about?" he whispered hoarsely.

"My mother was too drunk to be of any use. Mrs. Roberts knew I had assisted my mother so she called me. They snuck me in the house and up the back staircase." She paused to catch her breath. "The cord was wrapped around the baby's neck. I had never seen that before. I didn't know what to do. I tried unwrapping the cord but he still wouldn't take a breath."

He backed away from her. His face paled and mouth gaped.

"I am the reason your wife and child died that night. Not my mother."

Chapter 27

Colin backed away until his leg hit the table. It wasn't possible. They had all told him there was nothing that could have been done. It had been God's will that they died. All these years he had blamed her mother. They had told him Mrs. White delivered the baby. Mrs. White had even given him the heartwrenching news.

They had lied.

To protect Selina.

"Please say something," she begged.

He couldn't look at her. Her bedraggled look and tears would ensnare him. His wife and child might have survived if not for her. The room felt as if it was closing in on him. Without a word, he strode from the house.

He rode back to his house and stumbled into the study. He didn't care if he'd barely recovered from a night of drinking, it was not too early to start again. He poured a large glass of brandy and gulped it down. Then he poured some more.

"Have you heard anything?" Kate asked from the doorway with a worried look on her face.

"Get out of my study and close the door behind you," he said in a menacing tone. He didn't want to speak to anyone.

"Oh, God, what happened? Is she . . ."

"No, she is not dead. My wife and child are dead but the bloody wise woman lives on."

"What happened, Colin?" She walked into the room and closed the door behind her. "You need to stop drinking and tell me what happened."

"The hell I will." He poured another glass, gave her a salute, and drank it down. Nothing would ease the pain he felt in his heart. Everyone had betrayed him. "Get out, Kate."

"The hell I will," she parroted and then sank into a chair. "Sit down and tell me what happened. Did you see Selina?"

"Do not mention her name again."

"What happened when you saw her?"

"She told me the goddamn truth . . . finally."

"The truth about what?" Kate asked slowly.

"How Mary and my son died." He drained another glass before collapsing into a chair. "It wasn't her mother's fault, Kate."

"Then . . ."

"Yes, it was Selina's fault." He rubbed his hands over his face.

"Tell me what she told you."

He told her the story that Selina had revealed to him. As he spoke, his heart grew heavier.

"Wait," Kate said just as he finished. "How old is Selina . . . twenty-four?"

"Yes, but what has that to do with any of this?" He rubbed his rough jaw.

"She was only sixteen when this happened. Her mother was too drunk to do her job. And you have the audacity to blame Selina? She told you that she had never delivered on her own. God, Colin, she was only sixteen."

"Kate, they lied to me. Every goddamn one of them told me it was God's will. That God had taken them because he needed them in heaven. He didn't need them yet. She didn't know what she was doing."

Kate rose up from her chair and stared down at him in anger. "Of course she didn't know. Her mother was too drunk to help her. It wasn't Selina's fault. I'm certain she did everything in her power to save both your son and wife. You're a drunken fool for blaming her."

"They all lied to me. My servants, her mother, and even Selina lied by omission. She should have told me from the beginning."

"They lied to protect her from you. You are a complete and utter arse!" She stormed out of the room and slammed the door behind her.

Colin leaned his head back against the chair and closed his eyes. Even in his drunken haze, he realized Kate was right. He was an arse. They lied to protect a young girl from a duke's wrath. The servants had known that he would take his anger out on her.

And they were right. He had spent the past eight years blaming her mother so, of course, he would have done the same to her. He would have removed her from the estate. The only reason he hadn't ejected her mother was because of Selina. He couldn't do that to a young girl.

But he wouldn't have thought of her as a girl if he'd known that she had tried to deliver his son.

"I heard there was a commotion in here."

Hearing the soft tone of his stepmother's voice calmed him down. No matter how hard he had tried to push her away when he was younger, she had always been there for him. "Kate and I had a row."

"I figured it was something of the sort," she said in that light voice. "Would you like to talk to me? I might know a little more about life than your sister."

"I suppose you do." While he had been cordial to the duchess, he had never confided in her until now.

Once he finished telling her what happened, she released

a long sigh. "You cannot continue on this path of blame, Colin. She was only a young girl attempting to do something beyond her years."

"I know."

"Do you love her?"

"Yes," he admitted in a whispered tone.

"Then why are you letting this stand in the way of your happiness? What happened, happened. You cannot change the past. You spent eight years mourning a woman I don't think you loved half as much as you do Selina. I never saw you look at Mary the way you do her."

The woman was more intelligent than he had ever given her credit for. "Thank you."

"You know when I married your father, I knew he was still in love with your mother."

Colin looked up at her. "He was?"

She tilted her head and smiled at him. "Yes. He loved Elizabeth beyond words but knew you needed a mother. He picked me because he thought I would be happy just being a duchess. But that wasn't what I wanted."

"Oh?"

"I wanted your father's love. I fought for two years for it. Until he finally admitted that he loved me. It was the happiest day of my life. Losing him ten years ago just about killed me too. I understand grief, Colin. It can consume you if you let it. Don't let it. Life is too hard and too short to be miserable all the time. The happiest I've seen you was with Selina."

He closed his eyes again. His stepmother was right. With Selina, he felt whole again. "You are a very wise woman, Mother.

"It's about time you realized that. Now go to your wise woman and tell her how big a fool you've been and how much you love her."

"I will." He rose slowly. "But first I must change. I will not propose to her looking like this."

Selina spent the rest of the day in bed. Her heart ached, her body was tired, and nothing seemed to help. He had done exactly what she expected but still, she was disappointed in him.

She'd tried to tell herself this was for the best. Now, she could go back to her life as it was before he arrived. She would miss his tenants and servants terribly but Middleton's tenants would welcome her. Once they learned she had taken over from Tia. Tomorrow she would force herself out of bed and speak with the viscount.

But for the rest of the day, she intended on staying in bed and crying her heart out. How could she still love him after the way he treated her? It made no sense.

Tears soaked her pillow. She had been certain he loved her. He danced with her three times at the ball and told her everyone was talking about their betrothal. So how could he have run out like that this morning?

She heard a knock on the door but ignored it. If it was a tenant, they could send for Mia. She always covered for her sister when needed. By not answering, they would assume she was not here. She just needed today for her self-pity.

"Selina?" Colin's voice called to her.

God, no. She couldn't see him now. Why was he even here? Did he want to humiliate her? Tell her to never set foot on his land again? She had already assumed he would never want her near, which was why she left. Perhaps he would go away if she stayed quiet or pretended to sleep.

"Selina?" The door to her bedroom opened silently. She heard his footsteps coming closer but refused to open her eyes. The side of her bed depressed from his weight.

"Please leave me alone," she cried. "I cannot stand to see you so angry with me."

"I am not angry, Selina."

Hearing the tender tone of his voice only made her cry harder. "You should be."

His rough hand caressed her wet cheek. "I was a fool." He chuckled when she nodded. "I should never have blamed you for what happened. I was just in shock when you told me. I had lived the past eight years believing the version of the story that everyone had told me."

"They only sought to protect me."

"I realize that now. I just needed some time to sort things out." He lay down next to her and brought her close. "They all love you, Selina. Even then, they wanted you safe from my wrath."

She let her head rest on his chest. Hearing his strong, steady heartbeat slowly relaxed her. "I'm so sorry, Colin. I really did everything I could at the time."

"You were sixteen, as my sister reminded me. You had never delivered a child on your own."

"My first should never have been the duke's heir," she whispered.

"All children are important. Your mother should have been the one delivering or at least there to assist you. Not unconscious from the gin."

In her heart, she had always known that but it still hurt to hear him say it. "I know."

"Can you forgive me? I never meant to hurt you, Selina."

"I know," she said against his chest. "You were taken by surprise with my admission."

Strong arms lifted her up so her head was next to his. Looking into his beautiful blue eyes, she was struck by the love she saw.

"I love you," he said quietly. "You forced me out of my staid existence and back to life."

"I love you too, Colin. I have no idea how I went from completely disliking you and being terrified you would discover me living in your house, to love. I just couldn't help myself. And I tried so hard not to love you."

He smiled and kissed her gently. "Why did you try not to love me?"

"You are the Duke of Northrop. I am nobody. I knew there was no reason to think I could be anything but your mistress."

His lips parted hers again and then he pulled back. "You actually are someone."

Selina studied his eyes. "Well, yes, I am your wise woman."

"And according to Mrs. Featherstone, the daughter of the second son of a country squire," he said and then kissed the tip of her nose.

"Is that why you decided I was acceptable?"

"Sweetheart, I had no idea about your background until after I was shot. If you remember, I had danced three times with you at the ball. I was telling everyone there that not only were you taken, but I was too."

It hadn't mattered to him that she was nobody. Her heart swelled so completely she thought she might burst. "Did you ever find Mr. Wells?"

"Yes," he said and then lay back against the pillows and stared at the white ceiling. "I don't believe Mrs. Wells was involved but Mr. Wells admitted that he wanted you to feel some of the pain he and his wife felt."

"What did you do?" she asked fearfully. She knew he had a temper and wondered if he sent the man to prison.

"I told him how you cried in the rain that night. I also told him to find another place to live."

"You didn't have him arrested?"

"No." He sighed. "I understand his pain and even though he acted reprehensibly, I know about going a little mad after losing someone."

She nodded and looked away. She wondered what they

would do next. He hadn't officially proposed to her yet. Did he mean to go back on his unofficial proposal?

"Selina, do you think you would mind spending time in London with me?"

"After everything that has happened over the past three days, I never want to be without you. I will go with you to London and be your mistress."

He rolled over with a lopsided grin on his face. "Are you trying to wring a proposal out of me?"

"No, I just said I would be your mistress."

He stared into her eyes. "I am not looking for a mistress. I want a wife." He closed his eyes. "I want to try to have children."

She reached out and cupped his face with her hand. "You know there are risks with having children. I cannot guarantee the outcome."

"I know. But if you're willing to take the risk, I can too."

She moved her body closer until she was up against him. Closing her mouth over his, she kissed him soundly. "I believe if you force me to, I will be your wife."

"And my duchess."

"And your duchess," she added.

Epilogue

One year later

Selina closed her eyes as another contraction washed over her. They were definitely getting closer together now. She hated the idea of putting her husband through this but it must be done.

"Colin?"

"Yes, darling?" He looked up from the paperwork on his desk. "Do you need something?"

She had curled into a chair by the fireplace and now wondered if she should head for the bedchamber. "Perhaps you should send for Mia and her mother."

"Have you finally decided to tell me you're in labor?"

"You knew?"

"For the past hour. I sent for Mrs. Featherstone forty-five minutes ago."

She laughed softly. "I didn't want to worry you."

"I know. But I will worry no matter what." He rose and walked toward her chair. "Do you want to go upstairs now?"

"Not really," she replied, standing up next to him. "My mother used to get her new mothers to walk until they couldn't stand any longer. Would you walk with me?"

"Of course."

"Oh my," she said as another contraction slammed into her. "That one came much faster and harder."

Colin glanced down at his watch, praying Mrs. Featherstone would get here soon. When he had noticed his wife making slight moans and clutching the arm of the chair, he had immediately sent for Hart's wise women.

"They will be here in time," Selina said as she walked across the room with him. "Let's go on the terrace and get a breath of air."

They walked the length of the terrace twice before she stopped as another contraction hit her. She breathed in and out in deep breaths.

"That one hurt," she admitted. "Perhaps it's time to go to the bedchamber."

"Shall I carry you?"

"I need the walk."

As they reached the steps, the front door opened and Mrs. Featherstone and her daughter arrived. "Why isn't she in bed yet?" Mrs. Featherstone demanded.

"That's where we were going," Selina replied, unaffected by Mrs. Featherstone's harsh tone.

Colin helped Selina up the stairs to their bedchamber.

"And this is where you leave, Your Grace."

"I need to stay." He couldn't leave her alone.

"Your Grace," Mia said softly. "You will only be in our way and a distraction for Selina. She needs to work very hard over the next few hours to get your baby out. Please go to your study. Hart is down there waiting for you."

"Colin, wait," Selina said after changing into a nightgown. She put her arms around him and kissed him softly. "I love you. Please try not to worry. Everything will be all right."

"I love you, Selina." God, he couldn't lose her.

"Go, Your Grace," Mrs. Featherstone said as she helped Selina into bed.

He closed the door behind him as Selina let out a loud moan. This would be the longest night of his life. He walked down to his study and found Hart pouring two glasses of brandy.

"Here," he said, handing one to Colin. "How do they do this?"

"I have no idea."

The men barely spoke as the night wore on. A few times, Colin could have sworn he heard Selina's screams. Five hours later, Mia came into the room. "Your Grace, my mother would like to see you."

Oh, God. It was just like nine years ago when the maid had told him that Mrs. White needed to speak to him. He looked over at Mia's pale and drawn face. Dread filled him. It felt like hours before he finally reached their bedchamber. It was too quiet in there. He knocked lightly on the door.

"It's about time you got up here," Mrs. Featherstone said, opening the door for him. "You wife has someone for you to meet."

"What?" He glanced over at the bed and found Selina propped against the pillows holding a baby wrapped in a white blanket.

"Go to your wife, Your Grace." She picked up her bags. "Selina, I shall call on you in the afternoon to see how you are doing."

"Thank you again, Mrs. Featherstone."

She closed the door behind them, cloaking them in privacy. Colin walked to the bed and stared down at the perfect infant.

"Meet your son, Your Grace," Selina said with a smile. "He looks just like you with all that dark hair and those blue eyes."

Colin sat down on the bed and Selina placed their son in his arms. "He's beautiful." He reached out a finger and his son grabbed on. "Ten fingers."

"And ten toes. I counted." She leaned forward and kissed their son before kissing Colin. "Did you manage? I tried to hurry things along, you know."

He stared at the wife he loved and then moved his gaze to his newborn son. "I have everything I ever wanted."

Have you read these other fantastic
historical romances by Christie Kelley?
Available in paperback and as eBooks.

"Sometimes becoming a fallen woman
isn't as easy as it sounds. Oh! My!"
—Kasey Michaels,
New York Times bestselling author

One night is never enough...

EVERY NIGHT
I'M YOURS

CHRISTIE KELLEY

SPECIAL
PRICE
$4.99
$5.99 CAN
"Rollicking, sexy...
You'll enjoy this one!"
—Kat Martin
CHRISTIE
KELLEY
When desire's this sweet,
one taste will never do...
EVERY TIME
WE KISS

Something thrilling…Something secret…

SOMETHING
SCANDALOUS

CHRISTIE KELLEY

She's
all he wants
for Christmas…

SCANDAL
OF THE
SEASON

CHRISTIE KELLEY

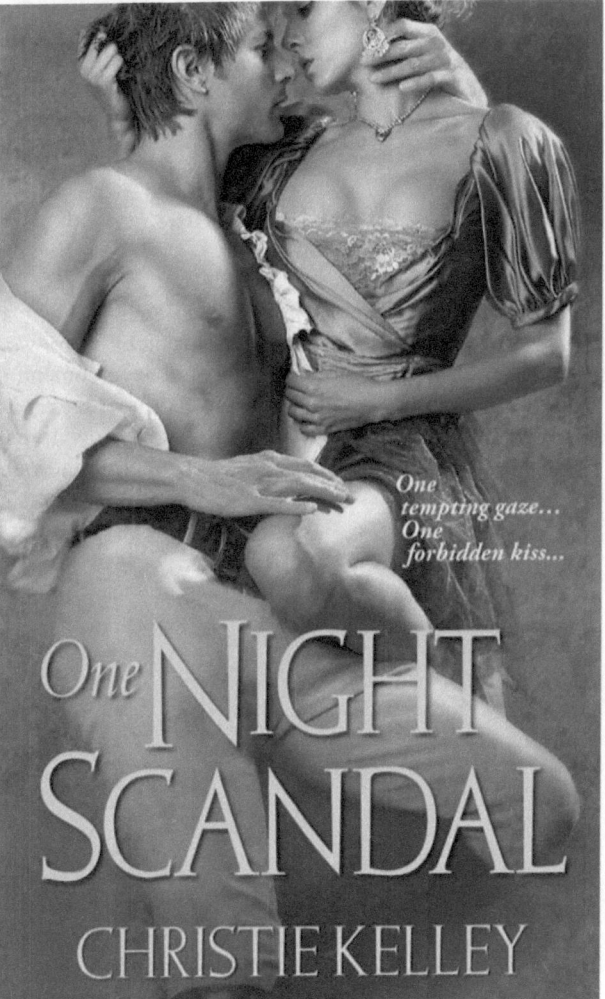

One
tempting gaze…
One
forbidden kiss…

One NIGHT
SCANDAL

CHRISTIE KELLEY

About the Author

Award-winning author **Christie Kelley** was born and raised in upstate New York. After seventeen years working for financial institutions in software development, she started writing her first book. She currently writes regency historical romances for Kensington and now lives in Maryland with her two sons. Come visit her on the web at www.christiekelley.com.